Pretty Girls Shouldn't Cry

Talia Atkins

Contents

They say your darkest hour comes before your dawn. But you have to survive the darkness first.

Author Note

Although this book is 'lighter' than my most recent releases, there are still some dark and twisted themes.

The darker themes in this book are more along the lines of deteriorating mental health, pressures of life, forbidden relationships and drug addiction.

Please only proceed reading if you're 18 and over.

Prologue

"Guys wait for me!" I yell out as I run down the long, trailing gravel road. My feet burn from the pangs of pain from the sharp rocks. The sun drenches me, blinding my eyes. I swipe the sweat away from my freckled face and keep trudging forward. I can see their backs, still moving a lot quicker than me. They both wear fishing bucket hats and hold their fly fishing rods like their lives depend on it. I look down at my bucket of worms and smirk, feeling proud that I get to carry the bait for the hooks. They never let me come fishing. Not unless I promise to carry their things. But I don't really mind because I love fishing at the lake.

My lungs start to burn as my short legs move faster, trying to keep up with their longer legs and quicker pace.

I make it down to the bank on the water's edge, where the boys are already sitting down, looking over their rods. Making sure their hooks and knots all look good, I'm sure. I'm learning a lot about fishing. Hopefully soon they will let me have a go at catching my own fish.

"About time little sis!" Bradey laughs. I look up into my brother's face and smile while holding up the bucket. "I forgot to grab my sandals out of the car before Mom left."

He scoffs and takes the bucket from my hand before openly rolling his eyes. I brush my strawberry blonde hair back and out of my eyes, ignoring his attitude. He's twelve now; it was his birthday last week. Mom told me sometimes big brothers can have a mean attitude toward their younger siblings when they hit puberty. I'm only two years younger than him and every time Mom tells me the negative effects puberty has on Bradey it makes me pray to god every night that I want to stay this little forever. I glance at my brother while he hooks a worm onto the hook and I cringe. Poor little worms never stand a chance in our back garden. His golden hair sparkles under the sun rays and his excited eyes gaze over his shoulder to his best friend.

"Nate hurry up, I reckon today we will catch the big one."

"Yeah yeah," Nate replies. I look at Nate, who is a head taller than my short brother but they are the same age. He has ebony hair that droops around his ears, his almost onyx-colored eyes crinkle at the edges as he glances at me. He chuckles and then whips a worm out of the bucket before he throws it at me. "Think fast!" He laughs as it smacks me on the forehead.

"Argh! Why do you always have to do that?" I squeal and jump back as the worm drops to the ground and lands at my feet.

He shrugs his shoulders and walks to the edge of the grass bank. I watch my brothers as they pull back their rods and then send the hooked worms flying into the water. A steady ripple runs over the clear water after a soft splash. Bradey and Nate are always together. They are together so much that Nate lives with us. Mom said I'm too young to understand. But I understand enough to know Nate's dad isn't very nice to him. Not like my dad. My dad is the best.

I peel my eyes away from the boys and skim over the withering worm on the crispy summer grass. After a second's hesitation, I pluck it off the ground and bury it into the soil at the bottom of the bucket. I pat the dirt softly when it's hidden and then find a spot under a small tree while I wait for the boys. I don't know why I bother burying the worm when it'll be fish bait soon. But I can't stand to watch it suffer like that. I cross my ankles and lace my fingers together as I perch them on my lap. I begin humming and hum louder when a small sparrow hops down to the branch just above my head and starts whistling a soft tune of its own. I love summer. It really is the best time in the world.

"Paisley," my name alerts me. I sit up and wipe my mouth. "Did I fall asleep?" I say groggily, already knowing that I certainly did.

"Yeah this is why I told Mom you shouldn't come fishing with us. You're a little girl!" Bradey scorns me then kicks my foot gently. "Get up, Mom will be here soon to pick us up."

Without hesitation, I quickly crawl to my feet and reach my hand out to carry the bucket.

"Huh! Paisley you can't carry this bucket. It's full of our fish, waaaaay too heavy for a small child like you."

"Hey you're a child too!" I say in a sullen voice while trying not to sob. Today is a good day. Not a bad day. My regular mantra normally helps.

"Nah I'm pretty much a teenager which means I'm an adult." He chuckles and sets off up the gravel path. Nate slowly follows behind him and I struggle to keep up with them both. Crunching sounds follow their hastened pace. My mood becomes worse because the stones are scorching hot now. Not only are my feet cut, they're burning with every step I take.

Tears slide down my cheeks as I give in to the pain. I scramble off the path and fall onto the grass huffing in air, not knowing how I am going to be able to make it the entire way up to the parking lot. While I examine my feet and run a fingertip over my deepest cut, a shadow casts over me, blocking out the sun.

"What's wrong Paisley?" Nate's concerned voice floats down to me.

"The rocks are really hot." I sniff with my legs curled under me now.

He crouches low and wipes a tear off my cheek before he smiles at me with empathy. "Pretty girls shouldn't cry," he placates me.

I push my bottom lip out and sulk. "Tell Mom to come and get me."

"As if. She will growl at me and send me back home if she knows I let you suffer. Get on my back," Nate orders me.

"You'll drop me."

He snorts while shuffling slightly so his back is to me. "Get on my back, Princess."

I stand up, wrap my arms around his neck and he stands straight. We start walking up the hill when I spot my brother looking down at us, shaking his head. He's going to beat me up for this later. He doesn't like me hanging out with his friend.

Chapter 1

So *very nearly perfect*, I think to myself as I eye the cupcakes in front of me carefully. I sink a little lower, so my eyes are level with the benchtop and I can inspect the icing on the top. I slowly move around, assessing every single one. The perfect swirl at the top of them all took so much time, but now I can confirm it was worth it. The icing is impeccable on all 100 of them. I stand straight again, placing my hands on my hips. I just need to put them on a platter in a patterned formation and they will be good to go for tonight's event. They are our team colors. Deep burgundy and white. We have our next cheerleading event tonight for the finals at the college basketball tournament. It's our men's team, the mighty Grizzlies against the Hawks who are our biggest rivals.

"Wow sis, you really going to do this every single game?" My brother, Bradey comes in and smirks while his eyes linger on my freshly made cupcakes. I follow his eyes and can't help but appreciate the shine on the buttercream icing.

"It boosts our team morale."

He snickers loudly and heads around the polished island to the stainless steel fridge. Pulling it open, he grabs his water bottle and drops it down into his gym bag.

As he comes up behind me, he tugs on the ribbon that is tied perfectly at the top of my ponytail.

"No, you do it because you want to be captain next year and are desperate to impress everyone," Bradey says quietly and then whips his hand around me and snatches a cupcake. He licks the icing off as he takes off through the kitchen.

"Bradey! They aren't yours!" I screech, growing flustered. I can still feel the rush of air from his fast descent when Nate strolls into the kitchen. All six feet of him. His dark hair is wet from his swim in our summer pool. Small tendrils glue themselves to his sun-kissed forehead. Mom and Dad adopted him officially on his thirteenth birthday, which makes him my second brother. Bradey and Nate are inseparable still to this day, yet they can't be more different. Nate is on the college's competitive swim team. He's a lot quieter than Bradey and he struggles massively with his grades. Mom and Dad have tried countless times to convince him to do tutoring, because if his grades drop too much it means he's off the swim team, but he always turns them down. Bradey, the cocky loudmouth, is an overachiever with his grades, although his teachers don't seem to like him very much.

My attention returns to my baking that is now less than perfect. I grimace at the gap in my cupcake line up and tend to agree with their assessment of him.

Nate looks over my cupcakes and pushes them together slightly so the gap is no longer. I let out a big sigh, while trying to hold in my frustrated tears. Or I'll cry, which means he'll ask me why I'm crying and I will have to admit that my monthly hormones are probably the fuel for the outburst.

"Thanks," I mumble instead while keeping my eyes low. Nate's fingers brush against mine as he tugs the ribbon from my fingers and moves behind me. He pushes my ponytail to the side as he slips the ribbon underneath and then ties it into a soft bow at the top of my hair tie.

"Anytime Paisley," he murmurs then slips out of the kitchen. He will be catching a ride with Bradey to school. I glare at his back, watching his toned muscles bulge against his singlet. Swimming keeps his shoulders and arms perfectly chiseled and he's free from any body hair. And most of all, he never calls me sis. He calls Bradey his brother, Mom and Dad his parents but I am always, simply, Paisley to him. Every so often he calls me Princess, but then as if catching himself he quickly goes back to calling me Paisley. He shows me kindness but I've never felt like he sees me as his family. I don't know why, but whatever the reason, it breaks my heart every time I let myself think about it.

After shaking my head to clear my pointless ill feelings, I take a deep dish platter and carefully place the cupcakes inside before placing them in the fridge.

I grab a notepad and pen and scribble a quick note on the bench,

MOM/DAD
PLEASE DON'T EAT THE CUPCAKES. PLEASE TAKE THEM OUT OF THE FRIDGE 10 MINS BEFORE YOU LEAVE FOR THE GAME. AND MY BROTHERS ARE DOUCHEBAGS.
LOVE YOU
PX

A horn blares through the house just as I write my initial at the bottom of the note. A wide grin spreads across my face because I know exactly who it is. I hook my fingers around my backpack and sling it over my shoulder. I pace out of the front door and down the cobbled pathway while admiring my best friend, Sara's car. It's a new Porsche in a sleek candy red. She's a year older than me, and I'm thankful that she wants to drive me most days because although I can drive if I need to, I'm not the world's best driver. My parents put more time into my cheer and dance training rather than practical skills.

"Hey rich bitch," I greet her as I slip down into the smooth leather seat. She rolls her eyes at me then swats my shoulder. Her fingers are heavily weighted with her selection of silver dress rings and shiny bands. Her fingers are finished off with white almond shaped gel polish. She's incredibly beautiful; she has bronzed skin which comes easily to her in summer, and deep brown hair with brown eyes. Her athletic build makes her perfect for tossing the smaller cheerleaders in the air.

"Because I don't pick you up from your cute gated neighborhood every morning." My eyes flick back to her face which is glinting with amusement.

"Because you don't drive your Porsche from your epic estate out of town." I look directly at her. We stare at each other for a moment before we both burst out laughing.

She presses the volume button on her steering wheel, turning up the music while we drive to school. I rest my hand out of the car window and wave my fingers through the brisk morning air. By afternoon, it will be a still, humid heat that will make my hair flair up with curly baby hairs around my hairline.

We pull up to the old historic-looking school we attend. Not the run-down historic kind of building but the come from money but has been around for many generations' kind. As we pull into one of the student parks, my eyes roam over the multi-colored bricks and painted white concrete pillars that frame the entrance. It's classed as a small-town college yet our roll numbers still do well at 620 students. We exit the car and I desperately try to ignore my brothers who are in a group with their friends leaning against their car two parks over. I feel their curious eyes on me, so I lift my chin slightly and walk side by side with Sara into school. I tug down my black bike shorts, feeling self-conscious. Sara smacks me on the backside and chuckles loudly, then pushes her way through the wide entrance.

"Your butt's grown," she says while leading me through the sea of school kids. We are a few weeks off finishing for our summer break so everyone seems even more riled up than normal.

"Yeah, it has grown and I haven't had a chance to buy myself some new shorts," I murmur as I happily follow behind. She is much better at being the leader in our group and not standing for anyone's shit.

"Why do you need bigger ones? Guys fizz over that thigh rubbing in the little shorts."

I snort and jog to catch up to her long strides. Since when did I ever care about what guys thought of me? I have my future set out and messing around with boys isn't anywhere near my plan.

"I have PE first. I'll meet you during break time!" I call after Sara as I weave left, heading out toward the gym. She throws her hand up with her back to me, giving me a wave. I spin and jog out toward the girls' locker room while shaking my head in awe. Everything about Sara is just naturally smooth and cool.

Chapter 2

I pull my school PE t-shirt over my head and stuff my bag full of books into my locker before slamming it shut. Blonde bouncy curls flutter past me with a strong scent of Baby Doll perfume. Kirsten turns to me and gives me a soft smile.

"We have a fitness test today," she tells me while pulling her hair back into a low ponytail and smacking her glossy lips together. Fitness test before summer break normally means track sprints. I don't mind running, compared to all the other sports aside from cheer squad. It's probably my favorite. But sprints with another group of girls is never like a relaxing jog through our local park. I let my eyes drop to the ground as I smooth my hair back.

Kirsten pushes her fingers through mine and pulls me out of the locker room. "Come on, you are fitter than all of us. Don't know why you hate it so much."

"I hate the sprinting part. Unless I'm being chased by a serial killer—I don't ever like to sprint. Not an entire track anyway," I grumble, knowing hormones, heat, and Bradey's cupcake stealing is making me irritable. The morning sun hits our faces, causing me to push my hand up so I can shield my eyes. We make our way toward the other girls and our waiting teacher, Mr Richards. He also coaches the basketball and athletics teams. He's an all rounder and for a middle aged married man, he's not too bad on the eyes either. His deep brown hair has a slight peppering of gray around his ears, and he has an athletic build to match. It gives all the girls here something to fuss over. I have seen many shamelessly throw themselves at him and others ogle from a distance.

"Nice of you two to join us," he states when we stop on the outskirts of the small group. I hang out at the back, ignoring his disapproving glare. The one and only time I want to be front and center is if it is for cheer which is the only place I feel confident. So hovering behind the tall girls and kicking at the dirt aimlessly is what I choose to do while the teacher talks. He lets the group know we will be running in two lots and have to complete two rounds of 400m in less than 3 minutes. I keep a passive face and tighten my burgundy ribbon in my hair. 3 minutes isn't hard at all. I should be able to keep a steady pace without stressing myself out and still make the time.

"Paisley and Kirsten, you two can go first since you enjoy turning up at your own leisurely pace. Another four of you join them. Go!" He claps as he says the last word. We head over and line up in our lanes. I look to either side of me, smiling at the girls that decided to go first with me and Kirsten.

"You coming to the after party tonight, Paisley?" one girl with blonde highlighted hair asks me. A friendly smile follows her question. I shake my head and scrunch my nose up.

"Sadly, not tonight. I'm in dire need of some study for exercise science. Science is the only class I am really struggling with and of all weeks, my science test is in two days."

"That's tough luck for real!" she announces and then turns back toward the track, getting into her starting stance. I nod my head and chew the inside of my cheek. Yeap real bad luck, but going to a party mid-week isn't the best idea for me anyway. I have only been properly drunk once at a mixer and the next day wasn't pretty. If I get too tempted to drink tonight, I won't be making school at all tomorrow.

"On your marks..." Mr Richards calls out, positioning himself beside the starting lineup. He bangs the two bits of box wood together and we all take off at the same time. Kirsten sprints in front of us all and I smirk. That girl will never learn. She burns out every time. We make the 200m meter mark with ease and I settle into a decent pace. I'm surprising myself but I have been doing more lengths in our pool this summer so maybe it has helped my fitness. That and the rigorous cheer routines for tonight's game.

Me and another girl are almost even as we gain on Kirsten who is starting to burn off and slow her pace. Another fifty meters and I'm right behind her.

"That better not be you up my butt Paisley!" she chuckles without looking back.

"Girlfriend, you are a slow learner."

"I know. But one of these days I want to pretend I can be an Olympic track runner and sprint this track in record time to get it over and done with." Her sentence comes out with a deep wheeze at the end. She's losing her breath.

"I see the logic, but it's not working very well," I say as I catch right up to her and run side by side. We fall into a quick run, and she works hard to match my pace. We pass the 400m and I side eye her with a smirk.

"One more lap then we sit back and watch everyone else struggle," I huff out. I stare ahead, trying to focus on nothing but my breathing when I see a group of guys leaning over the fence under the stadium seats. They wolf whistle loudly and chuckle while we jog past. I want to flip them the bird but I clench my fists and keep them tight at my sides. Kirsten's arm catches my attention as it reaches above my head, all the while we keep our pace. My eyes flick up and I burst out laughing. She read my mind and being more outspoken, she flipped the group the bird instead. Our feet continue pounding on the lanes when I risk glancing back over my shoulder. Nate is now there, with no shirt on and talking to the group that just whistled to us. The group walk away, as Nate turns and looks back toward me. Because I'm still running and not watching where I am going, I stumble and fly forwards. I manage to stay on my feet and keep running but I'm agitated now. I can feel eyes at my back and I grow red knowing that Nate and the class would have seen the reason for my stupid fall. Sweat beads across my upper lip as we come to the last 100m. Embarrassment, summer heat, and sprints don't leave me feeling lady-like at all.

As I make it across the finish line, I lean forward and clutch my knees with both hands. My back moves rapidly as I try to huff in large puffs of air. Kirsten mimics my stance and starts gasping for air beside me then pats me on the back.

"Easy peasy right," she giggles on an exhale. I nod and stand straight.

"Easy *fucking* peasy," I agree and look toward where Nate was frowning. He's still standing there, staring directly at me. I pace over to him now that the rest of the class is lining up for their turn, and his eyes narrow as I get closer. He's in loose basketball type shorts that are slung low on his hip bones and he isn't wearing a t-shirt. He glowers at me as I close the distance between us and I wonder what the heck his problem is. I should be the one that is mad. I was trying to focus on my run and him and his friends had to be disgusting horny humans as per usual.

I cross my arms over my chest when I come to a stop and Nate's eyes follow the movement. They flick back to me and he tilts his head, holding my gaze while he leans against the barrier fence. His toned arms ripple under the movement and I have to fight against the urge to reach out and drag a finger along his forearm to see if they are as hard as they look.

I clear my throat and lift my chin slightly. "Shouldn't you be doing school work?"

He smirks at me as if finding amusement in my words.

"Out here doing physical education just as you are," he replies in his deep voice. His tall body casts a cooling shadow over me but the way he says physical sends a thrill through me. It almost drips off his tongue.

"Your friends are gone, so I'm guessing you're meant to be back with your teacher."

He frowns deeply, then with a small flick of his head, he clears his ebony hair from his eyes.

"They aren't my friends."

"Well whatever they are."

"They're gone because I told them to stop staring at what doesn't belong to them." He almost sighs and stands straight once more.

"Oh, so you're doing the annoying big brother thing where you scare every male off? Guess what? I can handle myself!" I assure him in a scorning tone.

A look flashes across his features before his face grows passive. He starts slowly stepping backwards.

"Get yourself some new fucking shorts and some dignity while you're at it," he bites out and turns to leave. My mouth hangs open while I watch him jog off back into the men's changing rooms. *Fucking asshole!* I glance down at my bare legs and then head back to my waiting class, feeling more agitated. Other girls have smaller shorts than me and I can wear whatever I like.

"Everyone do some stretches then get changed and head to your next classes," Mr Richards instructs us all. I pull one leg up behind me and hold it by the foot while stretching my neck side to side.

"I don't know who's hotter. Your older brother or Mr Richards..." Kirsten whispers all giddily. I frown at her and roll my eyes.

"Nothing attractive about Nate."

"What's your problem?" she asks, giving me side eye now and following my stretches.

"Just sick of my brothers, I guess. Growing up in their shadow my entire life is getting tiring."

"Your brothers won't be here next year."

"I'm sure they will still find a way to control my every move."

Chapter 3

Hours later we are changed into our matching cheer skirts and tops. I smile back at my reflection in the locker room mirrors. I plant my hands on my hips and turn side to side, feeling proud. Sara comes up behind me and checks her hair and makeup in the same mirror. She's much taller than me so she can just do it over the top of my head. I smirk up at her, meeting her eyes in the mirror. She matches my smile while all the other girls around us share the same buzz of energy.

"Huddle together girls!" our captain, Lily, calls out. We all turn around and meet her in the middle of the room. It's crowded with us all in here.

"Right girls, this is our final big game before summer break. Let's go out there and support our boys. Grizzlies on three! One, two, three!" she chants out loudly.

"Grizzlies!" We all put our hands in and scream in unison.

We jog single file out into the gym. The atmosphere is addictive, the cheers are deafening, and we keep wide grins on our faces, which we have practiced countless times and wave to the crowd. My hands meet together as I give a small clap to our group to hype us up more. We create a tight triangle shape with the captain right at the front, leading our performance. I side eye Kirsten with a smirk and then look dead ahead with my game face on again.

"Big Grizzlies hear them roar!" the captain chants loudly.

"Big Grizzlies hear them roar!" we all chant back perfectly in time then clap twice. My hands drop back down onto my hips.

"Big Grizzlies, they have claws!"

"Big Grizzlies, they have claws!"

We clap three times. My fingers grip my hips as the tension coils within me like a snake desperately wanting to be let out.

"Watch out while they gnash their teeth!"

"Watch out while they gnash their teeth!"

"The trophy is theirs for keeps!"

"The trophy is theirs for keeps!"

"Goooooooo Grizzlies!" we all scream then the music starts. The 8 count runs through my head as we spread out from our tight formation. Our hands whip up, one at a time changing from hips to air and back again. The front row drop down onto their knees as the entire middle row and myself raise both our arms, run two steps then throw ourselves into a spin tuck. We land on our feet then clap three times, chanting loudly. I hold a smile on my face, but my knee has a deep throbbing in it from the landing I just stuck.

We jog backwards, four strides like we have practiced so many times, weaving back through the girls that are also getting off the ground now. We form a tight formation once more, and then Nellie eases into the middle, getting ready for us to toss her. Four of us make eye contact and nod, with hands connecting in the middle and energy buzzing between us.

I have a love-hate relationship with tossing. It's our biggest crowd pleaser, but also scary as shit to have this responsibility on our hands. It needs to be perfect every time because if it's not, it usually means someone gets injured badly. We drop our hands down and Nellie hoists herself onto them.

The routine from the other cheerleaders carries on around us as we prepare. Waiting for our moment, we bend one knee slightly and I grimace. That pain becomes more persistent with every movement. "5, 6, 7, 8" we chant between us and then throw Nellie high in the air. We look up at the same time, watching her tuck her arms and twirl elegantly in the air toward the ceiling. She starts tumbling toward us, and we brace with the knee lowered again, bracing for her weight. Her feet make contact and we hold strong. Her arms come out and the crowd cheers. We lower her and start clapping and cheering before we form two straight lines and march to the gym opening where our basketball players will enter the court.

We stay in two lines, facing each other as the players file out in a jog. My brother, Bradey, is the third one in line and he winks at me as he passes by. I roll my eyes and Kirsten elbows my ribs, giggling then carrying on like our interaction never happened. Once all the players are on the court getting the crowd revved up, the visitor team—the other team—make their way out. The Hawks have an eye-catching baby blue color kit with black lettering and a black and white hawk emblem. We stand tall and respectfully but basketball players still tend to tower over us. Their strong musk deodorant fills the air as their faces hold smug grins. They know they are the team we need to beat.

As the last of them walk past us, the second to last one catches my eye. He has deep blue eyes, with brown, thick eyelashes and ear length hair that is parted down the middle. He has a baby face but in a handsome way. He flicks his head sharply, tossing his hair away from his eyes and he winks at me while biting his lip.

My head follows him all the way until he stands alongside the rest of his team. The girls start moving but I'm glued to the same place until some of my teammates nudge me. Trying to get out of this trance, I shake my head and stride to our front row seats where we will watch the game.

Kirsten sits down beside me and leans close to my ear, whispering quietly so only we can hear.

"Put your tongue back in your mouth, doll."

I slide my eyes across to her, fighting my smile.

"He is fucking drop dead gorgeous. Too bad he's the competition."

She shrugs her shoulders while her horny eyes roam over the opposing team. "Only have to act volatile to them until the games are over," she murmurs.

The referee comes on and does a coin toss with the two captains and then the game begins.

Hawks have the advantage straight away, starting with the ball and getting a 3 pointer off it straight away.

I dig both my thumbs into my sore knee while intently watching the game. I massage it over and over again, trying to convince myself that it was just a bad landing. The Grizzlies catch up and get a good 3 points from my brother's best friend, Tommy. The rest of the game passes by quickly, with a range of cheers and ahhhh's.

Out of habit I straighten my ribbon in my high ponytail and stand up. We clap and cheer as full time is called on the game with a win to us by one field goal.

Some of the Hawks players come over to us, egging everyone on and shaking our hands. Getting the crowd stirred up comes with the territory of these big college games. The babyface boy comes over with another three and makes headway directly in my direction. *Act casual Paisley*, I grill myself. I try to look around, so my eyes divert everywhere, but in his direction. Rather than looking cool, sophisticated and casual I end up looking like a loser because he chuckles when he comes to a stop in front of me. My brows furrow together as my cheeks warm.

"Something on the ceiling we need to be looking out for?" his deep, yet immature voice asks me. My sight drops so that I'm looking straight ahead at his face. His vision peaks upwards and roams the ceiling, mocking me.

"Sad about the loss," I say, trying to taunt him. His face drops down to me so we are now eye to eye. His eyes wrinkle at the sides and his face morphs into that boyish, confident grin again.

"My mind might have been on something else tonight."

"I wouldn't admit that to your teammates."

He shrugs then his shoulders shake as he chuckles.

"Might be worth all the crap I'm going to cop later for it. Name's Leith," he says. I smirk at him and shake my head in disbelief. This guy sure does just dive right in. It's kind of hot though.

"Well nice to meet you, Leith," I murmur and start walking off. He lightly wraps his fingers around my wrist with a lust-filled look.

"We have a break-up party at one of the boys' houses on the weekend. You should come?" He almost pleads. I tilt my head at him, feeling my big bow flop to the side and rest on my ear. His eyes follow the movements.

"Grizzlies probably aren't welcome on your side of town."

"Nah, just a stupid rivalry, and you're not a basketball player," he encourages me. I can feel my near non-existent defiance dissolving.

"Can I bring a friend?"

"Bring two if you want. As long as you will come."

"What's the address?"

He repeats the address to me as his teammates start pushing him away and laughing while calling him a lover boy. I turn my back on him and walk away as Nate climbs down the grandstand seats and wraps his arm around me protectively. He glares at Leith over his shoulder and pulls me toward where the rest of the team are still standing and celebrating by the court.

I inwardly cringe and drop my head because Nate's tall and sovereign presence scares every man off that even bats an eyelid at me. But then I hear Leith's voice, distant but loud enough.

"Can I at least have your name?"

I bare my teeth with my wide giddy grin and throw over my shoulder loudly. "Paisley!" I snicker.

"Who the fuck is that?" Nate asks in a hushed yet scornful tone while he glares at him over his shoulder.

"Leith and he invited me to a party."

"Like fuck you're going..." he growls at me quietly as we get closer to our school supporters and team.

"Stop playing overprotective brother. I'm allowed to get a boyfriend one day."

I can feel Nate's dark gaze on me and his arm around me goes tense like a vise as the words leave my mouth.

My mom meets us by the court, holding the tray of my cupcakes. I take them from her hands and mouth a *thank you*.

"I made cupcakes for everyone!" I announce loudly.

Kirsten, Sara and some other girls each pluck one off the tray.

"Girl you are hilarious. But don't ever stop making these sweet things," Sara says while taking a mouthful of icing.

The basketball team surrounds me, taking cupcakes and leaving the tray bare. I smile proudly as I watch them all get eaten. Out the corner of my eye I see a burgundy Grizzly hoody weave through the crowd. I turn my head and watch Nate walk off and force the exit door open as he storms out. I shake my head and look at Mom, shrugging. She shrugs back and eyes the door that has now slammed shut.

I will never understand that guy, but it's probably better I don't try.

Chapter 4

I lie in bed the next morning, staring at the ceiling, trying to distract myself with the way the glimpses of morning sun bounces off the crystal chandelier that hangs from my matte white ceiling.

Forcing out a long deep breath I flop my arms onto my thick, baby pink comforter, not yet wanting to start my day. I don't want to face the reality of my life right now. My knee feels hot and tender, letting me know that as much as I wanted to pretend I was perfectly fine, that in fact I did some damage to my knee when I landed last night.

I gnaw at my bottom lip while I tell myself to be brave and try stretching my leg out to test it after a night's rest. As I tense my leg, ready to stretch it, I cringe in pain and let it relax onto my mattress once more. Tears well up in my eyes. For a cheerleader this is a killer, for a cheerleader desperate to be the next captain it's a complete game over. Even if I miss a few game nights and heal okay this will always be on the coaches' mind. Injured girls are always sidelined because the likelihood of that injury reoccurring is strong.

My hand flicks over to the walnut colored beside table and I pick up my phone to check my notifications. I hold the phone over my face, looking up into my flashing screen. I scroll through messages from the girls, still buzzing about last night's game and us pulling off a flawless routine. As I flick my thumb over the screen, going down the notifications further, my lips twitch as I fight a giddy smile that wants to beam bright. Leith has started following me on my socials and sent me a private message. I open it and giggle.

Leith: Is it creepy I found you just from your first name?

My fingers fly over the screen, tapping frantically as I reply.

Extremely. I may call the cops.

I intend to move on to my next messages, assuming Leith would be busy getting ready for school but I see he's typing. I hopelessly stare at the bright screen, still half asleep, waiting for his reply to be sent through.

My phone vibrates.

Leith: Can you get me arrested after the party this weekend?

It is a possibility.... Only because I want to partake in disgusting drinking games and consume free alcohol.

Leith: Fair Call. I'll be waiting for the cops Sunday morning while I am having the worst hangover of my life.

Perfect. I will tell them to look for the dying teenager

Leith: Handsome** dying teenager

Not vain at all.

Leith: Was just fishing for a compliment. My pride is questioning life right now.

I giggle quietly while gazing into my phone before I hear a forced cough from my bedroom door. I jump, just slightly because I didn't realize anyone had opened my bedroom door. My eyes meet Nate's and I arch an eyebrow at him.

"You not swimming?" I ask, genuinely curious because if he isn't swimming here in the mornings, he's usually already at the town pool doing lengths.

He leans one shoulder against the door frame and pushes his hands in his denim shorts pockets. His lips thin into a disgruntled line and I frown.

"Seriously, what is eating you at the moment?"

He shrugs a shoulder with a solemn look crossing over his features before he blinks a few times, looking over the length of my body. I'm glad I am covered by my blanket because the way he has been looking at me lately makes me feel so exposed.

"How'd your routine go last night?"

His question takes me by surprise. Not just because his deep, demanding voice trickles over a part of me that shouldn't feel *something*, but because he watched the entire performance. Like he has with all my other performances.

"Good. No fuck up's so that's something."

I drop my phone beside me, all of a sudden forgetting I was intoxicated by Leith's messages only moments ago.

Nate stares at me intently and then looks directly at where he knows my leg is under the blanket.

"How's the legs?" he asks in a *I'm not fucking stupid* voice.

My eyes widen briefly, giving away my surprise.

"How did..." I start, wanting to ask how he knew but he shakes his head, cutting off my words. Rage flashes through his eyes as he meets my own with a fierce look.

"With you Paisley, I miss nothing. Your eyes are a mirror to your every emotion and every fucking feeling," he says, making my mouth go dry. He has always been my brother's best friend and to me at least, my brother, but he's always been someone that has been an unconditional support to me. Through primary, middle school bullies in my pre teens, when my brother was a wanker he would check in on me. Little things here and there that always kept our private connection strong. Sure, he has his hidden personal life, but if something is wrong with me, he's the first to somehow know and first to support me.

As I stare at him with tears welling up in my eyes he speaks again.

"I saw the change in your eyes when you landed. How bad is it?"

My chin trembles and I sit up in bed. My hair brushes against my bare shoulder before it settles against my back.

"Not great. It's on fire this morning. I need to hide it from the coaches. I need to make captain next year."

He stays silent while drilling holes into me. I feel seen, exposed and fragile. I don't like feeling vulnerable in any sense of the word.

Finally, he shifts his position and steps into the room, coming over to the bed.

"Show me," is all he says in a hushed tone.

I slide my blanket back and hiss when I try to lift my leg out. Nate sits on the edge of the bed and pushes my leg back down, then tugs the blanket the entire way down to my ankles. My black, satin PJ shorts and singlet contrast against my white sheets and pink duvet set. His fingers drift over my knee and slide underneath. His touch sends a whisper of dark desire through me so I try to pull away from him.

"I'm fine. I'll ice it and be on my way," I assure him as I scream inside my head that I am sick and need therapy. I need to get away from Nate.

One of his hands grip around my calf muscle tightly and his head whips up, dark eyes meeting with mine intently.

"Don't be fucking stupid Paisley," he growls at me and uses his other hand to softly feel around my knee. He does it quietly, completely lost in thought while he gently feels the swollen, tender parts of my joint. I look down at it and grimace. It's swollen so I don't know how I can hide this from anyone.

"Is being captain really that important?" he asks me. I do a double take and frown.

"It's what I have been striving toward since I could walk."

"You try to please people way too much. Everyone at college are mindless fucks."

My mouth grows dry as I fight the urge to burst into tears. Then I finally find the courage to speak when I'm certain I can hold the tears back.

"It's all I have ever wanted. I am finally in a position where I can trial for an elite all star team and compete at worlds. Being captain for our college team will help even more."

"Yeah well, I don't think any of them deserve the pedestal you put them on. And one day you will realize cheerleading is just fucking cheerleading. It's not a make or break moment in your life."

I suck in a breath when he finishes speaking. His fingers gently massage my knee. I look over his black hair that almost hides his face from me. *Almost.*

A long breath escapes him and he places my leg back on the mattress before he gets up and pulls my comforter back over me.

"I'll try to get you in with my physio. Ice it while you eat breakfast and strap it today," he bites out then leaves my room. I am thankful, even though his kindness is usually wrapped with agitation and a hint of darkness. I know he has a good physio though. I have never needed one, but Nate got shoulder pain last swimming season so Mom and Dad hired the best for him to be able to heal quickly and win the state championship.

Awkwardly, I bum shuffle to the side of the bed and gingerly slide my legs over the edge. I rest all my weight on my good leg and then tip toe on my other foot, testing my weight.

A deep ache spreads through the muscles, settling right down into the joint. I suck in a breath and look up at the ceiling with my hands gripping my hips tightly. I blink rapidly while sending a silent prayer to whatever god may be out there listening to me right now. This entire year has gone perfectly so far. Why is the universe turning it all to shit?

Carefully, I limp out of my bedroom, and stumble down the staircase to the main living area, then make my way to the kitchen. It's only me down here. Who knows where Nate has skulked off to, probably the pool and from the sound of the shower, I'm assuming Bradey is in the shower.

Mom and Dad should already be at work. I grab a tub of yoghurt and muesli mix from the fridge and slide it across the granite island to where I will sit. Reaching down into the freezer beneath it, I grab out a gel ice pack and hobble over to the barstool.

While perching on the edge of it, I rest my foot on the small rail and press the gel pack onto my swollen knee. Thinking over my earlier exchange with Nate, I look around the expansive kitchen space. I'll grab tape when I finish my breakfast, but doing the physio means I need to talk to Nate again and get my appointment time. I don't like the thought of that.

Nate has always been one of my favorite people in the entire world. But as of late, lines between us are becoming a little blurred. I don't know if he notices the change in me whenever he's around, but I find myself more aware of his chiseled shoulders from swimming, his prominent V shape under his navel when his sweatpants and shorts hang low on him. And his secretive eyes that hold so many thoughts that seemed to stay locked up tightly.

Him and Bradey are as close as most best friends and brothers can be. But even then, from my observation, Nate doesn't tell my brother what shady thoughts loom in those desirable eyes.

Bradey walks in whistling loudly, pulling me from my intoxicating thoughts. I swing round quickly so my legs are tucked under the countertop and I fight with all my willpower to not cry out when the pain radiates through me once more.

"You riding with Sara?" Bradey asks me while looking through the fridge for breakfast ingredients. I glare at him, showing him I'm not stupid. He only asks about what I'm up to when he wants to perve at my friends. I have learnt that the hard way over the years.

"Well you won't take me, will you?"

"You could be a big girl and get Mom and Dad to just buy you a car." He shrugs as if it makes his selfish ways okay.

"Yeah, because it makes so much sense for all of us going in our own cars when we go from the same house to the same destination."

"I have after school plans, it's just easier you get your own ride."

"Mhmmm," I say while opening my muesli so I don't retaliate. It's fruitless. He doesn't give a shit if I get upset. Bradey grabs out a ready-made smoothie and side eyes me while he walks out.

"Your eating habits are becoming worse and worse Bradey. You need to eat solid food!"

"And you need to start worrying about someone that deserves it." He throws over his shoulder as he walks out the door. Nate jogs through the kitchen, grabbing his sports bag off the barstool beside me as he goes.

"I'll message you later with the deets, *sis*," he murmurs as he leaves, trailing Bradey again. The way he drawled out the sis makes me stare into his exiting back for the second time in twenty-four hours, hurt by the sarcastic statement in the word.

Chapter 5

I sit leisurely under a large oak tree with other girls on the college park-like grounds out the front. I received some strange looks today with my long, black linen slacks. Our school uniform is simple, with black bottoms and the school shirt that consists of t-shirts, blouses, knits and soft-shell jackets.

But wearing pants compared to my usual bike shorts or mini skirt at the start of a major heat wave draws attention from other students. I keep telling everyone I couldn't find any clean shorts or skirts but I don't how believable it is. I wonder what kind of scenarios they're all creating in their heads to explain my pants but I know they'll all be off the mark.

My strawberry blonde hair rests in waves over my chest, with my school bow tied neatly on the top of my head. I like my hair in the summertime. It gets natural blonde highlights running through it. In the fall, my hair looks more auburn, making me feel like a Halloween pumpkin in itself.

Sara and Kirsten shuffle closer to me, caging me in from either side. Kirsten tucks her converses under her butt while she smiles at me intently and Sara clears her throat. I roll my eyes and smile.

"This ought to be trouble."

Sara lightly brushes her fingers over her chest and scoffs, pretending to take offense to my statement.

"Why Paisley, that's not very kind."

I laugh and feel the heaviness of this morning melt away.

"Spit it out you two."

Kirsten turns further toward me and puts her hands together in a begging gesture.

"You need to go to the party this weekend, so we can go to the party," she finishes by giving me her best puppy dog eyes. I groan and twist some hair around my fingers.

"They are all from the opposition and imagine what shit we will get from the girls over that side."

"Fuck them, Hawks girls are trash." Sara almost spits out.

"Jesus, that's not very nice," I say, but I also can't disagree. We come across them at cheerleading competitions and they are a whole 'nother level of bitchy.

"We can ignore them. Maybe even talk to them nicely," Kirsten says encouragingly.

"Argh! Do you think Leith will look after us if we go? I don't know him well enough and I don't know. I guess I feel like we are throwing ourselves into the lion's den."

"He seems really nice. And we will take one of our cars so we can leave as soon as we need to if shit goes down." Kirsten once again comes in with the positive encouragement.

"Fine!" I agree, sounding reluctant but it didn't take much to convince me. I want to see how their house parties stack up to ours.

"Yes! We can get ready at your place, Paisley, since it's closer to their place."

It's my turn to scoff at Sara. I arch an eyebrow at her with a smirk dancing on my lips.

"Oh, wouldn't it be because you like to drool over both my brothers?"

She pouts at me. "I need to take one for a ride before they both leave college."

"Do you really need to or want to? Very different."

"Need! Experimental purposes."

"I don't get it."

"Well you see, Bradey apparently is really good with his tongue," Sara says in a rush and I throw my hand up so my flat palm is facing her.

"Stop right now." I gag.

"*Annnnnd* we have heard rumors about Nate but we don't actually know anyone that has slept with him. I need to see ya know, if he's as good as we all imagine, or a dud." She shrugs on the last word.

I shake my head and check the time on my phone, trying to get the image out of my head. And the instant jealousy when she mentioned having sex with Nate.

"Have you ever thought about sleeping with him?" Kirsten says from the other side of me, grabbing my attention.

"Who?" I ask, almost confused.

"Nate," she says like I'm being dumb.

"Ew he is my brother."

"No he isn't. He is a hot stray your parents took in but he isn't related to you."

"Don't call him a stray. That's mean," I say sternly. I could never see him as a stray.

"I meant it as a joke. But the second part is still true although you are right. We all see you as having two brothers. It would be weird."

"Well I don't look at him that way so it doesn't matter."

The bell rings out through the school yard before everyone starts standing up. I don't want to try and stand in front of the girls. My phone pings, distracting me. I hold it up to see that Nate messaged me.

"I'll catch up to you in class, just need to check my messages."

They all wave to me as they walk off in a tight group. I lean against the tree truck and slide my eyes from the leaving group and down to my phone.

Nate: Meet me in the parking lot in 10

I stare at the screen with my thumb hovering over the keypad. Being close to Nate doesn't seem like the best idea right now.

I message Leith instead and smile as I tap the words out and hit send.

What time is appropriate for you to get arrested after the party?

The typing words come up and I eagerly wait for his reply.

> Leith: After we have had time to swap our life stories and drink cheap liquor of course.

I start typing my reply, liking this easy going conversation with Leith when I catch Nate out of my peripheral vision. My head whips up and I stare at him as he paces closer to me.

"This isn't the car park," he barks at me.

"I could say the same to you!"

"Ten means now."

He leans down and pulls my phone off me and glares at the screen. He drops the phone into his back pocket before wrapping his strong hands around my dainty fingers and pulls me up. I grimace and chew the inside of my cheek while I fight pained tears.

"How you going to party this weekend when you can barely walk?"

"I can sit and drink."

Nate steps closer to me and pulls at a long wavy piece of hair before he flicks it back over my shoulder.

"Quite smitten with him, aren't you?" he says quietly. I swallow thickly, taking the risk of looking up into his brooding gaze. Big mistake because as soon as I do, I get lost in Nate's world again. I openly stare into his serious face before my attention drops down to his mouth. A lopsided smirk tugs at his lips before he runs his tongue over the front of his teeth.

I cough slightly and step back, away from Nate.

"He's nice," I mumble sheepishly.

"Who knew any old nice guy could have you falling head over heels?"

"Shut up, why do you always have to be a prick?"

Nate slips his hand around my backpack and slings it over his shoulder then nods his head toward the car park, gesturing for me to follow. I limp carefully beside him when he speaks again.

"Tell me does Mr Nice Guy know you have injured your leg?"

"No, why would it be any of his business?"

Nate's hefty shoulders shrug, showing his indifference. "Well guess I may be a prick but I'm the one helping you achieve your pathetic dreams. Mr Nice Guy probably cares more about shoving his limp cock in you."

My eyes widen and I trudge forward, ignoring the pain that screams at me. This is the most Nate has said to me in a long time.

"We're leaving in your brother's car," he says from behind me, with a hint of humor in his tone. He always seems to find it funny when I get angry at him.

I hate that he can get under my skin so easily.

"No shit, kinda figured. And he's *our* brother."

We step up to my brother's matte black jeep and I climb in when it's unlocked. Nate tries to help me but I brush him off.

Nate climbs into the driver's side, turning the key and letting the vehicle roar to life. Angrily, he pushes the stick into drive. He says nothing but his brows settle above his eyes and his silver band on his thumb taps on the steering wheel rapidly.

I stare out the window as we drive past the large lake toward the main township. My fingers lightly flex over my leg as I feel lost without my phone and remember that Nate took it. While I rest my other elbow on the window frame, I tap my chin, growing frustrated that I easily lost all thought of replying to Leith's message again when Nate was in my presence.

We show up to the Health Hub on the other side of our small town. It's one of two medical centers in Burke Town. It's a decently sized town but small compared to all our neighboring ones.

I slowly climb down and step onto the sidewalk, then limp through the entrance. The pale gray tiled foyer takes us to the front reception desk. Nate nods to the older lady at reception and she smiles sweetly at him then moves her gaze to mine.

"Miss Wilson, head to the second waiting room where the physio studio is."

"Thank you," I quietly say, because the initial waiting room for the GP is full. Nate leads me down the corridor before we get to a smaller waiting room. He sits down, and then links his fingers in mine and pulls me down so I'm sitting beside him.

He says nothing but flicks on his phone, mindlessly scrolling and watching videos.

"Can I have my phone?" I ask in a hushed tone so I don't draw attention to us.

He side eyes me and shakes his head then goes back to scrolling on his phone.

"Why not?"

He lets out a long sigh, not bothering to hide his agitation. "You can have your phone back after your appointment. Don't need you distracted."

"Do you ever get sick of being a dickwad to me?" I ask a little louder this time. An old man looks up from his home and garden magazine and scowls in my direction. I drop my gaze, growing embarrassed. Nate glares at the old man, staring at him in an uncomfortable way until the old man looks away.

"Stop doing that."

"Doing what?" I ask, confused by my brother once more.

"Letting people walk all over you."

"I don't do that. I'm just a kind person, you should try being at least friendly sometime," I suggest and pull my hand away from his so I can cross my arms across my chest.

"I'm friendly enough to you."

"Semi friendly and family doesn't count."

"Miss Wilson?" A young woman pokes her head out of her door. She looks early thirties max and eyes me expectantly as she pushes her glasses up the bridge of her nose. The clear, large frame on her makes her look trendy but professional. Nate stands first and helps me up and I let him. As much as I grow tired of his hot and cold ways, I'm not going to turn down help from the only person in my life that seems to know everything about me. Even if I know nothing about him.

I step forward, trying to angle around him but he steps with me, keeping his fingers tightly on my hand again.

"You don't need to come in with me," I bite quietly through gritted teeth.

"I need to talk to her about my shoulder while I am here." He looks down to my face when he talks. I nod once and trail behind him as we go into the room. That makes sense. Two birds and one stone.

I expect a clinical looking room, sterile of sorts. But as I shut the door gently behind me, I see splashes of bright colors amongst the gray and creme speckled pair of two-seater couches. There's burnt orange and blue rounded cushions on both couches, with abstract canvases on the walls in matching colors. The doctor is seated on the furthest couch, waiting for us so I sit opposite her with Nate, close to her large Monstera plant that's in a yellow pot. I look around, assessing the green and yellow vases on the coffee table before I finally focus on her.

"Good afternoon, I'm Kendra. What can I do for you, Miss Wilson?"

"Ah I hurt my knee last night when I was landing a front flip cheerleading." She nods as I speak and writes down notes on her Ipad. Nate leans back against the back of the couch, stretching one arm along the top. His white t-shirt and black shorts sag against the couch with him.

"Okay can you put any weight on it?"

"No, when I do the pain is excruciating."

"Okay can you roll up your pants? I will take a look."

I do as she says and she moves around and perches on the edge of her coffee table while taking a look at it. She stays silent while feeling around my knee.

"Because of how swollen it is, I wouldn't mind sending you for an ultrasound on it first to see what the damage is."

I nod gently, feeling solemn. She writes a referral and hands it to me. "Head on through to radiology around the other side of reception. They should be able to get you in while you are here and I will make another appointment with you when I have the results. But for now keep strapping it, arnica cream and use crutches." She moves to the side of her room where there is exercise equipment and grabs a pair of crutches from the cupboard.

"I can't use those."

"Your hand broken?" she says but sounds like annoyed sarcasm.

"No, I don't want the team knowing about the injury. I have practice this week, is there anything I can do to speed up the healing?"

"Not until you have had the ultrasound."

I stand up, using the couch armchair this time to help me and take the referral from her.

"I will be okay without the crutches."

She stares at me for a moment then arches an eyebrow "I'll make a note to say that you are going against what I advise. But do as you wish." She then turns her head to Nate who is standing beside me now. "How's the shoulder?"

"Yeah really good." His deep voice echoes around the room.

"Don't need me to look at it while you're here?"

"Nah I'm good thanks."

"Okay take care," she says. I look up to see Nate frowning. Mother fucker lied to sit in my appointment.

"Should go get this ultrasound done, don't you think?" He gestures for me to go first out the door. I glare at him angrily as I walk past.

Chapter 6

"Wear the pink and white floral dress," Kirsten insists while doing a full twist in front of my full length mirror. Sara slides fresh red gloss over her lips in the small desk mirror while making 'mmmm' sounds, agreeing with Kirsten.

"Is it too girly and cutesy for a college party though? I want to wear my oversized t-shirt and shorts." I say feeling unsure now and picking at the soft hem.

Sara stands up and pats her straightened hair down out of habit.

"Nope we are all going in dresses. Here, take a sip of this for liquid courage." Sara hands me an opened bottle of wine. It already has our lipstick marks on it. I take a huge drink and cough when I pull the bottle away from my lips.

"I fucking hate sav," I wheeze when I hand it back.

The girls laugh and then Sara takes a swallow and passes it to Kirsten. I toss my oversized t-shirt over my head and onto my large bed. Plucking the dress up with my freshly painted nails, I cry internally. If we were at our own guys' party I would feel more comfortable. But I'd rather be over-looked than draw attention to myself tonight.

Although if I went to one of our house parties, I would probably have my brothers shadowing me anyway, so why would it matter what I wore? I pulled the remainder of the strapping tape off this morning and spent half an hour exfoliating my legs and moisturizing them so no one could tell I had sticky tape on them for three days.

I wanted to pretend everything was okay, but the pain is constant. I told the team this week I have had migraines from hay fever so I couldn't do any tumbling and tossing safely this week. They seemed to be okay with that excuse. Although, I don't know how long that will last. My doctor wants me in to physio first thing Monday morning and I am nervous about my results after my ultrasound.

There's a part of me that knows this isn't just a pulled muscle. I carefully shimmy into the floral dress, trying not to pull at my painted eyelashes and freshly curled hair. Pangs of guilt stab at me that I haven't told my two best friends about my injury. They have always had my back, but there is an underlying competition between us. We all want to be captain next year. It's something we have all worked hard for, and although I don't think they would hold my accident against me, part of me is afraid the desire to be captain will overshadow our friendship bonds. I know how badly they want to be noticed by the coach and school.

As I run my hands over my bodice, smoothing the light fabric over my torso, I realize how much I love doing nice things for the people around me, yet don't really trust anyone completely. Except one moody person down the hallway. I haven't talked to him all week, and I certainly haven't told him about my appointment on Monday. But that's because my mind and body are on two very different wavelengths when it comes to him, not because I don't trust him.

"Get your runners on so we can get a photo!" Sara squeals and runs out the bedroom. She's already tipsy and I know exactly where she's headed. There are loud voices and then loud flirtatious laughing that becomes louder as they get closer to our room once more.

"One photo, stop being a spoilsport!" Sara giggles with a pretend pissed off Bradey on her arm. He loves the attention, especially from my friends.

He winks at me and then lets out a big sigh.

"Fine, just one photo." His deep voice scorns us three. Sara pulls me and Kirsten on either side of her and holds us by our hips. We all smile while Bradey takes the photo. He then does a reverse camera and takes one of his face photo bombing us. Sara snatches the phone playfully off him while I try not to gag.

"Here, take another mouthful. You're gonna need it," Kirsten whispers and holds the last of the wine out to me.

I wrap my fingers around the long neck, feeling a deep frown occupy my forehead. "Might need more than this."

"Let's go. I'm driving and staying sober tonight so I need to at least make this shit fun."

"I'll meet you all downstairs!" I say as they all leave my room. Bradey stops in the doorway and turns back to me.

He stares me down before speaking. "Be careful out there tonight."

"Nothing's going to go wrong," I say, feeling a little shocked he seems to give a shit.

"Crap aside, I know you're okay around our crew so I don't need to worry apart from making sure roaming hands don't land on you. With the Hawks I don't fucking know them, Paisley. And I don't like having to fucking worry."

He pushes off the door frame and walks away. I hear a door slam a moment later so I know he has gone back to his room. I hobble over to my bedside drawer and take out some pain killers then wash them down with the last of the wine.

I don't know how I'm going to handle a party tonight without falling on the ground in a crying heap but I do what I can to forget. I limp out of my room, enjoying taking the weight off my sore knee, before I have to go back to putting weight on it so my friends don't notice my hobble. I reach the top of the staircase and wrap my fingers around the stair rail before looking down the bottom of the stairs.

Nate is standing against the bottom rail, wearing a loose singlet and black washed denim shorts. His arms are crossed and I try desperately to keep my eyes on his face instead of squinting to admire every detail of those athletic arms. His black hair is messy over the front of his face with only parts of his face visible.

"You going to come down?" His deep husky voice sends a thrill through me.

I swallow thickly as I slowly walk down the stairs. My nose scrunches tightly on the fourth step when the pain becomes too much. Nate flicks his hair back, while his furious gaze meets mine. Two long strides before he reaches me and takes me under my shoulder. "How the fuck do you think you're going to party with these dimwits if you can't even make it down the stairs?"

"So it was a test?"

"Observation, Paisley," is all he says.

"If I ignore it for long enough it may just go away," I say pitifully.

His brooding temper shows with the tremble that rattles his body. Tensley, he settles me onto the ground level and slowly steps back.

"Do you think little lover boy will be able to help you tonight if you get too drunk and hurt yourself more?"

"I won't let that happen," I say carefully, not breaking eye contact so he knows how serious I am. His angry gaze rakes over my dress then slowly over the curled tendrils of hair hanging over where my breasts are before he drags them back to my face. I feel like I'm being stalked by a predator. I let my stare drift off to the large antique mirror that hangs on the wall above a potted palm plant and notice our contrasting looks. My light hair and pink floral dress couldn't be more different to his jet-black hair, black clothes and tense attitude toward me. I drop my gaze and turn to limp away and catch up with my friends. But Nate's long fingers wrap tightly around my wrist as he stops me mid step.

"Got your phone?"

"Yeah why?" I scowl at him over my shoulder.

"Any shit goes down, or you want to gap it, I'm the first person you call, okay?"

I stare at him for a moment, lingering on his parted lips that look like they may want to say more. Maybe some of those hidden thoughts and emotions he tucks tightly away. Then he drops my wrist and steps back and leans against the wall.

"Yeah okay," I agree with him and leave to find Sara and Kirsten.

Chapter 7

K irsten pushes the gear stick into park as we make a stop alongside a suburban curb. Large trees, with street lamps in between line both sides of the road. The street is lined with sleek cars and four-wheel drives from the young adults that occupy the footpaths, all heading to a large two-story house down the street. Nerves are starting to create a pit of confetti in my stomach.

My fingers grip the door handle and I slowly pull it, opening the door as I peer out the window at the streams of teens I don't know. With my phone in my other hand, I check it for messages and see Leith said he will meet me outside the house. I let out a sigh of relief. I'm glad because it takes away a small fraction of my nerves.

"This is going to be so sick!" Sara giggles, climbing out of the passenger seat and standing alongside me on the curb. Kirsten comes around, filling the dark night air with a beep from locking her car. The air is warm, the muggy June heat keeping us in a constant humid environment.

The three of us link our arms together and step down the footpath, sashaying around the patrons we pass. My smooth thighs rub together, greedily, the warm summer sweat feeling like a sticky layer. My eyes land on the soft blue tones of men's hoodies in a tight circle by the front mailbox as we get closer to the party house.

Leith's head turns to the side with a smirk on his face, as if laughing at something funny his friends said. He notices me, grin growing wider, warmer. I smile back, unlinking my arms from the girls and shyly flattening down my dress, feeling self-conscious. The entire group turns to us to see what Leith is distracted by and they all hoot and yell out greetings to us.

"The bear cubs are here!" a tall one announces and I instantly recognize him from the basketball game.

"More like Mama Grizzlies. We have a bit more bite," I tease back, feeling playful and grin. Leith surprises me, losing any shyness I thought he may have had, and steps beside me, throwing an arm around my waist. Kirsten and Sara move off to the side a little, making space for the new intrusion.

"Luckily I don't mind sharp teeth and claws," he says proudly.

"You going to show us how you birdy boys party or what?" Sara eyes each and every one of them as she speaks, the corner of her lips tugging, fighting her urge to smile. We make our way up the smooth concrete path, heading toward the crisp pale gray house with vibrant white trim. It's a huge house, not in a gated community but still in a good area. Music thumps toward us, enticing anyone in a ten-mile radius no doubt. Frankton is an hour away from Burke town.

We're neighboring towns, yet you would think we lived in different countries with the way our small-town colleges rivaled over the years. As we get closer to the front door that's wide open and overloaded with party goers standing in the threshold, my nerves start to ease. We aren't getting any funny looks, no bitchy comments that we shouldn't be there.

Leith's hand is splayed and pressed flat against my lower back as he steers me into the house. A beige tiled floor greets us first that has heavy traffic in it. We weave through the crowd until we get to a massive, open kitchen that is crisp white with turquoise tiles as a splashback behind the double oven and double sink.

There are people everywhere. The countertop is overloaded with blue plastic cups, puddles of cheap liquor that has been spilled and a few girls sitting on them. There is a group of girls lined along the breakfast bar, their bare legs hanging freely.

"Ladies, these are our friends. Make them feel welcome!" Leith's friend announces to the group and swings his arm out gesturing to us.

They wiggle their fingers at us, waving politely. It's not 'hey new best friend' kind of friendly, but it's 'I won't bash your face in tonight' friendly.

"Anyway." Leith smiles at me then looks back at the group before continuing, "This is Tucker, Wade, Cullen, Vanessa, Maree and Lyza! This is Paisley and her friends."

"Sara and Kirsten," I finish off, correcting him. The short flowy skirt on my dress flutters against my thighs as I spin in Leith's arm and smile at him. Our eyes meet and I feel giddy, his boyish grin matching my inner emotions.

"I'll get you a drink. Sara and Kirsten, do you want one too?"

We all answer "Yes," without hesitation. Leith and Tucker fill up a handful of blue cups from a big barrel keg on the ground beside the breakfast bar. Squeezing three in each of their hands in triangle shapes, they carefully creep back to us.

Kirsten takes a cup from Tucker's hand, giving him a flirtatious smile that I've seen before. She's not as out there and sexually open as Sara. She's coyer but has had a few boyfriends over the years. She's stunning, like all my friends. I think I'm biased because I think all my friends are beautiful because they have the biggest hearts. Anxiety sends my heart into a pounding state. And yet I make pathetic decisions to not trust them with my worries.

"Wanna play beer pong?" he asks her and she nods hopelessly at him. My head swivels toward Leith as he leans in to whisper in my ear, our faces become too close and I angle my face away from his. He breathes into my ear, "Your dress is nice."

I chuckle and look back at him. "Not normally a dress girl but here we are."

He bites his lip, gripping it tightly in his teeth before he lets it spring free again.

"And here we are," Leith finishes with a devilish smirk that nearly brings me to my knees. A guy openly flirting with me, not frightened of my brothers and not talking to me just to get them riled up. It's just me and him and a house full of vibing teenagers.

His fingers sweep out and capture mine in front of everyone, claiming me as his tonight. I trail behind him as he leads me to the huge lounge and out to the expansive patio. There is a narrow rectangular pool off to the left, framing along a high hedge. A high speaker with flashing LED lights coming off it is tucked at the end of the pool, blasting the latest Bryce Vine hit. I scope out the rest of the area, which is completely filled with drunk students and friends all dancing or standing in big groups yelling over top of each other, trying to have intoxicated conversations.

"You wanna sit on the lounger?" Leith's voice breaks my daydreaming.

"Yeah, sounds good."

He sits down and as I go to sit on the one next to him, he pulls my hips forcing me down onto his lap. A small squeal escapes me from the surprise as we end up in a tangled mess. A deep throaty laugh bursts from Leith when he unapologetically pulls me tighter against him.

"You know, I reckon I'm going to buy you a blue hoody."

I slap his arm with my brows furrowing. "I'll stick to burgundy thank you!"

"Nah, blue will make your ocean eyes stand out more."

"You can give me yours later on when I get cold," I jokingly suggest and he nods. His lust filled eyes roam from my face to over my shoulder and he tosses his chin up to whoever is behind me. I drink down my cup and place it on the ground beside the lounger. As I do, my skirt rides up higher and Leith pulls it down protectively as new voices boom behind us.

"Brother, sick party!"

"Always is, isn't it!" he proudly throws back at them.

I straighten up and lean my back against Leith's chest while pulling at my skirt as well. Leith's hand stays lingering on my thigh and I don't protest. It's comforting.

One of the tall strangers' slumps down next to us on the spare lounger while the other sits at the foot end.

"Hi," I greet them and give a pathetic wiggle of my fingers for a wave. They look older than the rest here, but not by much. Maybe Bradey and Nate's age. Possibly a little older and senior college students. They don't seem like athletic frat boys, more rocker outcasts. I assess their stretched lobe rings and pierced spectrums before one of them finally speaks.

"You Leith's girlfriend?" he asks loudly so I can hear his words over the speaker but his focus is on Leith, telling me the question was more for him.

"Not yet. But she will be," he says smugly, sliding his hands from my thighs to my torso while he pulls me firm against his chest. The smell of million-dollar cologne incases me in a tight lustful grip. I lift my head, stretching my neck back so I'm looking up into his face.

"Cocky?" I giggle with a raised eyebrow.

"Hopeful, cutie," he assures me.

The outdoor area becomes packed as the party moves outside. The dancing bodies are thick and rampant. Kirsten and Sara are smack bang in the middle, dancing with a group of girls they have befriended. I can't help but smile. I was so anxious about how tonight would go but so far everyone has been welcoming.

I twirl a tendril of hair around my index finger as Leith rests his chin on top of my head while talking to some more of his friends. Tucker's in our group and he definitely seems like the loud, social one. Every group has that one friend. Ours is Sara. They are usually the loudest yet somehow the most vulnerable and sensitive. Kirsten looks toward me, blonde hair flowing in the breeze as she whips her head around laughing. She waves her hand in the air, gesturing for me to go over to them.

I throw back my third cup, finishing the entire drink and involuntarily cringing as it burns in my mouth. Wriggling from Leith's embrace, I stand on my feet and head over to them. I slide in beside them, feeling slightly out of place since I haven't really had a chance to let my hair down and mingle yet. I'm still at the awkward stage of trying to spend time with Leith to make small talk and get to know him.

"Girl the Hawks can party all good!" Sara says, her words slurring as she leans right back, tipping a drink into her mouth from up in the air. Part of it dribbles over her lips and down her chin. I grip her head and send the tip of my tongue over her chin, lapping up the dribble, now feeling buzzed too.

"I wouldn't know what to compare it to because my lame brothers don't let me go to their college parties!" I shout once I'm done.

"You have been to some with us."

"Yeah but the tame ones where parents aren't too far away. My goal before the new school year starts is to go to one of the full-blown Grizzly house parties!"

Kirsten and Sara laugh loudly then Kirsten grips the tops of my arms and stares directly into my face with a devilish smirk. "And I'm not going to miss that for the world. I don't know who will whip your ass more, Nate or Bradey!"

I grin back, grinding my back teeth slightly at the same time. I hate that that one image of Nate whipping my ass leaves me with more curiosity than repulsion.

Hands wrap around my hips and I look down, recognizing Leith's blue hoody sleeves against my pink dress.

"Wanna come upstairs so we can talk?" he asks. I spin in his arms, wrapping my arms around his neck and tilting my head at him.

"Sounds shady."

"I promise I'll keep my hands to myself if that is what you want."

I chew my bottom lip and nod.

"Yeah, okay because I think we have to head home soon."

He pulls me through the thick crowd, through the stacker doors and to the stairway that winds up to another level. We follow the stairs, ignoring the couples leaning against the rails making out. We reach the top level and he drags me down the hall to the third door. It opens up to a room that has a twin bed, scotch dresser and blue Hawks colors hanging everywhere. A photo on the wall captures my attention. It's Leith holding a basketball. He turns to me, dropping his hand.

"This is your house?"

"Yeah guess it is," he says, then chuckles quietly under his breath.

"You never said."

He lifts one shoulder, shrugging it off. "Thought I'd try to make it as casual as possible."

"Where are your parents?"

"Gone away on summer vacay early."

"Huh."

"Huh?"

"I don't really know what else to say," I admit as I stroll around his room, fingering his ribbons and tracing indents on his school medals.

"Is it strange we are all nearly twenty and still live at home with our parents?"

I give him an absurd look. "No, their houses are big enough and who can afford their own place when they are still in college?"

"True. I don't know, I guess I'm getting itchy feet. I wanted to throw a big party at this house where I have thrown probably fucking hundreds to be fair, because I don't know if I want to go back to college after summer break."

"What do you mean you don't want to go back? What about basketball?"

"I have been looking at some bigger colleges, more of a chance getting noticed, ya know." His fingers brush stray strands of hair from my face, lingering for just a moment longer than needed.

"Yeah I guess I understand."

Leith pulls me to him in a warm embrace and rubs my lower back.

"More cheerleading opportunities too."

"I'm not moving across the country with a guy I've only just met."

"Just think about it. I really like you. It's almost as if I have met you too late."

"Yeah I get it. To be honest though, a boyfriend wasn't on my radar at all. I'm aiming for cheer captain next year so I need to stay focused."

Leith brings a hand up and rubs his thumb over my jaw-bone gently while staring into my face. He has nice eyes. Young, adventurous. Not moody and dark. I peep his lips, he mimics me, matching my movements.

His thumb pauses on my jawline as he pulls me to him, opening his mouth as it inches closer to mine. As our lips collide, and his tongue pushes into my mouth, massaging my own. We find a steady rhythm before his hand slides down my back and grips my ass. My knee comes up and hooks over his hip, holding him firm against my pussy. I can feel his erection hard against me. He grinds slightly while the assault on my mouth becomes more frantic.

The door swing opens, making the music blare louder through the bedroom.

"Ah sorry! Babe it's past midnight, we need to head back."

I pull back from Leith as I hear Kirsten's voice fill the room. My heart is hammering in my chest from a mixture of nerves and excitement.

"I'll be seeing you," I say all giddily and skip through the room, linking arms with Kirsten smiling.

"Ring me Paisley," I hear him call out as I leave.

"You shady slut," Kirsten chuckles as we jog down the stairs.

Chapter 8

I wiggle slightly against the soft fabric of the seat beneath me. Monday morning has come around too fast. I thought a few days would give me a reprieve and I would have a calmer mind set going into the unknown. But my stomach is in knots.

I purse my lips and sit on my fidgety hands as I contemplate crossing my fingers for extra good luck. *Does that actually work?* I always thought so growing up. After the party over the weekend, I spent Sunday in my room icing my knee and keeping it raised on my bed. It feels like it has a little more movement but too much weight on it kills me. It doesn't help that I overused it when I was with Leith because I was distracted with a wicked mix of liquor, painkillers and hormones.

I lean forward slightly, hands still planted under my behind as I look over my knee a little more closely. The swelling has certainly improved.

I tense when tanned muscled arms appear in my vision as they flop over the armrest casually. The puff of air from the instant drop of his body on the seat beside me causes his strong musk to brush over me, bringing all my senses to life. I want to be mad at my moody brother. But the instant he is near me I am more at ease.

"I didn't tell you I had another appointment," I mumble to Nate, letting my high ponytail sway over my forehead as I act nonchalant.

"Must have slipped your mind," his deep voice says, sounding bemused while he pulls his phone from his shorts pocket and starts scrolling on it.

I slowly look toward where he sits, letting my attention linger on his burgundy school t-shirt that only adds to the bronzed tone of his skin. His plain silver band hugs his thumb closest to me and I can't help but be mesmerized by it as he flicks his thumb over the screen repeatedly.

"Miss Wilson?" I snap out of my insane thoughts, giving the doctor a tentative smile. My throat feels dry and tight as I try to speak.

"Hi," I say but it comes out forced. I can feel Nate watching me and I can't help but wonder what must be going through his mind.

I stand up, Nate letting me do it on my own this time around. I walk into the room successfully, with only a slight limp. We waste no time sitting down. A strong smell of roses hits me. I eye the fresh long stem roses occupying the coffee table in front of me. I think from now on the smell of roses and my anxiety will always go hand in hand.

"So I have good news. You will be able to cheer next year," she begins and pushes her glasses up her nose. I fight the urge to tell her she may need to get them tightened because they seem to fall down a lot. But instead, I become zombie-like, nodding my head back and forth with a blank expression.

"Next year?" The question comes from Nate.

I turn my head slightly, look at Nate's profile and his god damn silky hair that hangs loosely around his ears. His strong arm tenses as he runs his fingers through the front of his hair and brushes it back roughly.

"You have a torn ACL, but not completely through. So with lots of rest and physio it will heal faster. No cheer or any physical exercise on it for six weeks apart from physio."

I suck in a breath and lean back into the couch, feeling defeated. "Six weeks? I can't be out that long. There's no way I will have a shot at becoming captain next year."

"Well, keep using it and you will do permanent damage to it. That's your options."

"Okay." I answer robotically and my face is strained while I try to hide my heartbreak.

"Good, rest it for another week and we can look at doing some physio next week. I will get the receptionist to make an appointment with you."

"Thank you, I appreciate the help."

"You're a young, healthy girl Paisley. There's no reason why this injury should impact your future so much."

"I know, I'm probably getting wound up over nothing."

Nate leads us out of the medical center. I trail behind like I always do, but following Nate around and letting him take the lead has never been a problem for me.

He goes to his car but I veer off to the small Mercedes parked across the lot. I'm thankful Mom let me take her car to school today. He looks over his shoulder, frowning when he realizes I'm no longer following. I keep walking, pulling the keys free and unlocking it. My fingers grip the door handle and as I start to pull it open, Nate's large hand slams down on the top of the door, closing it again. Getting a fright, I jump back slightly, then frown at him.

"What the fuck Nate!"

"Did you have a good time at the party?" he asks me, his face close to mine as he leans down into my space.

I cross my arms over my chest and tap one sneaker on the curb, growing more frustrated with this enigma.

"Yeah, it was nice going to a party where my brothers didn't watch my every move."

His eyes narrow down into slits and he bites his bottom lip. He releases it then shakes his head slightly.

"Someone as naive as you needs protection from the big bad world, Paisley."

"I'm not naive! And you were probably doing worse at my age."

"You know nothing on what I get up to."

"I know because you don't tell anyone shit." I match his stubborn fire, refusing to back down.

"The people that need to know, know."

"That simple huh?"

"Yeah it is."

"Well keep living your own life and let me live mine." I say.

"Did you fuck him?"

My eyes go wide as I draw in a deep breath. I can feel my cheeks growing more flush with his rude question shocking me.

"That's none of your business."

"Tsk tsk, oh I think it is. Did you fuck him or not?" His head tilts slightly while he runs his tongue over the front of his teeth showing me he isn't in the mood to play games.

"No I didn't."

"Good."

"But I might!"

"Aw, did you hit it off?"

"He's a nice guy."

"Nice guys come last. And nice guys aren't good at looking after what belongs to them."

"Well at least that nice guy will be coming regardless."

Nate chokes and then grips the nape of my neck, squeezing it tightly, but not enough to hurt me. It feels like a warning that I am walking on the knife's edge with his patience. Clearly no sense of humor this guy.

"If he enjoys having his cock on his body, he will leave you the fuck alone."

"This protective brotherly shit gets really old Nate!"

His fingers flex, the tips digging into my skin. It sends a shiver over me. I don't need physio, I need a *therapist*.

"Oh Paisley. Bradey may be my brother, but in no way shape or form have you ever been my sister..." he murmurs before letting my neck go. He stands straight and then storms off back to the car.

I let my fingers brush over the area where his possessive grip was only moments ago. I close my eyes as I fight the empty feeling I am now left with with him gone. His words are flying around my mind, loud and vivid. If he doesn't see me as his sister then what am I to him? Because he still keeps me at an arm's length, yet somehow on a tight leash. He always knows when I need him and how to help me.

Chapter 9

After I got back to school and sat through nutrition class, unable to concentrate, I came up with the decision that I'm going to tell my coach and teammates that I need to rest this week and then go on light duties until I am healed.

I'm so nervous I can feel the bile burning at the back of my throat. But I'm hoping it can be taken as a positive thing and I'll look like a good role model by making the responsible decision. I know plenty of the girls that have tried to push through injuries and then ultimately been pushed out of the team for lying and making the injury worse so they can't carry on regardless.

My shoes squeak as I follow all the girls into the large gym where we are due to begin practice. My fingers slide along the soft fabric of my bow, until the tips catch the ends of the loops and I pull it tight. Squaring my shoulders and letting out a deep breath, I head straight for the head coach.

"Hi miss!" I greet her, trying to maintain my fake confidence. A tremble begins in my chin and I shake my head just slightly then clear my throat, hoping it helps to keep that threat of tears far away from me.

"Ah Paisley, I was hoping to chat to you before practice. Come over here," she says while gesturing her arms away from the group. She turns and starts walking so I trail behind her. Maybe she already knows.

"Hey um, so unfortunately Lily has had a death in the family so she had to head back to England and I am unsure when she will be back. Will you be okay with being fill-in captain until she's back?"

As if I have been taken out of my body, it almost feels like I am hovering above myself and looking down to watch this all unfold. My head starts to spin. I lick my lips while praying for my mouth to say the right words. This was not part of the conversation I had rehearsed in my head.

"I can ask one of the other girls if you're not up to it. But it would be a really good way to stand out for potential captaincy next year."

"No, no problem at all. I can do it," I assure her and plaster a wide smile on my face. Those were not the right words that were meant to come out of my mouth and my cheeks feel like they may break.

Coach rubs the top of my arm giving me a pleased expression. The crinkle of either side of her hazel eyes lets me know that she means it too.

"I knew I could count on you. You have worked so hard for this big opportunity."

"Thank you. Can I just take a moment to go to the toilet then I will be good to go?"

"Of course but don't be long."

"I won't miss."

As I stride across the polished wood floor I ball my hands into fists. A whole day of worrying for nothing, because I have done the complete opposite of what I had planned to do. I am so mad at myself. I storm into the locker room, trying desperately to ignore the radiating pain from my knee. Fast stomping on it has nearly floored me.

I open my gym bag and pull my bottle of painkillers out. I'm not due for any yet but I will need to double up to get through a practice.

I throw back two large pills and swallow them down in one gulp. A slow steadying breath flows through my lips before I leave the locker room, desperate to show everyone that I am as strong as ever.

I march back into the gym and stand shoulder to shoulder next to the coach. She does five fast claps, making her usual attention-grabbing pattern. We all repeat the same chanting clap then give her all our attention, although I am facing the entire cheer squad, which is more intimidating than I expected. I've stood in front of them many times, yet now knowing I am with an authority of sorts over them makes my stomach churn. Especially with my secret I am hiding, I feel like a fraud.

"Right everyone, as some of you already know, Lily's had to go back to England where her family is based as she has had a bereavement in the family. Paisley is going to take on the temp role of captain until her return."

"Get it girl!" Sara calls out and the rest whistle and yell out their support. I smile back, the fraudster in me feeling stronger and stronger.

"Over to you girl," Miss says to me and takes a small step back.

"Right girls, let's start with one minute of stretches and then we will do warm ups then onto floor routines."

"No tumbling practice?" one girl calls out.

"Not today. I think we should really work on getting our timing perfectly in sync for floor."

"Sounds good Pais." Kirsten nods her head, agreeing. I wonder if my face looks like how I feel. Like I am about to combust at any moment. I look over the eager girls watching me for support and direction now and all I can do is swallow and clap my hands to get started.

After two hours of practice, we're having down time on the ground as usual. We do this regularly as a way to catch our breath and also team bond. For me, I am laid out beside the group, pretending to happily braid my long ponytail while letting out a scheduled fake giggle every now and then. But my leg feels like it's on fire.

My fingers tremble as I weave my hair tendrils, trying to hide the sheer agony I am keeping tightly inside of me. The pain nearly makes me nauseous. I kept giving it glances during practice and it doesn't look any more swollen. I know it's not noticeable unless you know to look hard, so I reason with myself that I haven't done any more damage.

"Right captain, are we free to go because I have someone to meet after school," Sara says while brushing off her shoulders with a mischievous smirk on her face. I turn my head to her, narrowing my gaze.

"Who?" I mouth and feign shocked silence with my mouth in an O.

"Tucker..." she loudly whispers and gasps with her hands over her mouth as she fights to hold in her giggle.

"Oh my god, Sara!!" I mock her.

"We're just meeting at Taco Bell to eat. Chill."

"Mmmhhmmm and I'll ask you tomorrow if you ended up in the back seat."

"Please girl, you should know me better than that. It would be front seat with me on top so I can get off nice and quickly."

"Hope you let him finish too."

"I couldn't give two shits as long as I do!"

We both burst into laughter before slowly standing. As much as I have tried previously, now I hiss at the pain and limp slightly.

"Jesus you okay?" she asks quietly beside me. I look up and watch Kirsten and the other girls filing out of the gym. I should tell her the truth but the words are stuck in my throat, with a suffocating effect. I fist my baggy t-shirt and try to slow my breathing and think of anything but the pain.

"I'm totally fine. Just sore legs because I went for a big run this morning as well." She looks at me for a long few seconds and I feel like withering under her stare. She knows me better than anyone, I should be able to tell her yet the selfish part in my human makeup keeps reminding me that she is my captain competition. I straighten up and chomp down on my cheek as we walk out of the gym.

"Well rest tonight because lil' miss captain needs to put us through our paces this week to be ready for the end of school show."

"Lily might be back by then." I fill the statement with girl power and friend support so it comes across as positive and supportive to our real captain. But the fraud in me screams, *you are fucking hoping she is back by then Paisley!*

Chapter 10

I carefully drop myself into the pool at home a few hours later. I only have my lace bra on and cheeky bottoms because my parents aren't home for another few hours yet and because, frankly, I didn't have the energy to change into swimmers. I paddle around in the center, where it is at its deepest, before I roll onto my back and start floating gently.

The late afternoon sun beams down on me, causing my breasts to grow hot. Having auburn hair and fair skin means I tend to burn quickly and sadly only gain a very tame tan. The endless supply of self tanner in my bedroom also proves my point. I use my hands to slowly paddle in the water, helping me float and also splash small amounts of water over the inferno spreading over the top of my body.

The current changes in the water are delicate, smooth almost, but I feel it. My body bobs in the water with a new flow to it. Hair tendrils fan around my face and move slightly faster. I flap my hands under me and move my legs so I can change position and float vertically in the water.

I am faced with Nate. Black hair frames his face, making him appear like the grim reaper. I try to back up but because I can't touch the bottom, he swims over to me in one stroke.

"Heard you nailed cheer training today lil' miss captain?" Nate taunts me but there's an underlining of disappointment.

"I'd love to know how you seem to know everything about me."

A deep dimple appears in his cheek as one corner of his lips curve up into a lopsided smile. He doesn't answer me. He never does.

I swim backwards a little, trying to create space between us because the change in our relationship lately is making me feel uncomfortable. So uncomfortable because it feels so fucking comforting being this close to him.

"What happened to the week of rest?" he asks me sternly while his brows frame his eyes tightly, letting me know how angry he is. Water dances over my lips as I float helplessly in the water. I feel like I'm at his mercy. But I keep my mouth shut, refusing to answer his questions. I back up again, just for him to mimic my movements once more.

He tilts his head, taking in my wet hair.

"I could lick those water droplets off your skin. I sometimes wonder if your skin tastes different to everyone else's. I imagine it does."

I blink slowly then pointlessly, I try retreat again. He comes closer, much closer this time. We are a mere millimeter apart. I watch the water cover his chin. I need to remind myself that I'm in a talking situation with Leith. He's good for me. He isn't my brother.

"Who are you dating?" The question leaves my lips quickly. I feel like a pathetic loser, desperately trying to catch breadcrumbs from the man in front of me.

He shrugs under the water, the movement reminding me that his muscles are strong and built for competitive swimming.

"No one. Everyone."

"Do you think it's fair you know everything about me yet I know nothing about you?"

He stays silent for a moment with his eyes drilling into mine. Then a slight nod from his leaves me surprised.

"You can ask me one question. One question only and I will answer truthfully."

I float around in the water as I process what he has given me. It's everything yet nothing at all. One question. Of all the things I know from Nate, or the little I know about him, I know his word is his word. I want to know so much. So many questions run through my head, yet they all seem insignificant at this moment. I need to ask him an important one.

His attention stays on me, never wavering as he stalks my movements in the water.

"Hi kids!" our mom calls from the veranda. I look up and see her under the clear light roofing, holding her briefcase. She's a child therapist and never home this early.

As if we had been caught in an intimate moment and doing something wrong, I cover my breasts with my arms and smile nervously back at her.

"Mom, you're home early," I announce. Nate turns his back to me, facing Mom. I look at the large back tattoo he got last summer and I chew the inside of my cheek again. I'll have no cheek left at this stage.

"I wanted to cook and have a family dinner at the table. It feels like I haven't caught up with you all for a long time."

"Sounds good Mom. I'll get out and come help you with dinner."

"That sounds nice baby," she says appreciatively. I watch her walk back inside in her pencil skirt and white blouse with straight strawberry blonde bob hair style. She always looks perfectly professional and very rarely we see her in slacks when she's hanging out with us at home.

I swim toward the steps to get out and pause at the bottom step. I look back to Nate over my shoulder, he hasn't moved and neither has his hungry attention. There is one half of me that wants to stay hidden in the water so Nate doesn't watch me walk away in my lace lingerie, and there is another half of me that wants to saunter in the house hoping that he appreciates the view. I slowly lick my lips and turn my head back to the door as my fingers clench the stair rail.

"I still have that question."

"One question. One honest answer," he confirms, his voice so low it sends vibrations over my body. I walk up the stairs and glide toward the house, refusing to look back but feeling Nate's heavy possessive stare at my back, stalking me the entire time.

An hour later, Mom and I place bowls of salad and a dish of chicken risotto on the table. Nate, Bradey and Dad are already seated. Us sitting together on our long formal dining room table is a very rare treat. It feels like I haven't seen or spoken to my brother, Bradey, much lately.

This school year has been a big changer for all of us. Bradey and Nate are on their last leg, while I'm still floundering and finding my feet. Nate has become secretive, but Bradey has just become cut off entirely from his family. He's not secretive in Nate terms, he's just distant. He is in his final year for medical sciences and needs to decide what he will be specializing in. Nate's is an English major. But I don't know what is next for him. I sit down next to Dad, who gives me a goofy smile. He's like a big kid. His thick black framed glasses, brown hair with thick silver on the sides makes his goofy smile seem cartoonish.

"How has my princess been going lately?" he asks while looking over the different salads we have prepared. I drool over the orzo pasta salad; it's my favorite every time.

"Good. I'm filling in as captain for Lily while she is on bereavement leave."

"Well I'll be, I knew you were destined for great things, Paisley. Have you been keeping up your extra fitness?"

I inwardly sigh as I think about my knee. "Of course Dad!"

"Well I'm very proud of you. And how's the boys?" he asks as lettuce falls from the fork and onto his plate.

Nate looks at Bradey subtly, so subtly everyone else would miss it but me. He gives him a strange look before shoveling food on his plate. "Great."

"That's good. And you Bradey?"

His face looks a little pale and he looks over the food again with a grimace. "Yeah, not too bad."

His sentences are short and sweet. Surprise surprise.

"You need to eat love," my mom says, looking directly at Bradey.

"I'm not very hungry. I would rather be excused."

"Bradey, we are eating as a family," Dad scolds him and drops his fork on his plate in anger. The shrill sound bounces off the walls.

Bradey gets up and storms off. Dad's chair pushes back as he goes to follow him but Nate stands straight. His frame towers over all of us.

"I'll take him some food and make sure he eats."

"Thank you Nate, please make sure he eats. He's looking pale." Mom says looking defeated.

"Maybe just a virus coming on, but I will do my best," he assures Mom. He picks up his plate full of food and takes off after Bradey.

"Well that was strange," Dad says. Now it's my time to be angry.

"For Bradey? No it's not. Unless you have been living under a rock, you would have noticed he has been acting differently all year."

"I think summer break will be good for him. Becoming the next top surgeon is stressful and tiring." Mom sips her red wine.

I snort then shovel pasta into my mouth. In between chews I force out, "You guys really think too highly of us sometimes."

And although they both smile at me and start eating, obviously thinking it was a joke. I am dead serious. My parents want the best for us and want us to succeed in life but sometimes their busy schedules and high expectations from us cannot be what is entirely best for us.

I still remember growing up and missing out on my friends' birthday parties because Mom and Dad said I had my weekend tutoring and extra cheer training booked in. I continue to shove food in my mouth and look up the hallway toward the lounge and large staircase, wondering if there is something more going on with my brothers.

Chapter 11

It's Saturday afternoon and I'm sprawled out on top of my bed in boy bottom shorts and a singlet with an ice pack on my knee.

Our girls' group chat is popping off and they are all ganging up on me. I smile as I read over the threatening messages. Threats of kidnaping and violence if I don't go to the party tonight. It's going to be massive. But my brothers are going and I know they are going to be overbearing and mood killers if I go.

I let out a big sigh as I stare at the ceiling. I ignore the tugging in my self-consciousness about how wrong it feels all of a sudden to call Nate my brother. Whatever he may be now, I need to stop letting them dictate who I see and where I go. Besides, I'm eighteen years old. I'm not a baby so why am I letting them treat me like one?

My thumb flies over my phone screen as I inform everyone in the group chat that I will come but they have to keep it quiet. I told them, if they don't, the consequences will be two rogue men raining chaos down on them at the party before the guys will bully them out of the party. Those boys all stick together.

I've hung out in my room all afternoon. I heard banging around in the boys room and shared bathroom while they were getting ready. I probably could have created my own swimming pool with the amount of times I wiped my sweaty palms on my shorts. My breasts press heavy against my thin, ribbed singlet while my chest rises and falls. *Grow some fucking balls Paisley!*

I'm acting like I'm thirteen and sneaking out of the house to meet a boy. But the scolding thoughts I scream to myself do nothing to placate my anxiety and the twisting in my stomach intensifies.

There's a knock at my door and I look toward it, watching it open slowly.

"What you doing tonight sis?" I meet Bradey's gaze and frown.

"Fuck all, you look like shit."

He shrugs one shoulder and leans against my door with one hand. "Too much balling."

"Maybe it should be you staying in tonight."

"Nah, no fun watching movies with you and Mom."

I can't help but snicker. "Just call me the good daughter."

A solemn look flickers in his dull eyes before he blinks rapidly and lets out a long breath.

"One of us has to make them proud," he says slowly then pulls my door shut.

I really can't keep up with this man.

An hour later I place my hair straighteners down on the dresser and run my fingers through my straight strands. Tilting my head side to side, I pout a little as I inspect my made-up face and fresh hair. I keep things simple with a green plaid pattern, pleated mini skirt, and tucked in plain white t-shirt. I flick my eyes down when my phone lights up and scan to read a message from Sara. She's parked out front. I brush down my skirt out of habit then nod as I walk out of my bedroom. Maybe I'm panicking for nothing, maybe they will all be excited when I get there. Maybe I'm full of shit.

We drive up a long narrow driveway that has maple trees framing the sides, giving it a natural tunnel like effect. I haven't been here before but I have heard a lot about the parties that are held here. Glendon is the captain of the basketball team and this is his property. Or more his parents'.

This is his start of summer break party. His last one was a party for end of mid-year exams, then there was a massive party for 'because they are celebrating their first win last semester'.

Well, I guess he just likes to find reasons to throw out of control parties.

The estate comes into view and my jaw drops. I would live forty minutes out of town if it meant living on a property like this. It's a pale gray brick house, with two levels and wide concrete steps that start on the gravel turnaround area and go right up to the double front doors.

Sara finds a spot to park and we both sit there and stare at the mansion. The music booms from the entire house and every so often there's a flash from strobe lights shining out through the glass windows.

"Are you getting nervous?" I mumble quietly to Sara while not taking my sight off the house.

"It'll be fun and looking at the size of the house, you could probably avoid your brothers all night."

I can't help but snort as I drag my attention away from the mansion and to my best friend's serious face. "Oh you're not joking?"

"Of course I'm not. Could be fun trying to avoid them all night."

"Mmmm well from what I have heard, it will be chaos inside so someone like me will easily blend in anyway. Just the way I like it."

"Yeah, the things we've heard. But I think a lot goes down that doesn't get spoken about. It's like an unofficial guys club where they get up to no good and guard those secrets to their graves."

"That's deep, bestie."

Sara flicks her hair back over her shoulder and regards me. The soft amount of highlighter on her cheekbones flash under the small car light. Damn her and her bronzed skin. The fake tan I have lathered on still has nothing on her picture perfect skin.

She shrugs her shoulder, causing her loose sleeve to drop off her shoulder. She's wearing an oversized t-shirt as a dress and of course she looks a million dollars.

"Yeah well, us girls just have to have each other's backs. Have fun tonight and fuck the boys club. They can keep their secrets as long as we aren't a part of them."

I give her a soft smile then pull the door handle open. She follows suit and we exit the car.

She's completely right and I am beyond lucky to have friends like her.

Sara links her arm in mine and drags me close to her then we walk toward the house.

"Have you heard much from Leith?"

"Yeah a little. We are going to try to catch up next week and then over the summer break. How's Tucker?"

"Meh, he's okay, we had fun but I'm not looking for anything more."

"You breaking hearts again my friend?"

"Always," she giggles, causing me to erupt in laughter. We pass by groups of people from school and clouds of smoke surround them. I scrunch my nose up at the strong smell of marijuana.

"Wholey shit, the cheer girls are here!"

"Why wouldn't we be?" Sara throws back to one of them.

"I heard Paisley was the only cheer girl that wasn't allowed at parties."

"Why the hell would you think that?" I speak up, feeling a little annoyed and plant my feet on the ground.

A blond guy looks at me with a smirk then chuffs loudly. "'Cause everyone has been told if they touch you they die."

"Where the hell do my brothers get off? Seriously, it was cute like five years ago, but now it's just pathetic," I say strongly, feeling pissed off. I knew there would be a drama regardless.

"Not brothers. Just your parents' adopted pet," he chuckles.

"I wouldn't call him that. Apparently he drowns people in pools," a tall guy from the back says.

My eyes grow wide and then when I have composed myself, I frown deeply. "Nate isn't like that."

"I heard the swimming team loves getting up to sick shit." The tall one at the back voices again then takes a toke on a joint.

"Yeah well he ain't here tonight anyway."

"I thought both of them were here." I frown and look off toward the street feeling confused.

"Bradey is, but Nate doesn't come to these parties that often. He just turns up to grab your brother when he gets too messy."

"He sure is your brother's keeper," a girl says and takes the joint from someone else.

Sara pulls on my arm and drags me up the concrete steps. "You are already letting people get to you."

"But if Nate doesn't come to parties very often then where the fuck does he go?"

"Girl he is probably out fucking groups of girls like pussy is going to become extinct."

"Yeah maybe," I murmur back as we finally cross the threshold. A part of me becomes sad because I was so close with my brothers growing up. Sure, they didn't always treat me that nice, because I was the annoying little sister, but we did everything together still. Holidays, fishing, food fights at the dinner table when Mom and Dad weren't looking. And sleepovers in the lounge on the weekends when we would binge watch Friday the 13th and The Chainsaw Massacre. Although Nate doesn't treat me entirely like family, not knowing *anything* anymore hurts.

The flooring my feet hit are large, textured terracotta tiles that spread out through the entrance way. The main area is a big open space, with a few white L-shaped couches, side tables with vases and a narrow runner up toward what looks to be a kitchen. I crane my neck to the right and see an archway into a dim lit room, then to my left, finding a winding staircase that goes upstairs.

"Fucking hell this is impressive."

"It's just a house, and white couches with parties doesn't seem very bright,"

"Sorry, miss gated community," I say sarcastically but show the humor on my face. She responds by slapping my arm lightly as we proceed to walk further into the house. I look around at the crowds of people from our school. Most I recognize. But not all.

I don't see Bradey yet so I let out a steady breath. I do see a bouncing blonde out of my peripheral vision, jogging toward us.

"Kirsten!" I announce.

"Legends! Come over here. The whole squad is playing drinking games."

"I am sober driving," Sara says, almost with tears in her voice.

"I can drive too!" I speak up.

"No, I like driving my baby and I don't like hangovers. But I'm going to get FOMO."

"We could sleep in your car tonight. Could be cozy," I suggest as I see all our friends coming into view.

"My Porsche is my baby. But damn it's an uncomfortable one."

"Uber back to town, come get the car tomorrow!" Kirsten says as we reach the group.

"Sara! Paisley! Sit down. We are playing red or black." One of our squad friends yells in excitement.

I slump down on the couch with the girls and Steff passes me a can of premix gin. I flick it open and take a long drink.

"So captain, you're up first. Red or black?" another one of our friends asks me.

"Red," I say, staring down at the deck of cards on the glass and marble table in front of us.

"Black. DRINK!" she laughs after pulling out a card. I take another long drink.

"With pleasure," I gasp when I'm finished and let out a big burp.

Sara, who is sitting opposite me, looks over my shoulder and her face drops then her eyes flick to me. They look sympathetic.

"Oh fuck," she says under her breath. I turn my head, looking over my shoulder and locking eyes with Nate.

Chapter 12

He's in a plain black hoody, basketball shorts and sneakers. His face is thunderous as he walks straight over to me. Everyone moves out of his way. As soon as he reaches me, he leans down and scoops me up under my upper arm, dragging me to my feet.

"Nate what the fuck are you doing?!"

"I could say the same to you. You shouldn't be here Paisley."

I end up over the back of the couch and on my feet again, standing toe to toe with him. I look over the girls who are staring at me with their mouths open but say nothing. Fucking traitors!

"It's a college party and guess what? I go to college."

"Move your ass, we're fucking going!"

"I'm not going anywhere with you."

"Paisley don't play games." He is so close I can almost taste the venom in his words on my own tongue.

"I'm here with my friends, not harming anyone."

"You don't get it do you. It's the ones that will harm *you*."

Nate's swim partner comes over and whispers in his ear intently. I scowl further because Nate's grip on my arm is still solid so I am stuck in place while they have a private conversation.

His friend leans back and Nate nods slightly then glares down at me.

"You want to be a big party girl," he bites out then lets go of my arm "You party all fucking night then, but mark my words.

If anyone here touches you, I will throw you over my shoulder and drag you out the door *after* killing them."

"So you're going then?"

He snorts loudly and shakes his head while he walks away from me.

"You fucking wish!" He throws over his shoulder. I squeeze back into my spot on the couch and rub my arm, where red rings are appearing from his tight grip.

"You okay?" Kirsten asks and the girls all lean forward so they are closer to me.

"He just gets stranger and stranger," I huff and pick my drink back up.

They lean back and we keep playing the game.

I run my fingers through my long strands of hair as I shuffle back into my seat a little more. My chest rises and falls, over and over and growing more rapidly. I am so angry and the more I realize I have played the good little sister for so long, I get even angrier. Mom and Dad are so busy with their own lives, they don't know and also don't care that Bradey and Nate cause hell in my life, all the while they do whatever the fuck they want.

My skin prickles as the anger spreads through me, almost consuming me. I finish my can and grab another, cracking it open instantly.

There's a ruckus behind us with deep booming voices that are hollering and laughing.

"Baller boys," one girl assesses as she watches them. I almost fold into myself when I realize Bradey will probably be with them. If he and I start arguing it will turn into a full-blown wrestling match on this glass table.

My praying for invisibility is fruitless because Bradey and his team come crashing into our space. The boys lift half the girls up before they sit down in their place, making the girls sit on their laps. The rest of them drape themselves over the armrests and back of the couches. Bradey sits on the arm rest beside Sara and throws his arm over her shoulders while staring at me.

"Heard you were here."

I shrug my shoulders and nod to Kirsten who is now holding the card pack.

"Red," I say.

She pulls up a card and smiles. "Lucky, it is red. But drink anyway." She forces a giggle. I know she's trying to brush away the tense feeling as much as I'm trying to ignore them.

"What happened to your movie night with Mom?"

"I decided I wanted to hang with my friends."

"Oh well don't come crying to me when you see someone fucking on the benchtop or kids passed out on the lawn drunk."

I frown deeply at him. "Why are you being such a dick? I'm not a five year old. People fucking doesn't worry me at all. And I'm sure I've been drunk before too."

He scowls then downs his whole cup of liquor. He biffs the cup across the floor, making it hit someone's foot who is dancing with friends on the tiled area.

"Fuck off Bradey," the guy yells then keeps dancing.

Bradey's lips tug into a smirk as he eyes the guy that he had hit. Bradey looks wired and like he wants a fight with someone. I brush my long fingernails through my hair and stand up. I'm going to drive myself mad trying to guess what the fuck is going on with these men in my life.

"Aw you leaving so soon? We're about to play spin the bottle." I hear Bradey's voice behind me. I flip him the bird over my shoulder and weave through the thick crowd. I slip my phone out of my bra, intending to ring Leith. I scroll through my contacts until I find his number then hit ring as I ascend up the stairs, quickly trying to get away from as much noise as I can. I walk up a long hallway that has people sitting down, making out and some passing out. The responsible part of me is concerned that it's so early in the night, yet they are already passed out drunk.

I get to the end of the hall because it's the only shut door. I open it and slam my back against the door as Leith answers the phone.

"Hey baby cakes," he greets me. I close my eyes and smile.

"Hey, what are you doing?" I ask, but I can hear his friends in the background.

"Just at the courts having a late-night game. Where are you? It sounds loud."

"Came to a party but I'm getting over it already."

I slowly open my eyes and let out a long breath now that I am feeling calmer.

"You could come across town and see me?" he offers. But I don't answer him. I can't. My words are caught in my throat as I stare at the scene in front of me. My free hand covers my mouth but my eyes can't be peeled away.

"Babe you there?" Leith asks me.

"Is that your lover boy?" Nate's tense voice fills the silence in front of me. His eyes are locked with mine, while his large hand grips a guy's head as it slides off and on his cock. As if Nate can see the thoughts running through my mind, he grips the man's head harder. Parts of his hair falls through Nate's fingers while Nate savagely fucks his face faster.

"Paisley!!" Leith's voice booms in my ear.

"Yeah sorry I'm here," I say weakly. I can't stop staring. *Is Nate into men? Is that why he has been so distant?* I need to leave but I can't. My mouth becomes dry and my panties soak through while I watch the erotic scene play out. I rub my bare thighs together as a tingle spreads through me. My eyes slowly roam back to Nate's face. His gaze runs up and down the length of me slowly. His hooded eyes match his bottom lip that is being painfully bitten between his teeth. His hips move faster, while gagging sounds escape the man on his knees.

"I ah, I will, ah—I will call you back," I stutter quickly and hang up.

"I should go," I murmur but my words don't match what I want to do at all.

"Don't fucking move," he snarls. Nate looks down while pulling the male's head away from his cock.

"That taste good?" he asks the man on his knees. The man swallows and smirks.

"Always tastes fucking good."

My hand grips the door handle.

"Don't move Paisley," Nate grinds out again. I like this too much and I shouldn't. I don't know how I should be reacting so running from an uncomfortable situation seems like the most logical thing to do.

Nate's massive, hard cock is pointing directly toward the ceiling. It glistens under the soft bedroom light from the saliva and pre-cum coating it.

"Lick it slowly," Nate whispers down to the man, who he still controls by his hair. He pulls his head closer to his hard cock again where the male grips his cock in one hand and then slowly slides his tongue up the entire length. A quiver runs up my spine. I clench my thighs tighter as I watch his long tongue run over the bulging veins on Nate's cock.

"How wet are your panties?" His commanding voice captures my attention once more. I meet his watchful stare but my cheeks grow flush. I don't want to answer his question.

He smirks at me then guides the guy's mouth onto his cock again. He moves his hips, fucking his face quickly. Nate's vision stays on me though, roaming my body, lingering on my harden nipples and bare thighs, as if he's fucking me in his head. I can't help but envision that it is me on my knees, pleasuring Nate. Tasting his cum in my mouth. Sexual frustration starts to erupt in me. I run my hand up my stomach, strategically rubbing my palm over my nipples to make me feel better. Nate's view latches on to the movement and he groans loudly while using both hands now to hold the head on his cock right to the base as he rocks and comes down the other man's throat. My hand desperately rattles the handle while I silently will it to just spring open already.

I hear the click and then pull it open and I dash out of the room, slamming the door shut behind me.

I run downstairs, trying to find Kirsten or Sara again but I'm met with Bradey being hauled off a bloodied guy. His knuckles are covered in blood.

I go to run forward to find out what is going on but Nate is behind me in an instant and pulls me back behind him.

"Stay away from him Paisley. I will handle it."

"But—"

"Not now. Just fucking listen to what I am saying," he growls and heads toward Bradey. He drags him to his feet and yells at his friends. "Help me get him in the fucking jeep."

They drag him over the tiles while Bradey is yelling and swearing unintelligible things.

Nate locks eyes with me and then they slide over my shoulder. I see his boyfriend behind me.

"Get her home." He glares at me then says loudly, "And make sure she fucking stays home this time."

His boyfriend puts his hand heavily on my shoulder and I try to shrug it off but it's no use.

"You his fucking slave now?"

He chuckles close to my ear. He's close to my height, but has chestnut brown hair and olive skin.

"Nah, just his friend. Let's go or my *friend* might dump me." He draws out the 'friend', making me scowl.

"Do friends suck each other's cocks?"

"Sometimes, obviously."

I huff and head toward the door.

"Obviously," I say and roll my eyes. Sara and Kirsten are already outside on the gravel area.

"Jesus, that was intense," Sara says, looking worried.

"Tell me about it. I'm going to head home now to make sure he is okay."

"Sure I'll drive you," Sara says.

"It's okay, this nice man here is driving me."

"I prefer Lance," he says behind me.

"Stay at the party and have fun for me, okay?"

"Are you sure?" Sara asks while warily watching the new stranger.

"Yeap. Positive."

Sara and Kirsten group hug me and head back inside. I'm slightly jealous of them but in the same breath, what happened upstairs is a secret I will hold close to my chest and it goes down as the hottest night of my life.

Tonight has been all kinds of shades of fucked up.

Chapter 13

I creep into Bradey's room the next morning. The curtains are still closed and he's under a top sheet, with his leg hanging over the bed. His pillow is stuffed on top of his head, as if he needs it to block out the world and sleep. I stand at the foot of his bed and look around, feeling sad. There are old basketball posters sellotaped to his wall, and a small hoop by his desk with an overflowing rubbish bin underneath. My attention slides back to Bradey and I sigh when they focus on his raw knuckles. Something is off with Bradey and I wish I knew how to help him. This weird space between us feels unnatural.

As if magic energy surrounds me, changing at the new presence, I can feel him behind me. Nate is the other unnatural feeling in my life. His presence consumes me and it shouldn't.

"Will he be okay?" I whisper quietly. My throat throbs as I hold my tears back.

Nate steps into the room, lurking behind me while he looks over my shoulder at Bradey. "He will be if I can help it."

"And if you can't?"

"I don't want to think about that. It can't be an option."

"Are you going to tell me what's going on with him or is it male business?"

"It's not my business to tell. Nothing to do with the sex of the persons whose business it is."

"I heard you college boys have a secret club of sorts where fucked up shit happens and you all stay tight lipped."

There's a soft scoff behind me.

"If there is, I'm not a part of it. I don't blab secrets no matter who they are."

Bradey shuffles under his sheet and his hand reaches up toward his pillow. I can't have a conversation with him yet. I do what I am good at a lot, I side step Nate without looking into his face and leave the room.

I hobble downstairs and grab a glass of water to wash down my painkillers and anti-inflammatories for my knee. I'll be back at school tomorrow and promised the girls we would do a full routine practice because we have a football game this Wednesday and with it being the last week of school before summer break, we need to go out on a high.

I slide onto the barstool and shovel the handful of pills into my mouth before swallowing them down with some water. I hear footsteps behind me so I stuff the pill packets in my sweatpants pocket.

"Morning love."

I look up to Mom and smile. "Hi Mom."

"How was the party last night?" she asks me while pulling her box of granola out of the pantry. I watch her pale green, silk dressing gown sway as she moves.

"It was good."

"You weren't home too late?"

"Nah thought I should have an early night so I'm well rested for practice tomorrow."

The porcelain bowl pings as the granola gets poured in.

"Hopefully Lily stays away for a while so the coaches can see your full potential as captain."

My mouth hangs open as I take in Mom's blatant insensitive comment.

"Mom, Lily deserves to be here and deserves to be captain this year. I feel sad that she was missing last week because someone in her family *died*." The last of the sentence comes out a little bitchy but I am short fused at the moment.

"I know, that's not what I mean Paisley. I think it's just a good opportunity you have been given."

"Well what if cheerleading isn't in my future? What if this is as far as it goes."

"Don't be silly. You've trained hard for this. I can see you in big stadiums dancing, baby."

"I could get injured," I counter, testing a theory I have always known.

"Unless your back is broken, there are no injuries you can't work through. Pain is mental."

She strolls out of the kitchen, whistling away with her bowl gripped in one hand. Mom is a great psychologist and can be a loving parent. But Mom and Dad have always been like this. Because they are both successful and high achievers that is all they have ever expected from us as well. We have been pushed and pushed our whole lives. Now that we are adults, I feel like we aren't all eager to go in the direction they want us to go in. My mind shifts to Bradey briefly, wondering what he wants to do. We haven't talked properly in so long that I have no idea if his goals are still the same and if he is still happy.

Then I think back on my own conundrum. I want to be cheer captain next year, I want to dance in big stadiums and make world class teams. But if that wasn't to happen, I would have my parents' disappointment hanging over me for the rest of my life, so I would never be able to accept it and move on. I would be stuck.

I climb off the seat and go to the lounge where I park up on the couch and flick the TV on. A bare chested Bradey comes and slumps down next to me. He hangs his head over the back of the couch with his eyes closed.

"Hungover?" I ask while trying to keep it casual and scroll through Netflix. As I keep flicking sideways through the top ten movies, I peek sideways to see if Bradey has moved yet. He hasn't. His breathing drops into a steady rhythm before a soft snore slips from him. I turn my head and look over him while sighing. *I guess him coming to sit by me is his way of showing me he misses our closeness too?* That is what I hope anyway.

Nate comes and sits on the other side of me half an hour later. Bradey is still snoring and I leave him to it. I want to be close to him without us fighting. I want him to wake up and tell me all of which he chooses to hide from me.

"What we watching?" he asks while wrapping a damp arm around my shoulders.

"Elite," I say while staring into the flat screen. He scoffs but settles back. Small water droplets roll down his bare chest. He must've been swimming.

Nate pulls me harder against his chest, trying to get me to lay on him.

"What's changed with you?"

He pauses breathing, becoming still like a statue, then he slowly lets out a breath again. "We can't act like kids anymore, pretending things are different. It's exhausting."

"I have a kind of boyfriend."

He chuckles. "I have a kind of boyfriend too I guess."

I lay my head down on his lap and press play on the next episode of Elite. "I'm also kind of your sister."

"Well again I don't see you as my sister. So we're good."

I giggle quietly and then we both fall silent with just the sound of Netflix and Bradey's soft snore filling the space.

I force myself to focus on the TV and not the fact that I saw what is beneath my head. A thin layer of fabric separates me from his big cock. If I pulled down his waistline and turned my head just slightly I could have my own taste on it. Would my lips stretch far enough around it? I tried to give someone a blow job once, but me and the boy were sixteen and he prematurely ejaculated all over my face. It made me never want to touch a dick again after that.

I feel his cock twitch under me, turning into a semi. I gasp and try to sit up but he holds me down.

"How's the knee?"

"Sore."

"Mmm well prob shouldn't be doing cheer practice and running off to parties."

"I didn't run. I drove with Sara."

"Sarcasm is really beneath your intelligence." Amusement drips from his tongue.

"Sarcasm is the best form of defense in uncomfortable situations. You cannot change my mind."

"I would never dare try to change that mind of yours."

I roll my eyes and turn over so I'm looking up into his face. He looks down at me and moves a strand of hair away from my face. "I would say sarcasm is beneath your intelligence but..."

His chest vibrates as he chuckles under his breath. We stare silently at each other. His dark hair slides over his forehead, covering his thick lashes.

"I look into your dark eyes and see so many things I desperately want the answers to," I whisper.

"And I look into your pale blue eyes and almost see a version of me in them that's not fucked up. I like how you have always looked at me."

"You're not fucked up."

"But I am. I can feel my dad's evil blood running through my veins. I don't want it to be there but it is."

"You're nothing like him."

"You don't know me very well, remember?"

"I know your soul."

Nate runs a thumb over my forehead lightly and licks his lips.

"Don't talk to me about my soul. It will lead to nothing good."

I can feel him closing off again. So, I try a different approach.

"Are you gay?"

He takes the inside of his cheek in his teeth and purses his lips before answering, "Do you think I am?"

"No I guess not."

"Some things are just the way they are."

Chapter 14

Streams of burgundy and white fill the field grandstand seats while our squad begins stretches on the field. I sit down on the bench seat where our football team will be seated. This is their side. Across from us I see a lot of green and black. This is the last game before the football guys have a big summer break but it's also a friendly game. Well, it's labeled one. It's a club playing us, not a college in another town.

I look down at my swollen knee. Tears prick at my eyes while anxiety starts to build in me. Training on Monday killed me. I don't know what to do. It's like the walls are closing in on me and my lungs are being squeezed in a vice. I hang my head and let my shoulders roll in while I hide my deep, desperate breaths. I should have been honest from the start. But my entire life, from the moment I could walk, my parents wanted this for me. They have spent thousands on my training, one-on-one coaching and pageants and dance class every other weekend.

It morphed into me wanting the same thing. I need to be captain next year, or giving up the childhood I was jealous of all my friends having would have been for nothing. I see the disappointed faces of my parents flash behind my closed eyelids and I gag, vomit threatening to pool at my feet. I swallow and raise my head slowly while I seek out Sara. She's talking to a small group of girls but her focus turns to me, as if she can feel my eyes desperately seeking her out. She comes jogging over.

"You okay?" she asks.

"Can you get one of the new girls to take my place with the tumbles tonight? It can be a good practice run for them."

"What if they fuck it up?"

"They won't. I think I may be getting a tummy bug so I don't want to risk flipping."

"Okay girl. I got you!"

She nods and rallies the girls around her. Some of them give me questioning looks but they listen to Sara. I watch the group while feeling a tear slide down my cheek. I should have been honest and given Sara the chance to shine as well. She's a natural leader. She has an energy about her that everyone wants to be around, a commanding yet gentle voice that everyone responds to.

I hear the squeak of the small metal gate behind me then Nate sits down beside me.

"What the fuck are you doing at a football game?" I ask. I ignore the fact his cologne encases me in a strong erotic hold.

"I love football. It's my favorite game. Have you been taking your anti-inflammatories?"

"Yes, every day. They don't do shit."

"Not when you don't listen to your specialist and rest the fucking thing. You're ruining your body for people that don't give a shit about you."

"I'm ruining my body because it's my dream."

"If you think hard, I think you'll realize whose dream it is."

He runs his fingers over my knee, causing me to pull my head up and look around to see if anyone is watching our transaction.

"Calm down. You will make it obvious."

"I think I made a mistake," I mumble quietly while hanging my head again. I feel completely defeated.

"No shit," he bites out.

I stand up.

"I don't need your cocky shit right now," I sniff and straighten my shoulders. Nate stands at the same time and grabs my ponytail. His fingers work my ribbon and then pull it tight.

"Can't have a loose bow or everyone will really know something is wrong."

I step away from him, trying hard to keep an invisible line between us. But the once solid line is becoming blurred, dissolving away with every kindness he shows me. Nate is the only one that knows what is going on in my life and he's been more supportive than any of my family ever would have.

The seats are full, with only a few stragglers in the aisles. Both teams begin their final warm up on the field so we all huddle.

"Massive thank you to Sara for stepping in and rearranging things. My tummy is feeling a little queasy so I just don't want to risk any upside business." I try to pass it all off casually as a joke.

Kirsten giggles and nods. "Yeah I'd rather not have your vomit all over us. Don't worry, we got your back Paisley. You've been solid for years so we know you wouldn't pull out unless you had to."

My reply gets cut off from my emotional lump in my throat. Why did I ever think I couldn't be honest with these girls? I've been doing cheer with them since primary school.

"Right let's get it girls," Sara calls out as I struggle with speaking still.

We create our formation and clap in unison a few times when the music begins. We start with our basic counts, slowly working our way into our routine. I get to the point of our sphere shape when I spot Mom and Dad in the seats. They never come to my friendly performances. My head starts to spin as sweat beads on my forehead. They'll wonder why I'm not tumbling.

The rest of the routine goes like a distant dream playing out in front of my eyes. I keep my face blank, eyes trained on an empty space in front of me and count over and over in my head. I could do this shit with my eyes closed if I ever needed to. All the girls around me are smiling and cheering but I can feel my face locked solid. Sara and the new girl run and tuck into a round-off, followed by a back handspring. Everyone cheers. As soon as they both land perfectly I breathe a little easier.

We start clapping loudly and yelling out, "Go Grizzlies!"

We walk off to the sideline as the teams take their places on the field. I can feel my parents' disappointed vision on me. Nate is off to the side leaning casually against the chain link fence like he's a moody sex god and Sara keeps giving me a curious side glance. *Does she know I'm not sick?*

I rub my hand over my chest as it tightens, the muscles feeling restricted. My knee throbs with a heat ebbing deep within the joint. I desperately try to follow the game but I can't. The more I try to find something to distract me the more my heart pumps faster, slamming loudly against my rib cage. My mouth becomes filled with acid, and although I swallow over repeatedly, it keeps pooling in my mouth. I look for a way out. I need to finish the night with the halftime performance but I can't. My brain keeps telling me to run. Run from everything that is making my soul feel heavy.

The whistle blows, our team scores again. Absently, I clap my hands, feeling like a zombie.

I look sideways, down the barrier to where sky blue colors stand out in the sea of burgundy. Leith, Tucker and another friend wear blue singlets and baggy basketball shorts. He's leaning back against the hood of a Mercedes. He lifts his chin at me, giving me a soft nod, eyes crinkling as he smiles. RUN! my brain screams at me. I regard Nate and he shakes his head no. His stare has become an onyx black that terrifies me.

"What the fuck are they doing here?" Kirsten hisses when all attention goes to them.

"Just ignore them," Sara says, but she too watches the group of Hawks standing there acting casual but they have no business here. They are our greatest rivals and at a football game where people have been drinking and are already fired up, it'll end in disaster. I change my weight slightly as my knee burns hotter. I look over my shoulder to Mom and Dad and they're both glaring at me while whispering in each other's ears. They look livid. Confused and livid.

RUN! I hear in my crazed mind again. Tears well up, wetting my lashes. I walk past the bench seat, grab my small side bag that has my phone and belongings in it and take off toward Leith.

I don't look back. I can feel the heaviness of the stares behind me. I don't want to stay though, and face all the questions coming my way. Not from my parents and not from Sara who I'm fairly certain knows I don't have a tummy bug. I get to Leith and he pushes off the hood and strolls over to me like he owns the place. I lean over the fence and wrap my arms around his neck, pulling him into a kiss.

"Wanna get out of here?" he asks.

"You couldn't have picked a better time," I reply. I start to climb over the fence but Leith and Tucker lift me under the arms and pull me over in one motion. I walk to the car, about to sink down in the back seat and ready to be hidden from the world when I see one of his friends across the lot talking to Bradey. Bradey hasn't seen me. But they're huddled tight together.

"What's my brother doing with one of you?"

Tucker and Leith look over with grim looks.

"That your brother?" Tucker asks.

"Yeah."

"Hmm, just swapping ball skills, I'm sure. Let's get the fuck out of here," Tucker says and climbs into the driver's seat. Bradey takes off back to his car. I climb into the back with Leith, shaking my head. Every time I think I have seen it all, my world keeps getting more fucking strange.

Leith throws his arm around me and I lean against him. He kisses the top of my head and it feels sweet. But being here, snuggled up against him doesn't leave me with the same heat and desire I get when I'm around Nate. It's not distracting enough for the turmoil I am feeling.

"Pull into Chicken Palace," Leith instructs. His deep voice makes his chest vibrate against my cheek and I close my eyes. Willing myself to feel something more than a cute crush on a nice guy. It's hard to let things develop at a normal rate when you have someone in your life that gives you forbidden feelings that consume your very being. Everything compared to that is miniscule.

A few minutes later we roll into the parking lot. Tucker climbs out and slams the door behind him. As I'm about to open the door, Leith puts his hand on top of mine.

"Want to have some time alone together since we don't see each other much?"

The feeling in my gut tells me exactly what he is insinuating. I chew the inside of my cheek as I think about what I should do. I don't feel like I am overcome by hormones and that I want to jump his bones. But I *do* want to forget. I want to forget the world around me. I look into his handsome face and cave. I pull my hand off the handle and lace my fingers in his. Our intertwined hands rest between us. My skin doesn't burn with need at the slightest touch, but he's good for me. He's who I *should* want.

Chapter 15

The back seat is small but we make it work. Things don't move all that naturally. They are awkward and I am self-conscious. My determination will make this work though. Leith's muscled body is pinning me beneath him, his erection pressing into my thigh. He rocks his hips gently while rubbing my breast in his hand, showering my neck in soft kisses.

"I need to put a rubber on," he says as he sits up on his knees and pulls a condom out of his pocket. I sit up on my elbows and watch him take it out of the packet.

"Here let me," I offer with a nervous smile. I take it from his hands, careful not to slip off the narrow back seat. How do movies make this look so romantic? I grip his cock and slide the rubber over his length. This brings back nostalgia from health class with Sara. I force those thoughts away. There's no way I'm going to let him know I'm on the verge of a mental breakdown and that I'm a virgin. This is just another annoying part of my life I want remedied.

Once the rubber is flush with the base of his cock I lie back down again. Leith hovers over me, nudging at my entrance with his tip. He slides his hand between us and rubs my clit a few times. He snakes his hand over my hip, where it lands back on my breast. He inches his cock in and I grit my teeth.

"You're not wet enough." Leith pulls the tip of his cock out, spits onto his hand and rubs it over his shaft. "Let's try this again."

He pushes it in again, the friction stings at the walls of my vagina but I spread my legs more, hoping that will help. He gets the entire way in and pulls out a little before pushing back in completely again. There's a deep stinging in my pussy and I suck in a breath. Leith is reading it all wrong though.

"Good isn't it babe? You're so fucking tight," he groans and pumps into me faster. A few more thrusts and his cock spasms inside of me. Leith drops his head into the crook of my neck as he waits for his orgasm to pass. His heavy breathing brushes against my skin, making goosebumps erupt over my skin. Leith sits up and pulls his cock out. As he takes off the rubber he frowns. There is an uneasy feeling growing in my gut, fueling the anxiety I already have. I don't feel loved or taken care of like I had hoped.

"You got your fucking period?" Leith biffs the full condom out the window and onto the pavement.

"No, I didn't get my period."

"Well there's blood on the rubber. Maybe it was my big cock, doing damage," he says all arrogant.

Tonight was meant to be my distraction, to try and make me feel better, but I feel worse and I don't like Leith's attitude. His lack of affection toward me and my body has left me feeling used and empty. I didn't expect fireworks but I know Sara says she orgasms every time she has sex, and at the very least gets wet for her sexual partner.

All his friends climb back into the car and they all give us funny looks.

"Where to now?" Tucker asks as he starts the car.

"Can I please get dropped off at home?"

"Don't want round two baby?" Leith says with a grin.

"Round one that good huh?" His friend on the other side of me in the back seat says between mouthfuls of fries.

"The best. But we are made for each other so I would expect nothing less," Leith announces to everyone. I want to find a hole and run and jump into it. I sink down into my seat.

"Nah, I just want to go home. I have school tomorrow."

"Sweet babe. Two more days of school then we have all summer together." He pulls me against him.

We park outside my house and I see that the top bedroom lights are on but dark downstairs. I've already checked my phone and I don't have any messages from anyone. They all hate me.

"I'll see you later," I say to Leith and climb out of the car. He climbs out after me and pulls me into a kiss. It feels all wrong. This isn't what I want anymore.

"See ya babe." He smirks and slams the car door shut. Tears saturate my bottom lashes before they start flowing down my cheeks. I can't fight it anymore. I dash for my door, wanting to be hidden away in my room. As I go to open the front door, Nate rips it open and blocks the entrance. His shorts hang low on his hips and he's completely naked from the waist up. My sad gaze roams up his chiseled torso, over his small scattering of new dark chest hairs and up to his furious face. I cry harder. My body and heart want the man in front of me. My brother.

"Did he hurt you?" he hisses at me.

I shake my head. "I need to go to bed."

Nate grips my neck and spreads his thumb out so it presses my chin painfully, forcing my face up so we're looking into each other's faces.

"Tell me the truth Paisley. Did he fucking hurt you?"

I cry harder. The sobs are loud and ugly but Nate doesn't let go. I can see he is having his own battle. If I say yes, will he go after Leith? I know the answer to that. But Leith didn't hurt me. I hurt myself by making a string of bad choices.

"I'm a stupid girl. That's all."

"Don't ever call yourself stupid."

"I've made a mess of my life."

"It's nothing that can't be fixed. And nothing was intentional. You're the best person I know, Paisley. You bring the best out of everyone."

I sniff loudly but the tears keep coming.

"Do you love him?"

"I don't know. I thought I could."

Still gripping my neck, Nate brings me up to him, where he brushes my lips so lightly with his own. My whole body is ablaze with need, an inferno with longing, a desire that swallows me whole, only to spit me out broken.

"I will accept him as your first love, because I plan on being your last."

I swallow and meet his possessive gaze. Nothing in that determined stare tells me he isn't being truthful. He means every single word. My emotions are already frayed, and disappointment runs through my usually warm veins so they feel icy and pained. I viciously shake my head, feeling my tight ponytail loosen with my ribbon hitting the sides of my head. I can't do this now. Not with Nate. I don't think I can do this *ever*. I am a bad person through and through. I always thought I was a good person but I'm untrustworthy and selfish.

He grips either side of my head and holds it tight so I can no longer shake it.

"What the fuck happened tonight Paisley?"

Tears run down my cheeks as I gasp for air. I expect him to shake the answer out of me, demanding the truth. I expect him to be as disappointed in me as everyone else is. As I am in myself. But instead, he pulls me to him tightly and rests his chin on my head.

"I will kill anyone who hurts you. I'll kill myself if it is me causing you this pain."

"Don't say that," I whisper through a choked sob.

"I only ever speak the truth, you know that."

"How can life change so quickly?"

"Don't let life get you down. It's a series of small events that have snowballed into a big emotion." His fingers lightly run up and down my spine while he speaks words he seems so sure of.

"I fucked up tonight."

"You will be okay."

I push against his chest and look up into his face. I then walk toward the staircase and mumble, "I need to ring Sara."

His next words make me pause on the bottom step.

"Did you fuck him?"

Fresh tears run down my cheek as I think about the back seat of Tucker's car. I thought it was what I needed, I thought that getting my virginity lost and over and done with would help.

"Yes," I mumble and keep walking. I don't look back because it would shatter me if I did. It was a part of me that I wish I had saved for Nate but I never wanted to admit that. I still don't. He may not be blood related, but he's still my brother and we'll still be condemned.

I make it to my room and pull my phone out of my small bag. I scroll through my messenger app, looking for our bestie group chat but I can't find it. I frown as I try to manually search it, but nothing pops up. I message Sara privately, my thumbs flying over the screen and my stomach in my raw throat.

> Hey, can we catch up tomorrow before school? I need to talk to you.

> Sara: No thank you

I stare at the screen, feeling sodden with a single tear dropping onto the screen. I wipe it away and reply.

> Please, you will understand when I explain everything.

> Sara: I understand. We all do. You faked a tummy bug so you could take off with a Hawk boy. See you at our final training tomorrow. X

I read the message three times before I click the screen off and drop my phone to the ground. It all looks as bad as my head had made it out to be. They all hate me and think I'm an unloyal slut. I drag my hand slowly down my face and close my eyes as hurtful and unwanted flashbacks storm my mind.

"Paisley put one more tissue on the other side," Sara's sweet voice tells me while finishing on a giggle. I rip another tissue from the box, roll it in my hand and stuff it into Moms bra that is now hanging off my shoulders. Sara and I stand in Mom's full length mirror, with panties on, long crew socks and an oversized bra each. I smile widely as I turn from side to side, showing my two missing front teeth.

"I wonder if my boobies will get as big as Moms when I am older." I ponder and catch Sara's gaze in the reflection. She grips the bottom of the bra she is wearing and pushes it up, so the white tissues squish together, giving off the look of cleavage.

"When we get boobies we have to make sure we buy our very first bra together."

"Yes we have to. We have to do everything together for the rest of our lives." I agree.

She turns to me, dropping her tissues from her bra and squeezes my hands excitedly. I grip them back and we jump up and down before swinging each other around in a circle. "Let's marry our boyfriends at the same time too. We can wear matching dresses and walk up the aisle together," She squeals and smiles at me, showing her new adult teeth starting to grow in the same spot I have just lost my own teeth. I smile back at her, feeling like she's the only person I will ever need in my life. She's the best person in the world.

Chapter 16

I step into the gym feeling like enemy number one. The girls openly stare at me when I slowly walk in trying to act nonplussed. I don't want to hide away in the shadows but I also don't want to act arrogant because I know I fucked up. It's a tough balance. My walk is casual, yet careful, slow, yet not slow enough to make myself look scarce. I'm halfway across the court and I feel like I have an awkward robotic walk, making my legs lift and stretch out as if controlled by a puppet master. Kirsten takes a step back from me as I near their group, so she is snug in the middle of the cheer girls. Sara holds her position and crosses her arms over her chest.

I clear my throat and run my hands through my long ponytail, gliding over the straight ends as if it is my lifeline.

"I want to apologize to everyone for last night. I owe everyone an explanation," I say loudly but there's a soft quiver to my voice. My heart is hammering against my ribs again, my ears are thumping so much, I am certain everyone around me can hear the sound. Can they smell my fear along with the nervous pounding of my fragile heart?

"We only have an hour's practice so why don't you just get on with the lesson, *captain*," Sara drags out and looks over all the girls like she's rallying a gang.

"Okay I guess we can start with some stretches and then go through a routine," I mumble pathetically. I'm showing my weakness, which makes me look guilty too. If I was a dog I would have my tail between my legs and my ears hanging low, and I kind of feel like a dog right now.

We begin doing some stretches with the coaches standing back. Watching my performance, no doubt. I try to let the uncomfortable emotions run their course, let go of what I can't control but I feel the accusing glares from my team, like they're throwing knives and I'm the bullseye.

We turn the music on and with my instruction, we work in small groups. We have most of our performances down packed so I figure why not work on fine tuning our strengths and positions in the team? I'm a coward because this also means I'm not with Sara. She's with a few girls, helping them get faster with their tumbles because that is her strength. I stand back, watching over the small groups in the gym when I catch my head coach walking toward me. I keep my face angled forward but as she nears, my heart races faster.

"Can I have a word with you Paisley?" Her voice is clipped, and nauseousness rises within me.

"Yeap sure," I murmur and follow her to the far side where large college banners hang. I hug my sides as I trail behind her, my eyes lingering on the proud display. Regret is the dominant emotion at the forefront of my mind and heart. I only have myself to blame for my turmoil.

My coach spins on her heels and faces me with her arms crossed tightly over her chest. Tilting her head, she licks her teeth in a pissed off manner.

"Do you care to explain why you let the team down last night?"

"I am so sorry. I have some personal things going on, and I guess..." I pause as I finally admit to myself the reality of what I experienced. "I had a panic attack and took off when things got too much. I'm ready to face it all now and I will never let it happen again."

"No you won't, because you are no longer the captain. Lily won't be here for half of next semester and we have asked Sara to fill her spot. You not only let all the girls down but you also let yourself down. We all expected better from you, Paisley."

"But I just had a bad mental health day. It won't happen again. I won't let it," I plead.

"That's a very sad and pathetic excuse. You are lucky you are still on the team. Now I want a full run through of the routine and then we will announce Sara as new captain."

I stare at the disappointed face in front of me and absently nod. Can a panic attack and dip in your mental health be a sad excuse? Can it not be good enough? Should I have lied once more and come up with a better excuse. I turn, almost robotic, and walk toward the group while I hear my head coach's booming voice behind me.

"Girls, we are doing a full run through for the basketball final game routine next semester. Get into position."

They all scramble with big smiles on their faces. I watch all of them, with a darkness now a light sheet gently touching my once light and fluffy persona. I make one fuck up and I'm thrown to the side. Memories of endless cupcakes for my cheer squad and offering to iron their cheer skirts on the weekends while they party come back to me. Now I wish some of them would hurt themselves so they can see how it can become a lonely spiral where your actions are not ones you are proud of. I chastise myself for thinking such thoughts, but these foreign feelings are becoming more vocal in my head.

We get into position and I roll my shoulders while stretching my head side to side. I look beside me, to where I know my once best friend is positioned. She side eyes me and frowns then looks ahead. I look forward once more and am met with Nate in the far distance, leaning against the open door frame and his arms across his chest. He shakes his head slightly. It's so subtle I should have missed it. But I take in every single thing about Nate whenever he's in sight. The broody, dark male is my shining light. His presence has been my light in the darkness. He knows I shouldn't be doing this right now, but I need to prove to these girls, even if only one girl forgives me, that I still take this seriously. I can worry about my knee tonight; I will double up on pain meds and rest it all summer break if I need to. *I can get through this.*

"Go Grizzlies, hear them roar!" we all chant and clap our hands. "Watch out for their deadly claws!" It echoes off the high gym walls. I count the steps in my head, looking ahead, never missing a beat. I'm solely focused on every single count in my mind. I take three large steps back, let out a held breath and then skip forward and launch off the ground, throwing myself into a double back tuck. I collapse to the ground as my feet hit the floor. My knee gives out with excruciating pain. A scream tears hoarsely from my throat as my entire body trembles. This is the worst pain I've ever experienced.

Kirsten comes over, hands flying over me and words coming out of her mouth but I can't process exactly what she's saying. The coaches crouch low beside me and I grip my knee, tears sliding down my cheeks.

"We will call an ambulance," the assistant coach states.

I shake my head quickly. "No, I am fine."

"You need to get it looked at." The head coach looks at me with fear.

Yeah I wasn't fired from the squad because everything aside, I'm still one of their strongest squad members. Now her brain must be scrambling with what it means if I can't compete.

"Shouldn't you be in class?" the assistant coach asks, looking up at Nate's approaching figure. I close my eyes and cry harder. The pain is getting worse.

"I am where I need to be. Now fuck off," Nate's deep voice growls loudly. He crouches low and pulls me against his chest before standing tall again.

"I have her, get the fuck out of my way," he warns everyone then slowly heads toward the exit.

"It's bad," I sob into his chest. I hate needing this man the way I do, but in my moment of need, I cling to him so tightly that I fear I may stop breathing if I let him go.

"I'm taking you to the hospital. Then I will tell you all about how I was right once again." His spicy cologne envelopes me. Is it family ties that make me feel like I'm in a safe cocoon, or is this the strange feeling I've been experiencing lately? Feeling this way is all kinds of wrong, yet the more I fight it the more I realize it's every bit perfect for me, and he may be the only guy that gets me. He may be the only guy that I *want* to get me.

Chapter 17

We drove to the hospital in his large wheel ute. It's matte black with black rims, but it doesn't get used much because he rides with my brother most days. The way he gently put me into the vehicle is a complete contrast to how he spoke to the team. It's also a contrast to the haunting way he seems to track my every movement and watch me with a look, letting me know he isn't sure if he wants to devour me or torture me. Maybe both at the same time.

After waiting half an hour to be seen, I'm now lying on a hospital bed in the emergency department. Nate's fingers clench mine tightly. It's the only indicator that he feels anything, because the rest of him is still and silent. He sits back in his chair with one leg kicked out in front of him while he scrolls on his phone. Every now and then he looks up to the pulled curtain to see if whoever is walking past is stopping to check up on me, otherwise he says nothing. What a moody, silent enigma.

"How's your kind of boyfriend?" I ask, trying to distract myself from my swollen knee that is now on an oddly shaped angle.

Nate raises his head, peering through his black strands of hair. He tilts his head slightly then looks back down to his phone.

"How's your fuck buddy?" His words bite out as his fingers clench my hand a little tighter.

"So you can rub nasties with whoever you want but I can't?"

"I don't rub nasties, I get my cock sucked."

"Well I'm glad I got rid of my virginity. You and Bradey controlled my love life for too long."

"Clearly for good reason," he scorns me, words like acid, but still, he keeps his head pointed down. "Were you nice and wet for him? Did you enjoy coming all over his pathetic tiny dick?"

I try to pull my hand from him as his words fuel a deep anger within me but he refuses to let it go. He hit a soft spot, because with all my confident gloating, his words hurt me because I did neither of those things when I lost my virginity. It was nothing like movies or romance novels portray.

I chew the inside of my cheek and choose to turn my head and look at the blank white wall rather than Nate's face. I can't stand it. As soon as his face leaves his phone and lands on me, I feel the weight of it.

"Did he taste your pussy?"

"Nate, stop. You can't ask those questions."

"Answer the fucking question Paisley. I've had to struggle with the fact he took what was meant for me. At least tell me he treated you well."

I know what he means. Leith hasn't done anything to hurt me, but he was selfish in that situation and with all the thoughts in my head about that moment would look like, that wasn't it. But I blame myself, how did I think it would go with running off and doing it in the backseat of a car? My cheeks warm as the silence between us grows. His demanding stare grows wilder.

"You can't be angry about something that has nothing to do with you."

"Oh Paisley. You should know by now I don't get angry. I'm pretty fucking good at fixing all the wrongs in the world though."

I whip my head to the side, meeting Nate's penetrating gaze front on. A deep furrow forms between my eyes.

"Don't hurt him."

His lips tug at the corners, turning it into a smirk that isn't a happy one. It's malicious.

Nate chooses silence but the energy in the room tells me nothing is promised.

"How do you always know where I am? Every time I need you, you appear, and sometimes when I don't..." I mumble the last part. A scoff leaves him as he settles into his seat more.

"You didn't think I wouldn't have put a tracker on your phone the moment Mommy and Daddy got you your very first one."

The curtain pulls back and Mom, Dad and Bradey walk in.

"Baby we got here as fast as we could. I just saw the doctor on the way in and he will be here shortly," Mom says before she pauses then looks at Nate. "Thank you for messaging us. But you can go now."

Nate looks confused and I glance between them all. Bradey stares apologetically at Nate before his shoulders slumps as he looks down.

"I would rather stay here if it's all the same to you," Nate says slowly.

My dad clears his throat then wraps his arm around Mom's waist.

"We found the drugs in your bedroom. We have packed your bags already and they are waiting by the front door. You need to be gone before we get home."

My mouth goes dry and lungs burn as I hold my breath. My sweaty fingers grip Nate's hand harder. Drugs? He doesn't take drugs, I would know. "I want him to stay. He's no druggy."

"It's not up to you. We won't call the cops if you leave without a fuss."

Nate stands slowly and slips his hand from mine.

"Don't go! They can't make you."

Nate looks at Bradey then shakes his head as he gazes down at me. He brushes the hair from his eyes.

"It's okay. I'll check in with you later. This was always going to happen."

"You don't take drugs. How can you say that?"

He snorts and looks at Mom and Dad.

"Not the fucking drugs. Them...My place as their son was always conditional. See that's the thing, they love you and Bradey unconditionally. They would never kick you out if you fucked up. Me? I am a fill-in son with a lot of conditions. They say they love me, until I fuck up. They love me as long as I don't outshine you both. But I have to shine just enough to be good enough to be their son." He walks out through the curtain and I am too choked up to call after him. Mom takes his spot on the seat and tries to grab my hand but I rip it away and hold it against my chest.

"How could you do that to him?"

"I will not have a drug user in my home." Mom spits at me while crossing her arms at her chest.

"Is what he said right? Would you have kicked me or Bradey out?"

She side eyes Dad then nods. "Of course." But her words come out weak, dismal and full of shit.

Conditional love keeps running through my mind. I never thought of his position in our family like that. To me he would always have a place in my heart. The doctor walks in, holding his clipboard and blue ball point pen in his other hand.

He starts talking but I can't take in his full sentences. I want to chase Nate. What if he leaves and never comes back? Through my spiraling I hear the words surgery, long recovery and the sighs of disappointment from my parents. I lay my head completely back against the pillow and cover my face with my hands. My long manicured nails scrape my scalp while I heave in breaths.

"It's okay Paisley, we'll get a second opinion, your cheerleading career isn't over."

I speak against my hands that still shield the heartbreak that is written on my face. "Do you realize it's more than just my knee? I've fucked up so much that I have no chance of being captain and the only person that knew how to comfort me is gone from my life."

"If the college wants to keep receiving our donations they will pick you for captain. And you won't be seeing that Hawks boy again."

That causes me to slip my dampened hands from my face. Not because I desperately need to see Leith again but because of the way she is speaking to me as if I am still a child.

"You know I can technically do what I want. I'm eighteen."

"Paisley, you still think like a child. Look at the embarrassing performance you put on last night." Moms disapproval of me is apparent with every word and displeased look she gives me.

"I had already hurt my knee so I couldn't perform properly."

"And my point stands."

I stare into my mom's face, looking for some sort of empathy. Understanding of the slightest, just a fucking hint. But there's nothing.

"How have you and Dad always been this way yet we have never noticed?"

"Been what way?" she asks as she leans back in the hospital chair. She tucks her bob behind her ears and crosses her legs. She wears a high end, tailored navy blue suit with plum matte lipstick. Her image has always shown impeccable professionalism.

"More concerned about us being highly successful rather than healthy or happy."

"Successful is happy. Succeeding in life and making something of yourself is how you be happy."

"Do you really truly believe those words that come out of your mouth? You're meant to be a shrink."

"I am a children's counselor. It's not like I work in a psych ward. I still am allowed an opinion on how life should be."

"An opinion, exactly. It's just that. Do you think me, Bradey and Nate are truly happy?"

"You will be when you are cheer captain and dancing around the world, and Bradey will be when he is a world class surgeon."

"And Nate?"

"He takes drugs and brings drugs into our home. We gave him the best opportunities and he fumbled them. I no longer want to talk about him."

"He's cut off? Just like that?" I bite out and swipe away a lone tear

Mom purses her lips together then clears her throat. She looks at Dad and changes the subject. "I want another doctor to look over Paisley's notes."

"Of course dear."

"I want you all to leave, I am tired," I mutter.

"You are due to go into surgery to repair your ligament."

"Ligament?"

"Yes, it seems you completely tore a ligament and have a small fracture but that should heal okay."

"Unlucky," I mumble. As much as I try my mind can't keep up and get past the fact Nate apparently uses narcotics.

"I still want to be left alone. Eighteen, remember? I will call you when it is done."

"Paisley..." Dad warns from my other side. His sleeves are rolled up, showing his aging arm hair and Rolex watch. I shake my head and stick to my guns. I feel like I've been backed into a corner.

"Out now," I say again, stronger this time.

Bradey is leaning up against a small piece of wall, one leg folded behind him so his school sneaker is flat against the wall under his behind. "You can stay. I want to talk to you."

As if he was expecting it, he nods and doesn't try to argue.

With a scrape of the chair, Mom stands up and paces out of the small cubicle with Dad trailing behind her. Her heels click on the corridor flooring before it becomes a faint echo.

Bradey slowly creeps over and sinks down onto the seat. My brain starts going into a hysterical state as I internally joke about it's now becoming the hot seat.

"Do you really think Nate is on drugs?"

"No, not him. Me."

"You?"

Bradey drops his face into his hands while shaking his head side to side. He looks back up to me with pleading bloodshot eyes.

"Mom and Dad can't find out." His voice quivers.

"How long has this been going on?"

He lifts his shoulders with what looks to be weighted boulders.

"It started out as just the odd line at parties, then gradually grew to buying a whole bag for myself at parties, then I don't know, I guess it became during the week as well and now I need it to get through the day."

"How did Nate get roped into this?"

He sniffs loudly then rubs his eyes. He's been looking off for weeks but now it all makes sense.

"He saw me doing lines at the parties and would look after me at the end of the night. I guess it became our little pattern. Routine if you will. Then he found out how bad it got so he told everyone in the basketball team to cut me off."

"What about the college piss tests for team events?"

"Nate or whoever was clean."

I am in a state of disbelief.

"Don't look at me like that. There is so much worse that fucking happens."

"You need to come clean and tell Mom and Dad."

"Stop worrying about your precious fucking Nate. He'll be fine and I'm going to get clean while I am on summer break with Mom and Dad."

"I don't think coming off a drug addiction is that easy." I point all my anger and resentment toward him.

"It is for me because I know I can give up if I want to. I just haven't wanted to."

"You have this all figured out, don't you?"

"Stop trying to act like your perfect high and mighty self. You admitted before you had already hurt your knee but have been lying to everyone about it."

"That's completely different. I'm no drug addict."

"So judgmental Paisley. Should I ask Sara if she thinks ditching the team for some Hawk cock is okay by friend standards?"

I glare at him and pull myself into a sitting position. "When did you turn into such a nasty person? I've always done everything for everyone. I go through one bad patch and everyone ditches me the first chance they get! Fuck you all and get the fuck out of my cubicle!"

"Gladly. And if you try dob me into Mom and Dad, I will tell them all about Nate's fun, nighttime pool side activities which will get Mr Perfect kicked out of college."

Bradey stomps out, throwing the curtain to the side as he pushes through it. I sit there stunned, completely alone and wondering who the fuck everyone is anymore. Including myself.

How did life go from picture perfect Stepford wife families to drug addicts, whores and well, Nate. I have no idea who he is and what he does. Yet somehow he's still the closest person to me that I have in my life. There may be a lot of mental and psychical distance between us but we have a connection on a deeper level. I can feel it and I know he does too. We don't need words. But I do need him in my life. I glance at my phone that sits on the small trolley beside me, but as I go to reach for it the doctor and a few nurses walk in.

"Good afternoon Miss Wilson. You need to be nil by mouth for another few hours before we can proceed with the surgery, but we do have a space for you tonight."

I nod carefully and look down at my leg that's in a full brace.

"What's the recovery time?"

He lets out a sigh and laces his hands together behind his back. "You're young, fit and healthy so with time and physio you could make a full recovery. But you have completely torn your ligament from the landing and you have fractured your knee as well, so you will always have a chance of restricted movement in your knee. We won't really know until further into your recovery."

"We will take you to a private room on the ward where you will wait for surgery. If it all goes well you should be discharged tomorrow." The doctor carries on as two nurses stand on either side of the bed and tap the wheel brakes off. They start pushing me out of the small cubicle and all I can do is lie back and stare at the sterile white ceiling and flashing fluorescent lights with nothing but regret and self-loathing over my actions.

Chapter 18

"A re you comfortable enough?" Mom asks for the fifth time in the span of one hour. She fusses over the blankets that are propping me up against my headboard again.

"Mom, I am fine. I just want to sleep this grogginess off."

"Okay I will check on you again at lunch time. You should try to eat."

"Sure…" I murmur and pull my hair from its messy bun so the unruly tendrils flow over my shoulders. I massage my head with my fingers, trying to remedy my pounding head. I feel like shit.

Once my door finally clicks shut and I am left alone, I turn my phone on. Notifications start blowing up, but as I scroll through them all I notice there isn't any messages from Nate. There are about twenty from Leith. I click on his name and scroll through the string of messages.

Leith: Morning Beautiful xx

That was from yesterday morning, the day after our back seat rendezvous.

Leith: Hey you okay?

Leith: You going to sleep with me then give me the cold shoulder?

Leith: Tucker spoke to Sara, you off the squad and everyone's hating you? What's going on?

Leith: Why are you acting like I have done something fucking wrong?

Leith: Sweet as, I see how it is now. You just used me?

Leith: Heeeey, Tucker said you're in the hospital. Sara said something about karma? Are you okay and sorry for my previous message.

Leith: Please message me back when you can

Leith: Hey, it's been two days… maybe you are just ignoring me?

Leith: Okay, I'll catch you later Paisley.

I feel exhausted once I have got through the roller coaster of messages. Karma? Kicked off the team? Using him? For what? The sex was horrible.

I decide to rip the band-aid off and ust message him back.

> Hey I have only just turned my phone on. I have been in surgery and only just got home. I have some family shit going on right now so can't do a relationship right now. I hope we can still be friends.

I read it over again before I send it. Old habits die hard, because instead of sending a scathing message back I am being Mrs Nice Gal.

His reply hits back instantly and I suck my bottom lip in while shaking my head.

> Leith: Who said we were ever in a relationship?

He's projecting, I keep telling myself that at least. He's also an immature piece of shit and a mommy's boy that can't fuck for shit. My eyes dart around as I internally scream the added on sentence as if someone would hear me.

There's another message that has me confused. It's Kirsten. This could be really, really bad or just a little bit bad. But either way I can't see what she wants to say as being anything good.

> Kirsten: Hey you up for visitors?

> Not really. I'm pretty tired.

> Kirsten: I won't stay long. Just want to check in x

I drop my phone beside me and close my eyes. I'm not falling for their shit. Sara's probably sending her my way to do her dirty work and rub her nose in my failing life.

I wake to a shifting of weight on my bed and murmured voices. I squeeze my eyes shut harder, I feel them scrunch and then a soft, girly giggle follows.

"Paisley, acting was never your forte."

I open one eye and my half-asleep blurriness lands on vibrant blonde hair and a concerned face looking at my wrapped leg.

"I thought I said no visitors."

"Well I ignored you. Your toes are really chubby. Is that normal?" she mumbles and pinches my big toe. I wriggle them, trying to make her stop.

I open both eyes and look down at my foot. My toes are purple and fat. "I don't know. Maybe I need it elevated more."

Kirsten jumps up and grabs a pillow then carefully lifts my leg at the ankle and slides another pillow underneath. The pain intensifies and causes me to hiss and grip my thigh.

"Sorry."

"No, it's not your fault." I half scoff when the words leave my mouth. "It's actually all mine."

"Don't say that. God, people fuck up. Not like we are all perfect. Although we like to judge like we are." She smiles sadly then climbs over my legs and lies beside me. She rests her head on my shoulder.

"Why are you being nice to me?" I feel suspicious, skeptical that she could be here out of kindness and not with an ulterior motive.

"Because we are best friends and I would need you if I was ever in a low point in my life."

"Sara will hate you for being my friend." Suspicion is replaced with regret. When did life make me so pessimistic?

Kirsten lets out a big sigh and starts braiding a small piece of her long hair. "Sara is just hurt because you didn't tell her every detail of your life. She's angry because I think she always thought if you had shit going on she would be the one and only person to know your secrets. But Sara needs to realize we aren't little kids anymore. We're adults and we're all heading in different directions. She'll get over it."

"Different directions is right. No more cheerleading for me."

"You can cheer again."

"Mmmm I don't think so. But yeah, I should have been more honest but I didn't know how at the time. I guess it snowballed." My voice hitches.

"Snowballed is right. Well you know you can tell me anything."

"I don't even know where to start."

"Start at the beginning."

"Sheesh it feels like a lifetime ago yet it has only been mere weeks."

Silence falls between us as my mind races with events and every touch, look and word Nate has spoken to me. My insane decision to let Leith put his dick in me to solve all my problems, and my knee that has decided it doesn't want to help me reach my dreams. And about my parents that care until they don't need to no more.

My chest rises as I suck in a deep breath and then smile, feeling a strange type of freeness come to me.

"Well I think I may be in love with my brother. I'm no longer a virgin, got Leith's spit in my vag and I hid my sore knee because I was worried the coaches would think I was weak and now my slightly torn ligament is a fully fucked knee."

She sits up, her eyes glowing like an excited child. She spins on her ass and faces me front on.

"Okay it sucks about your knee. But brother and Leith! Catch me up."

"I don't know, shit with Nate has gotten so weird. But there's just this wild energy between us. He says nothing at all yet it feels like he is saying everything at once."

"Does it not feel weird that you grew up with him? He was there through all your tummy bugs and probably when you pissed your bed when you were little."

I slap her arm and laugh. "I know, I know. I saw him as nothing but a brother until recently."

"Well he *is* hot and not your blood but it still feels creepy. But theeeen in a kinky taboo way it's also kind of hot."

"Like the forbidden fruit."

"Mmmm like the forbidden fruit," she agrees while nodding her head. "What about Leith? He's such a nice guy."

"Was. He shoved his cock in dry, then pulled it out, spat on it then rammed it in again. I think Tucker still talks to Sara too and it just caused a stupid mess."

Kirsten turns around and lies back down beside me. It's nice having her here, and I've told her everything I have been holding in and yet she hasn't screamed at me from disappointment and hatred.

"So why leave us the other night? Was it your knee?"

"I don't know if I can pinpoint it. I think too many little things had happened and it caused a panic attack I suppose. When Leith turned up I saw a way out of the whirlwind in my life. Turns out I just made another mistake though."

"Fuck Leith. Fuck them all. You are so smart and pretty. You can do whatever you want. You could travel the world if you wanted. Not be held back by cheerleading."

"Cheerleading is all I know and all I have wanted to do."

"I know, girl. I can understand why you're unhappy. You are grieving the future you had all planned out."

"Wow I never looked at it like that. *Grieving...*" I say the word slowly as I let it sink in.

"You have plenty of time to discover the new you. It can be fun and exciting when you are over the shock."

Something in me changes. Amongst the disturbing emotions there is a new spark. It's small, almost threatening to be extinguished by the storm swirling around it. But it's there. I cling to the small glimmer of hope and it brings a soft excitement in me.

"I don't know what else I like doing. But it's not to say I can't discover something."

"You are great at loads of things."

Kirsten leans down and pulls up my throw, placing it over top of us both.

"Well tomorrow we can brainstorm. Tonight let's watch some movies about mysterious grumpy men and you can pretend they're Nate."

I smile and bite my bottom lip. "Did you hear about him getting kicked out? I nearly forgot about it with being distracted talking to you about everything else."

"Mmmm a lot of people at school have been buzzing over it. No one knows where he's staying. Have you talked to him?"

"Nah he hasn't messaged. But again, tomorrow's problem," I confirm and rest my head on her shoulder. My heart feels a little lighter right now and I want to bask in it.

Chapter 19

With all the pain meds I'm on, I slept through most of my last day of school. I've ignored social media because it will be inundated with happy start of summer break posts. I ate chicken noodle salad for dinner alone in the kitchen. I pull a pillow out from under my head so I only have one now and lie flat. My silk PJs feel better than what I was in last night. The shorts and button-up t-shirt top are easy to move in and keep me cool. I close my eyes, ready for another night's sleep. As a loud yawn stretches my cheeks painfully, and a soft steady snore follows only moments later.

It's still dark when I am awoken again. I lay in complete darkness aside from the soft orange glow of my salt lamp in the corner of the room. Goosebumps cover my body as I feel a charged energy in the room. It's a dangerous one, a blanket of thick perilous energy.

My fingers slowly feel around for my phone while my eyes dart around as I contemplate screaming for help. By the time someone reaches me I will be dead though. As my fingertips tap my phone, it rips away from me, the movement of clothing so close to me causing a small scream to burst from my lips before a hand smothers it, muffling me.

"I've never been so hard in all my fucking life. I thought your smart mouth awake was the hottest thing in the world, but watching you sleeping with the thought of sliding my cock in you while you are unaware does things to me I should be ashamed of." The words breathe against my ear before sharp teeth nip at my earlobe. "But I'm not ashamed."

The voice is one I recognize. A voice that can nearly make me come just from simply hearing it. It's probably the most words I have heard from him for a while.

Nate speaks again. "I am going to remove my hand and you will come with us, if you try to call out for help, well you may not like what happens," he threatens me. Us?

"You hear me?" he whispers again. His hushed voice sends a shiver through my body. I nod.

As his fingers slip away, I burst out, "How did you get in? Who's with you and why, how could you?" I have so many questions that it all comes out in a fast jumbled mess.

"Quiet, Paisley. Last warning. And I have had ways in and out of this house for years. It ain't no fucking Fort Knox, and my kind of boyfriend and his kind of boyfriend are here. Get up Paisley, we're going for a drive."

"Like fuck I am going with you anywhere! Jesus Nate, maybe I was wrong and you are on drugs!" I hiss out, looking around. I can't see them. But now I know they are here, somewhere, observing all this and it throws a cold bucket of ice over the heated pleasure I felt before.

"I was hoping you would put up a fight." I hear the excited taunting in his voice. I can only imagine the smug smirk playing on his lips, paired with dark, wild eyes.

"Why are you doing this?"

"I'm fixing the injustice," he growls before his strong, muscular hands wrap around my neck. I tap on them violently but it's no use. My airways are cut off and I get a slight tingling in my mind.

"I won't hurt you. Trust me. Like you always have," he says before my eyes flutter shut and I pass out.

I wake up to dim lights that are perfectly lined along a high ceiling. I try to sit up but my arms are held behind me and I'm laying back against a lounge chair. I hear the soft humming of a machine and hushed voices. As I blink rapidly and look around, waiting for my eyes to adjust properly, Nate's face comes into view.

He runs a finger down my cheek before it slides to my chin and pinches it.

"You deserved better than what you got. I need to make this right for you." His words are firm, non-negotiable, but his eyes seem like they're searching mine for some hope or understanding. *Understanding for what?*

"Paisley, what the fuck is this shit?" The strained voice echoes off the walls. I wriggle myself to a sitting position, my leg has a fluffy folded towel under my braced leg. So *kind and thoughtful,* I sarcastically grind out in my head as I look around at my surroundings.

I'm in the college pool building. My lost gaze lands on Leith. He's on a small plastic chair with bound hands behind him.

"Nate, what is he doing here? You've lost your fucking mind!" I spit out and again try to push off the recliner to try to stand up. Me and Leith need to leave whatever messed up shit Nate is trying to drag us into. Whatever hands hold my arms, loosen so I can move a little more.

Nate stands tall beside me with his arms crossed over his chest while he stares daggers at Leith.

"Don't tell me you feel sorry for the pretty boy. He's not a very nice person."

As I go to stand up straight, a heavy hand slams down on my shoulder and pushes me back down. I flick my head up and lock eyes with Nate's little boy toy. "*This is insanity!*" I'm yelling, going from angry to worried now. My heart is racing, hearing it pound in my ears like a frantic drum.

"No, the insanity is that you lost your virginity to someone like him." He says so low I barely hear him while dipping his head in Leith's direction then continuing. "The insanity is that he got offered such a special gift, yet he wasted the gift because he's a selfish little prick. He couldn't even make it good for you. I'm going to show him how he should have been with you." Nate turns and faces me now. He runs his tongue over his teeth before his lips tug into a mischievous smirk.

"I'm going to show you what you deserve and how your first time should have been." He tilts his head while his chest rises and drops rapidly under his bulky arms.

A deep frown runs across my forehead and I swipe my hand over my eyes. I'm feeling major whiplash from being in a deep sleep to being in a nightmare with my once brother—now hopeless crush—at the center of it. This is the dark side of Nate I had been desperately wanting to see, the part of his life he kept hidden from me. I wanted to know everything about him, but now I wish more than anything I could go back and be naive with my erotic dreams tucked away safely in my head.

"Nate, I stuck up for you about the drug thing. Now I'm starting to think it's all true, because you either have to be on a narcotic high right now or you're clinically insane."

Nate walks around the front of me, like he is stalking his prey. His eyes are the color of a gloomy shadow, hiding pain and deadly secrets in the depths of them.

He leans down over the foot of the lounger, placing both his hands on either side of my legs and flexing on his broad shoulders.

"You want me. Your soul sings to mine every time we are together. You have tried to be a good mommy's girl for too long. The rebellious, free spirit inside of you is desperate to get out. Let go and embrace your true nature."

I shake my head from side to side, refusing to let him be right. But some of his words resonate with the core of my being.

"Not like this," I murmur into his face that is now inches away from mine.

"Exactly like this. You fucked up letting him put his cock near you. He fucked up being a selfish little boy." He whispers the angry words against my lips. His teeth nip at my bottom lip, pulling it out while he playfully nibbles on it.

"You are a fucking psycho!" Leith yells behind Nate. I shamefully drop my eyes, because for ten seconds I forgot Leith was there, tied to a chair.

Nate puts his hand around my throat and forces my face back to his.

"From now on, every time you show me you feel sorry for that weasel, I will cut a piece of his body off in front of you."

Nate stretches tall again, casting a long shadow over me. I let him see the pleading in my eyes but he just smiles at me.

He turns and casually strolls over to Leith before his arm whips out and wraps around his neck. Nate places his mouth against his ear and whispers slowly into it. I can't hear the words but Leith's face changes, becoming angry. He nods once when Nate is finished his sentence then relaxes against his seat. Nate nods to the two guys behind me then one grips my shoulders and Nate's boy toy comes around and lurks in front of me.

"Don't hurt me. You won't get away with it." I try to reason with them.

He chuckles and squints his eyes at me. "We aren't here to hurt you. We're here to show you how good fucking for a woman like you should be."

Chapter 20

I stare at two faces in front of me. Their hungry, predatory looks send shivers through me.

"You can't force this on me." My words hitch at the end of my sentence while I suck in a breath through my softly parted lips.

Nate slips off his shirt and throws it beside him. My shoulders are still in a tight vise grip from his friend who I recognize from the school swimming team. Lance copies and takes his tight singlet off, revealing scattered tattoos of numerous random images across his torso. Nate closes the gap between us and crouches down by the bed.

I watch his lush lips part. "Tell me you haven't dreamed of this? Tell me that deep down you don't want to come all over my tongue? Tell me you want me to stop and I will, but I'll also need to extract my revenge in another way if that's the case." He slides his eyes toward Leith when he says that.

"You're deranged. You know that!"

The corner of his lips tug into a lopsided smile. "Oh I know, I came from two parents who put a capital E on evil. It's in my genetics."

Nate leans over me, and I slam my back down against the seat, tensing instantly. I want to keep a gap between us, but I am their prisoner and...their prey.

Nate follows my movements, lowering himself on top of me so we are millimeters apart.

His heavy breathing is all I can hear as he dips his head and slides his sizzling tongue up the length of my jawbone. When he reaches the base of my ear he lets his fast, hot breath coat it before saying, "If I had it my way, I would have sucked your clit and eaten your pussy for hours before even thinking about putting my cock into your virgin cunt."

My cheeks blush as heat fills my body. I feel so *ashamed* of myself. I keep using the fact I don't want Leith hurt as my excuse to not put up a bigger fight. But god, the dirtiest parts of me want him so badly. My body ignites with a fire I just can't seem to feel from anybody else.

"But you disappointed me Paisley. So it means we both suffer. Just for a little longer at least." His words come out slow. I'm confused as he climbs off me again before saying loudly, "Lance, show her how good you are with your mouth."

Lance's hooded eyes roam over my body, making me feel self-conscious. I'm still in my sleeping wear and my wrapped leg is keeping me in place, which means I can't run away. Would I run though? I *should* want to run as fast as I can. I swallow thickly, my dry mouth making it seem like an impossible task.

"You can't want to. You want Nate."

But all he does is lick his lips and give me a sadistic expression.

He tugs at my smooth shorts and panties, gliding them down my thighs. He stops when they get to the top of my knee brace and raises his determined face to look at me. Before he carefully lifts them over and pulls them off.

I growl and lean forward but the hands on my shoulders squeeze tightly and pull me back.

"Just one little taste," Lance murmurs as his hands pull my thighs apart. My bulky leg makes me feel unsexy yet he doesn't seem to notice at all. His eyes are on one thing only and that one thing is my pussy. I chew the inside of my cheek, my breathing quickening when his head nears my crotch. *I shouldn't want to feel sexy*, I remind myself. This is rape. Maybe sexual assault. Orgasms against my will? I keep downplaying the situation as his breath flows over my damp lips. Something about being their sexual prisoner has me soaking wet and Lance has noticed.

His eyes raise up between my legs and he watches my face through his long eyelashes. With a smug smirk he says, "He was right about you." Then he sends a sizzling lick up my wet clit.

I suck in a shameless breath and look over to Leith, almost begging him to forgive me for being a horny betraying bitch. I'm fucked in the head because I don't want to fight this, it feels too good. Lance's warm lips gently suck onto my swollen clit where he starts a steady suction motion on it.

My lips purse into an 'o' as a soft moan escapes me. My eyes close while my fingers claw at the seat material on either side of me. He nibbles on my clit gently, causing me to rock and buck against his mouth.

Nate fills my view while he stands directly behind Lance. The bulge in his shorts steals all my attention while shivers run through me from the pleasure between my legs. I clench my muscles while his tongue flicks over my clit. I'm getting close. My cheeks warm as Nate pulls his erection from his shorts and starts stroking it slowly, up and down.

His thick fingers squeeze firmly, making his cock flush an angry red. Lance slowly licks up my core, taking all the wetness I have to give. He groans then ravenously pulls my clit into his mouth once more. While he sucks, his tongue massages against my sensitive spot. As the orgasm creeps up on me, I grab his head with both hands, and rock against his hot mouth. A whimper leaves my lips as a shiver runs up my spine and my core muscles spasm.

I lean my head back against the lounger with my eyes closed while the last of the orgasm finishes. I'm too scared to open my eyes and face the men in front of me. A fresh flush of embarrassment scolds my cheeks. Fingers run across my damp forehead, moving the wild strands of hair from my face.

"I like how your hair gets natural blonde highlights in the middle of summer," the deep voice says so gently. Lovingly. It's Nate's voice. I slowly open my eyes to see him leaning over me, but they feel tired. The vortex of contradicting emotions is depleting any energy I have.

Nate's firm fingers slide up under my singlet and massage my bare breasts.

"You've made your point," I say quietly but it sounds pathetic. Even I could laugh at that response. But my lips stay closed in a thin, tight line.

"No, I don't think so. Point is made when I say it is."

I quiver with heated need as Nate kneads my breasts possessively.

"Let me go home you sick fucks! I don't need to see your incest orgy!" Leith's voice bounces off the high walls once more. My head snaps to the side, meeting Nate's dark gaze. He's right. Although he isn't blood related, he is my brother of sorts.

"That's your problem. You care way too much about what people think," he draws out as his hand slides over my bare stomach and slips between my saturated lips. Two of his long fingers press up into my pussy, slowly running them in and out. He scrapes his teeth against my jaw and then pulls the soft skin of my neck into his mouth, sucking hard as his fingers stroke in and out of me painfully slowly. My breasts press against his hard chest every time I suck in a deep and desperate breath. Nate bites on my bottom lip before he lets go and presses his lips against mine. I part my lips, knowing this is our first kiss, something I have secretly thought about for so long. Pulling back just a little, Nate hesitates for a moment and takes in a few shallow breaths.

"This right here..." he whispers against my damp lips. "Is only for me to penetrate from now on..." He emphasizes his order by pushing his fingers deep in me again and holding them there. I can't help but look up over his head to where Lance is still fixated on me.

Nate understands my silent question instantly. He shakes his head ever so slightly. "Oh he can taste you when I tell him to. But he knows the rules. No penetration."

There's a moment of hesitation before he slams his lips down over mine. He parts his lips and snakes his tongue out, pushing it into my mouth. I match the rhythm he's creating and wrap my arms around his neck. I want and need him closer. This feels right. It should feel wrong but like my heart has known my entire life, everything when it comes to Nate and myself is perfectly right, even if the circumstances are wrong.

His fingers move in and out of me faster, stretching me more and more. Losing control, I flex my fingers and then run them down Nate's bareback. I can feel the satisfying scrape of skin beneath my sharp nails. He matches that same energy by pushing a third finger inside me and sucking on my tongue. I'm completely at his mercy.

The hands on my shoulders move down, running over my collarbone and landing on my breasts. He pinches my nipples, sending an electric tingling to my core. As my muscles clench Nate groans into my mouth. As he pulls back, he says, "You're so fucking tight. I can't wait to feel those tight muscles strangle the cum out of my cock." Warm fingers slide up my naked thigh, running up and down it, tickling my soft skin. Lance, I realize. All three of them explore my body greedily with their hands. Nate breaks our kiss only to move down my body, slowly kissing my torso as he goes. He licks just under my belly button then dips lower. His lips caress the inside of my thigh gently, pressing kisses with every breath he takes. He rests one hand beside my hip, careful to not hurt my fragile knee, while he wraps his forearm around my thigh on the other side. He's strong, and he's showing off all his upper body strength to me and the men. He licks my clit, making me jolt with scorching desire. Lance was good, but with Nate, everything seems so much more radiant. My previous quivers have now turned into sensations of earthquakes, threatening to open up and swallow me whole.

He looks up at me while he swirls his tongue over my swollen slit. Lance moves to sit beside the lounger, while his swim partner matches the movement. Both of them push my singlet up, so it's around my neck and they fasten their teeth around my nipples. They nibble on them, one each, teasing my nipples until they look like vibrant raspberries.

Nate swipes his tongue through my entrance again, taking all my cum into his mouth. As he pulls away, he stretches up and pulls Lance's head to his glistening wet lips. Lance's tongue snakes out and traces along the crease in his lips before he pushes his tongue inside Nate's mouth. Lance's eyes are closed, while a groan rumbles in his broad chest. He's enjoying my flavor on Nate's tongue. I look down to Lance's pants and notice the erection pressed hard against his sweatpants, I slide my eyes to the other side of me and see his swim partner's cock bulging against his gym track shorts.

My fingers clench, with my fists opening and closing. I want to touch them. As soon as I do that, they will know I am theirs. That they have won and my willpower and common sense is lost forever. I lick my lips as my eyes rise again, taking in the passionate kiss in front of me. I rake my hungry eyes down Nate's torso and admire his bare cock that is still on display out of his shorts. The sight of the bulging veins in it and pre-cum shining on the tip undoes the last of whatever pathetic excuse for common sense I had.

While my eyes stay on his cock that seems to call my name, I slide my hands beside me, across the lounger on either side and trail my long fingers, softly over both men's hard cocks. His swim partner stops playing with my breasts and swaps a look with Lance who has now broken the kiss.

Nate pulls away from him with an arrogant expression. "You're ours now." He lowers his head between my legs once more.

His swim partner and Lance abruptly pull their pants down and shuffle closer to the edge of the seat. I clasp my grip on them both and start stroking them up and down slowly. They both tease my nipples again and suck my breasts firmly, covering every inch of them in hickies. A loud moan tears from me and Nate sucks on my clit hard. I try to close my thighs on his face when the sensation becomes too much but he forces them apart and continues. My thighs fall apart when he flicks his tongue over my clit and inserts a finger inside my pussy again, stroking it in and out.

My hands glide up and down the cocks on either side of me, my strokes grow harder, and faster. I squeeze hard, knowing I won't hurt them. The harder I grip the more they rock against my fist. My hands move faster, more eager with each stroke. With the savage assault on my nipples and Nate working my g-spot, I scream out and come hard against his mouth. I rock against him, bucking my hips.

Nate pulls back and pushes two fingers deep inside me, while the last of my orgasm spasms around him, coating his fingers. He pulls them out and rubs them over his shaft. His breathing is heavy, like he is struggling for control. Will he fuck me now? I don't know if I am ready for that.

Lance and his swim partner come in unison, coating my bare stomach while it shoots out rapidly. Nate is quick and rubs his fingers through the fresh cum and spreads it over his cock as well. Lance smiles at him and moves around, pulling his pants further down so they are around his knees. Understanding dawns on me as he bends over.

I suck in a breath and cover my mouth. His swim partner moves away from me and crawls over to them, like a panther, ready to take his prey. He stares down at Nate's cock and wanks him quickly, pulling it.

"Fuck," he growls as he comes again and shoots it on to the opening of Lance's ass.

Nate inserts a finger into his ass, pushing the fresh cum into it, lubricating every part of it. His swim partner, kneeling beside him, pushes his finger in Lance's ass when Nate takes his out. The other man pokes the opening slowly before Nate grips his own cock and pushes his hips forward to close the distance between him and Lance. His swim partner removes his finger and Nate edges close, nudging the opening with his tip. He swirls the tip around the opening, massaging the cum into the rectum.

"You want daddy's cock?" Nate whispers to Lance.

"Yeah hurry the fuck up would you?" he chuckles in reply. The corner of Nate's lips twitch as he pushes the head of his cock in. Lance groans loudly and claws at the concrete ground. He arches his back and pushes his ass closer to him. Nate slowly pushes his length in halfway, then slowly glides it back out before thrusting back in again. He pulls back and thrusts in again, faster this time and going deeper, nearly to the base.

He thrusts in and out a few times before baring his teeth and moaning. The whole pool building echoes with Nate's pleasured cries as he pulls out and comes all over Lance's back.

I stare at the scene in front of me, shocked. Nate angles his head toward me and swipes his tongue over his teeth.

"Time to get you back home to bed, sleeping beauty."

Chapter 21

"Do you want to try and come downstairs to eat?" Mom's hushed voice whispers close to my face. I groan, still half asleep, and pull a pillow from beside me and smother it over my face.

"Did you not sleep very well last night?" she asks, sounding concerned. For a moment I'm shocked, because she never sounds concerned. Then the shock comes from my heated memories from last night. The car ride back home was the worst. It was silent, yet I could feel Nate's eyes on me every time he side eyed me whilst driving. They weighted me down like an anchor.

I stared out the window, subconsciously tapping my nails on the window frame, trying to figure out where I go from here.

"Come on Paisley. Moving around might help you heal quicker and then you have a chance at cheering next year."

"And there it is..." I mumble angrily and throw the pillow from my face to the side of the bed.

At least my muddled thoughts about Nate are no longer, because they've been replaced with resentment toward my overbearing mother again.

She flicks her arm out and holds it out with an expectant look on her face. Soft sunlight streams through the curtains, making her red hair look more vibrant. I can't help but look down at my long, messy strands, comparing them to my mother's color tones. I find myself comparing our physical looks a lot lately.

Trying to find any subtle resemblances that may indicate we will end up being the same person one day.

I know that's irrational but when you lived a rigid childhood because your future only has one path, possibly because of the way your parents raised you, you'll wake up one day and see what you really look like for the first time. I don't want to be robotic like Mom and Dad. Her version of success and happiness differs from my own. But that's been a new development. Knowing I will struggle to get up on my own, I slip my hand through her bent arm and pull myself up.

"I can walk with the crutches."

Mom nods and scrambles to my drawers where my crutches rest against. Nate fills my mind again, and the fact he easily carried me in and out of the house. I clear my throat and look ahead as I slowly make my way out of my room. It's not as hard as I thought it would be. My leg feels scarily heavy though.

I slowly make my way down the stairs and across the tiled floor, where I proceed to head to the large dining table. Bradey and Dad stop eating as I sit down on an empty seat.

"What?" I snap. I don't want to be here with any of them. They're all frauds and malicious people. Dad very slowly drops his eyes down to his phone and keeps scrolling while sipping his hot coffee.

"What are your plans today brother?" I shoot at Bradey. He scrunches his nose up and shovels eggs into his mouth.

"Not much," he says through a mouthful of food.

"You going to see your best friend?" Everyone pauses what they are doing and swivel their heads my way.

"I have a lot of studying to try cram in before we go away for summer holiday."

"You can take your study on summer holiday. And Nate always comes on summer holidays with us. Has anyone asked him to come as well?"

"Paisley, that's enough! He is an adult now, he can make his own decisions and while he is choosing to make terrible ones, I don't want him in my house," Moms cuts in while leaning on the table. Her face looks fierce, no part of it at all shows remorse over her decision to kick him out.

"This is fucking bullshit. I knew you were heartless but didn't realize how bad."

She grits her teeth angrily, and drops her elbows so she is closer to matching my level.

"And you have spent too much time with him. We made a bad decision bringing him into our home. Like father like son I suppose. You need to stop fraternizing with him."

If only Mom knew the extent of the time I have spent with Nate. My taboo thoughts made me feel ashamed but after all I saw and experienced last night I grow anxious.

"The words that just left your mouth are the vilest things you have ever said. I'm not going away on holiday."

She stands straight and sucks in a breath. Bradey and Dad's eyes flick between us both.

"We are leaving for Greece in a few days. I have organized all your medical needs all morning."

"I would rather be here. On my own."

"With him."

"With your other son. Yeah."

I grab some toast, toss them on the plate in front of me before slipping out of my seat. I then slowly make my way up to my room, gripping the plate carefully. After putting it on top of my bedside drawers, I use both my hands to lift my bandaged leg up on the bed then shuffle up against my pillows. I slide my phone screen with my thumb so it unlocks, then snag a toast and take a big bite of it. While I'm chewing on it, I see a new message from Nate.

> Nate: You hear from Leith. I'm the first person you tell.

My heart sinks as the toast in my mouth becomes so dry it feels like I'm chewing on coarse sandpaper. My brain thumps hard, becoming a whirlwind of heavy thoughts. My chest tightens. *How could I forget about ringing Leith last night?* I don't think anything could fix what happened last night and I'm honestly surprised he hasn't called the cops yet. I forgot about someone's well being, someone that was dragged into a horrible nightmare because of me. I have so many heavy yet lucid thoughts consuming my life at the moment that I forgot one of the most important things.

Is he okay?

Nate: Don't ask about him or I will do something you wont like.

Nate: Or you may like it.

Answer me

Nate: I did. I answered fairly. Don't ask about him again. Only time I wanna hear about lover boy is if he messages you

I stare at my phone and scrunch my nose up while I reread his messages. How the fuck can he think I will just roll over and do what he says.

Maybe I am sick of doing what everyone says. Maybe I want to act eighteen rather than twelve.

Nate: This should be interesting.

Want to meet me at Burke Towns Chalet tomorrow night?

Nate: You need to rest your leg

Knew you were a pussy

Nate: I'll make the booking for 7pm don't be late Paisley

I glare at the screen then think over my *on a whim* plan. I miss Sara. At this moment, I really miss my best friend. Everything aside, I really think she would be proud of me for getting up to mischief. It's always her while I'm on the sidelines cheering her on, in awe, but not wanting to do anything myself that could tarnish my family's perfect A+ image.

Kirsten sent through some memes last night. I send back laughing emojis to the ruthless ones about people with bad knees trying to have sex. Do I reply and tell her it's doable on a lounger by a swimming pool? I sit up straight and tie my hair into a messy top bun as I bite my lower lip, contemplating letting Kirsten in on my new secret life. *Fuck it.*

I'm doing something questionable on the other side of the law tomorrow night. Wanna be my sidekick?

Kirsten: Murder?

I snort and tap on the screen, writing out my reply

Sexual assault at most.

Kirsten: I'm in x

Chapter 22

My sneakers squeak loudly as I walk through the tiled foyer at the chalet. It's nestled on the outskirts of town, on the waterfront of our big lake. I hobble with one crutch under one arm and in my other hand is a beautiful gift bag, with a red ribbon hanging off it. I stop in front of the front counter and greet the receptionist with a big and friendly smile.

"Hi ma'am, welcome to the Lakes Chalet. How can I help you?"

"Yes, so this is an odd request. My boyfriend has booked us a room for the night and we are meant to be meeting here at 7pm. It's our anniversary you see, and I want to surprise him. I'm hoping I can be let into the room early so I can set the room up with flower petals and balloons."

"I'm sorry ma'am, if the room is under your boyfriend's name then he has to check in himself."

I was expecting this. I drop my gaze and pout out my bottom lip, just a little so it looks like I'm holding in a cry.

"His name is Nate. That's what the room name is under." I lift the gift bag so she can clearly see it. "I broke my leg last week and he hardly left my side. I just want to do something nice for him," I say, forcing a little quiver in my words. She stands up and looks down at my leg.

"That looks sore," she murmurs and sits back down.

"Oh it is, I should be resting it, but there's only so much rest you can do ya know," I finish with a soft smile.

She sighs and drums her nails on the desk.

"Do you have any proof you do actually know this Nate?"

I drop the bag and slip my phone from my big pocket in my oversized hoodie. I find a cute photo of us, with his arm around my shoulders at a family BBQ. No one, from the outside, can tell it is a brother and sister hug for the camera.

I hold the screen up so she can look at the photo. "This is the man that you will see walk through the doors tonight. I promise."

"I could lose my job for this, you know. But here is a spare key card for room 112." She winks and then answers the phone. "Hello, the Lakes Chalet, Tori speaking."

I bend down, grab the bag and hobble off toward the elevator. As I near the entrance, I turn my head and nod toward the large palm plant. Kirsten's head is poking out, waiting for me to give her the go ahead. She jogs over and we quickly slip into the elevator as soon as the doors slide open.

"Room 112 baby!" I giggle and spin the card in my fingers. She cackles and grabs the bag from my grasp.

"Oh I like this side of you."

"I thought she was going to play hard ball and say a straight out no."

"Nah, with one leg and that cute innocent face, I think she feels like she is pretty safe with you not running off stealing things."

I snort and glance down at my toes. They look a little blue and I frown.

"God I am unsexy. Look at my toes."

"Yeah you can elevate your leg and rest while I try to make the room look romantic. I still can't believe you had three hot guys getting hot and heavy with you with a leg in a big brace. You are a champ."

"Oh my god, you make it sound like it was a marathon or something."

"What I am picturing in my head, it probably was like a marathon."

"Exhausting, yes, especially when my body was coming down from the hormonal high. But if my leg wasn't broken I would have probably made it more like a marathon."

The doors slide open and we both laugh as we head down toward the end of the corridor, looking for room 112.

Room 110...

Room 111...

"Here is ours," I say and slide the card through room 112's door lock. The small light turns green and I turn the handle, pushing the door open at the same time.

The room is beautiful. All the rooms here are. They look over the lake and have fresh natural colors for the decor. With off-white walls, green and gray bedding with large white plush cushions in the center. It ties in nicely with the nature color scheme .

"Go sit down. I got this girl," Kirsten says as she slides past me and puts the bag on the small oak table in the corner of the room. I climb onto the bed and put a cushion under my leg.

"Are you sure you want to do this?" I ask Kirsten again. I have asked her so many times since she first said yes last night. I watch my toes as I wriggle them.

"Shut up Paisley. He's the hot swimming god that bests every single person he comes across. There is no fucking way I am not doing this. And I know how much he cares for you so he will never hurt us back."

"I wouldn't count on that. I have yet to see Nate being put in a situation where he isn't in control."

I watch Kirsten rustle through the bag and pull out a box of black rose petals. She spreads them from the door to the bed, and pulls out a bottle of pink, raspberry vodka, placing it on the table. She then grabs out two pairs of handcuffs and attaches them to the headboard on the other side of the bed. She runs a long silky black blindfold through her fingers then drapes it over a chair by the small table. Kirsten looks at me, meeting me dead in the eye, while she unscrews the lid on the vodka. She takes a long pull then holds it out to me. "Your turn crutches."

I take it and throw my head back, savoring the burn of the alcohol down my throat. Coughing erupts from me as I pull the bottle from my lips.

"That's intense, yet a crucial element," I wheeze out and punch my chest, as if that'll help sedate some of the uncomfortable burning.

Kirsten then slides lacey garments from the bag and turns to me with a smirk, letting the garments hang off the tips of her fingers.

"Time to get prettied up."

Half an hour later we stand side by side, in front of the round mirror in the small bathroom. My long strawberry blonde hair softly hangs over my breasts that are covered in a skimp, lace bralette.

"You always do the best curls," I murmur to Kirsten.

She runs her fingers through one of them, loosening it slightly.

"Women kill to have hair your color." She pats her own hair down at the top, getting rid of the last of the wispy flyaways.

"Getting called fanta pants and angry ginger in primary school makes me think being a blonde is a lot nicer."

"Awww it's okay," she assures me and adjusts her deep red bra with a mischievous smile.

"Fanta pants," she whispers under her breath. I turn on her, ready to give her a piece of my mind when I hear the door handle jostling. My eyes go wide and I look at Kirsten.

"Show time, angry ginger," she chuckles then pushes me out the door, closing the bathroom door after me. I lurch forward as my injured leg doesn't have the same lightweight pace as the rest of myself.

I briefly glance down at my bare torso and vagina that is covered lightly in the same deep red panties that Kirsten wears.

The door pushes open and I lock eyes with Nate instantly. His expression tells me he's surprised to see me like this. *Perfect.*

He smooths his facial features and leans his shoulder against the door frame. His sweatpants hang loosely around his waist, and his black singlet clings to his muscled frame. His dark hair is roughly pushed back away from his face. "Aren't you resourceful?"

"You're bringing out either the worst in me. Or the best. I'm unsure." I run my tongue along my lower lip as I drink in his broody stature.

"I'm bringing out the truth in you. The real you that deserves to be free." The words roll off his seductive tongue in a deep voice.

I feel the lick of moisture coat my panties as the desire I feel for Nate consumes me like it always does. Can I follow this plan through? Or should I spend the entire night licking every hard, chiseled part of his body? Nate steps toward me and slowly closes the door behind him.

He nods down to my leg then asks, "How's it feeling?"

"Good enough…" I murmur, intoxicated because I can smell Nate's cologne now. It's spicy, yet fresh and it overwhelms me. Nate steps forward again, circling my hips this time with his long arm, while brushing my hair softly with his other.

"Your hair always seems softer than everyone else's, your eyes always seem brighter." His fingers, ever so slowly, brush over my bare collarbone. "Your skin always seems more delicate." He says the last words as if he is in pain.

His brows furrow while his dark eyes follow his fingers movements slowly. His fingers linger over the soft skin above my breast, then run down between them, snaking over my nipple, then down my bare stomach. Goosebumps erupt over my skin and a tingle spreads over my swollen clit. I'm filled with a desperate need for the man in front of me. There's been other people, there have been games. But it will always only be him that my body and soul are connected to on this intense level.

He steps forward, pressing his hard body firmly against me, forcing me to step back. He repeats the process, until he has me backed up against the bed. He lifts me up and carefully places me down on the bed. He spreads my legs apart so he is nestled between them. His hard cock presses against my pussy. Only our thin layer of clothing prevents us from doing what we both need to do. He moves his hips back and then rolls them forwards, causing his erection to rub over my damp, thin layer of lace. A moan escapes me. *Oh Nate.*

His fingers clench around the nape of my neck and hold my head in a secure hold, bringing his warm lips to my own. My lips part, inviting him in, although if I didn't he would just take what he wants anyway.

His tongue massages my own while his hips roll against my crotch. *Nate.*

It shouldn't but as always, it feels perfectly right.

He breaks our kiss, with the tip of his nose brushing mine he breathes heavily in my face.

"You have always been mine," he whispers deeply.

"What about Lance? What's he to you?"

His chest vibrates as he fights a chuckle. "He's my friend. And my friend has benefits when I need benefits."

"Does he know that?"

"Of course. He's in love with someone else. Do you want to know something?"

"What?" I ask, feeling anxious. This is vulnerable, full of emotions. It's making me feel guilt ridden for what I had planned.

"Despite what you think...I have saved myself for you," he says. I'm left confused and it shows on my face.

"I've never been with a woman before. You're the only one I want. Ever. No other woman could ever compare to what I feel for you. I only want to ever feel your pussy. And if you never felt the same way about me, then I would die a virgin."

"I don't know if you can class yourself as a virgin..." I say, trying to cover my heart fluttering with a weak joke.

He pinches my chin and lifts my face to meet his hungry gaze.

"This isn't a fucking joke Paisley. It's you or no one else."

I remind myself why I am here. *Leith.*

"This feeling consumes me. Sometimes it almost hurts me so much I feel like I am about to be torn into a million pieces."

"I know," he agrees, eyes searching mine.

"Why did you kidnap Leith though?" I ask. I need answers. But when the energy in the room changes and Nate holds his breath, I realize there is no way I am about to get answers.

"Has he messaged you?"

"Of course not. Although I expected him to go to the cops."

"You need to stop seeing people in black and white or good and bad. Bad people can do good things. And good people can do very bad things. The line isn't so fucking vivid, it's blurred and circumstantial."

"Which one are you?"

The corner of his lush lips twitch then he runs his tongue over his teeth.

"Maybe only god can tell me the day I am dead." He pushes me back, so I am flat on my back. His fingers crush over my panties and he groans.

"So wet for me," he breathes.

I close my eyes and let myself enjoy his fingers roaming my body, his touch leaving sparks. Could Leith truly be a good person that does bad things? Could I? I chew the inside of my cheek while I dance with the idea. Life has done a complete 180 on me, and letting go of my girl next door persona empowers me with a dark thrill.

I open my eyes and place my hands on either side of Nate's face.

"I want to be in charge tonight. Get on your back," I say it strongly.

"Not happening. I am always in charge."

"Give me one night?" I beg in my cutest voice.

"One night where I give up the control? I don't know, having control over you is my favorite part of my days."

"One night," I whisper and trail my fingers down his chest, then wrap them around his hard cock through his pants. He thrusts in my grip.

"One fucking night."

Chapter 23

We change positions. Apprehensive, Nate lies on his back with his head on the pillows. I can't straddle him with my leg, one point I had overlooked. But I still awkwardly stand beside the bed and glide my hands into the waistband of his pants. As soon as I wrap my fingers around his cock, his hips buck.

"Let me handcuff you?"

"How am I going to fuck you on my back? You know you want my cock in you," he states. It sends a thrill straight to my needy vagina.

"All in good time," I purr while grabbing his wrist and pulling it above his head. I fasten the handcuff around it and then repeat the process on the other side. He looks sexy while he's completely at my mercy. I lift his singlet up and run my nails sharply down his skin, leaving red marks. Will he think I am weird if I lick his skin like ice cream?

I stroll over to the chair, where the blindfold is, thankful my knee is taking my weight okay and pluck the black blindfold off the chair. As I make eye contact with Nate, I delicately slide the blindfold through my fingers.

"Only you could ever make me give up control. It's always been you, Paisley," Nate whispers while his arms rest above his head. His arms flex as he speaks, not letting me forget he is completely at my mercy.

His words have me faltering for a moment, but I keep my cool composure and make it to the side of the bed. The Paisley he knows is gone. He's expecting something completely different from me.

He has always been my pillar of strength, but kept me in the dark at the same time. He's been there when I needed him, but never let me be any more than a burden. I needed more, from him, from everyone. Someone can only be picture perfect for so long, before cracks start to appear, their armor that protects their heart and soul starts to diminish and crumble.

I climb onto his lap and cover his eyes with the blindfold, I say nothing as I slide the elastic over the back of his head. His silky strands of hair run through my fingers so smoothly. Oh, how many times I have wanted to run my fingers through his hair while telling him that if I have him, I don't need anyone else. Fantasies for little girls.

While his eyes are completely covered, I look down to his full lips that are gently parted. Quick breathes flow through them. Is he nervous? Excited? Does he just want me to be his next conquest? I lean my head down and brush my lips against his, tasting his breath, wanting his essence to be inside of me. Maybe if I breathe in his corrupt being, it will allow me to finally cut the ties of this guilt and regret I carry for those that don't deserve it.

I pull his shorts down, tugging them hard over his waist. He lifts his hips as I pull to make it easier for me. Once I have them over his ankles, I throw them to the side of the room and crawl back up his body. The cool breeze from the open window blows over my near naked skin, giving me goosebumps. I swallow thickly and remind myself to stay strong. He deserves this, even if I want to finally have him all to myself. I straddle his hips and rock gently, grinding over his large, hard length.

"Feel good?" I breathe down into his face.

"Everything feels fucking good with you. Heightened. Over-whelming. *Perfect*," he murmurs and raises his hips to meet the careful rhythm I am creating.

"What about Lance? He seems to mean a lot to you."

A crease line appears across his forehead and he shakes his head, disagreeing with me.

"It's not like that with him. It never has been. We are friends."

"Friends that fuck? Do you even like girls?"

"No I don't," he answers.

I lean my head against his, chuckling. "Like I thought."

"I like you. I love you. When will you get that?"

"But Lance too?"

"He's a friend, Paisley. Fucking is just fucking."

Jealousy erupts in me. Taking over the betrayal and reason I was originally here for revenge.

"You have opened up parts of yourself and life to Lance that you won't even let me have a glimpse at!"

"Paisley, why are you doing this? Tonight is *our* night."

I sit up straight, squaring my shoulders and massaging his shaft with my crotch again. Thankfully the thin layer of lace fabric is stopping me from letting it glide inside me and this all turning to shit.

"Where are you staying now?"

He grows quiet and I see the motion of him chewing the inside of his cheek. I want to slap it. I know where he is staying.

"Point made." I climb off him and walk to the bathroom, opening the door and nodding to Kirsten who is leaning against the vanity, filing her nails.

"Still time to back out?"

"How bad is this going to go?"

"I don't know. I thought I knew him but maybe I don't. He did kidnap me."

I hear the pulling of the handcuffs against the headboard.

"Paisley what the fuck is this shit? If you're angry about the other night, fucking talk to me."

Leiths face floats through my mind. "Fuck it?" I say to Kirsten nervously.

"Fuck it!" She smirks at me.

"Then let's go get a cheap bottle of liquor and drink it at the lakefront."

"Deal."

We both quietly walk out of the bathroom and I lean back against the window frame as I watch Kirsten climb on top of Nate. She rocks her hips against his bare cock.

"Paisley?" Nate's voice comes out shocked. I stay silent as I watch with a detached feeling coming over me. A manic smile crosses my face while I watch Kirsten grind against him, looking down over his covered face.

"I've heard you have been a little bit mean to my girl?" Kirsten asks quietly. God she is good at this.

Nate's jaw flexes before he spits out, "Get the fuck off me."

"Naw, don't you want me to use that hard cock for my own pleasure? Don't want to be used and abused?"

"If you value all you hold dear to you, you will get off me."

"Empty threats. And I quite like exactly where I am," she answers and uses a grind of her hips to put emphasis on her statement.

"Paisley, you need to stop this game playing because you won't like where this ends."

I roll my eyes and push off the windowsill. Kirsten climbs off him and moves down the bed, gripping his cock in her hand tightly as she nestles herself on all fours. I move up and remove the blindfold from his face. His furious expression is met with my humored one, which only angers him more.

"Do you think I like being kidnapped by you freaks?"

His face goes as cold as steel. "Yeah actually, if memory serves correctly, you enjoyed it a lot."

My bottom lip pouts in fake sadness. "Naw, well I'm here just to repay the favor."

Kirsten licks the length of his shaft, from base to tip, causing Nate to buck his hips and hiss loudly.

"Fuck off Kirsten," he scorns her. My eyes linger on the slick line up his cock and bulging veins.

"He looks like he is enjoying it, doesn't he Paisley?" she says, giggling at the end.

"I want a taste," I say, moving to where Kirsten is. I don't grab his cock though, I grip the back of Kirsten's head and pull her face down to mine. My tongue traces the outline of her bottom lip, before Kirsten's lips part, letting my tongue slide in. I slant my lips over hers and massage her tongue with my own. Nate pulls at the handcuffs once more but we ignore his fruitless tries. I pull away from Kirsten and smirk at her.

"Let's tie this up," I whisper into her flushed face.

Kirsten drops her head back down over Nate's hips and takes his length into her mouth. She glides her mouth up and down it slowly. I push up Nate's t-shirt and nip at one of his nipples. His body erupts in goosebumps, making me pleased.

"Paisley you know you are making a big mistake. I've tried to tell you." His warning is so quiet. Like a secret moment between the two of us. It feels more personal. I ignore him and swirl my tongue over his other nipple while using two of my fingers to pinch his other one. His breathing is growing quicker, His hard chest moves under my face. The chest that gives the best hugs in the world.

I push myself off him, running from the emotions that will make me the weak doormat again. I lean back, with Nate raising an eyebrow at me. He knows. He always fucking knows. He knows my heart and feelings before I even do.

Nate frowns deeply with his cheeks growing flush. I look down at Kirsten who licks glistening pre-cum off the tip of his cock.

"Ohhh, you're getting so close. Do you want to cum? Do you want to release your pleasures all over us, yet tell us you didn't want this?" I say.

"I don't fucking want this. If I blow my load it's because I can't help it, not because I want any of you."

"Ouch that hurts," Kirsten chuckles while slowly stroking his cock. His face is strained and a new happiness over-whelms me.

"Never ever did I think you wouldn't be in control," I mur-mur while I glide my hand down, over his abs and onto his cock. Kirsten removes her hand and massages his balls.

"I'm always in control. Even if you don't think I am. I won your very fucking soul." His strained words are forced out between his gritted teeth.

I grip my fingers firmly around his cock, squeezing as hard as I can. I glide my hand up and then down to the base again. "That good? You want me to slide my hand over your big dick until you cum all over my fingers?"

"If you stop now, your punishment may be worse," he hisses. His neck muscles bulge. His body has taken over the battle now. He doesn't want to be in this situation, but he's so close, he needs a release. The exact situation I was in. But I'm not as nice. I remove my hand, with Kirsten following suit.

"Paisley..." he growls.

My long fingernails walk up his hips and dance around his naval.

"Beg me."

Nate glares at me, keeping his mouth in a straight, hard line. I slide my nails down his torso and back to the base of his cock. I slowly work his cock again with my hand while Kirsten moves around the bed and teases her clit. He glances at her and then back to his cock. His teeth bite down on his lower lip while pre-cum accumulates at the tip of his cock once more.

I stop my movements. "Beg me."

His face becomes deadly, with his black hair falling over his forehead. Teeth marks still indent his lower lip.

I lean down and lick the beads of cum from his head and let out a moan. "Beg me," I whisper this time and run my tongue over the tip of his erection.

"Please." The deep voice fills the room. Never *ever* did I think he would actually beg. I clench my needy muscles, feeling empowered and fucking horny. If it was just me here, I would have climbed onto his cock right now. If our situation was different. But it's not. I ignore the tingling spreading through my body and lick the tip again. "Please what?" I ask as I move my head away.

"Paisley," he bites out. My name sounds delectable on his tongue.

I shake my head. "Nope. Please what?"

"Please suck my cock and let me cum down your throat."

I smirk at him before I open my mouth and take his cock in my mouth. I glide my lips over it, letting my tongue run over the hefty veins.

As I squeeze the base, I bob my head up and down, taking in as much of his cock as I can. His breathing fills the room as Kirsten teases herself. As soon as his balls tighten again and I taste the salty pre-cum once more, I pull my mouth from his shaft.

"Paisley!" Nate yells. His dick is an angry red now. I swipe my thumb over my mouth and smirk at him.

"Kirsten, I'm bored now. We should go."

She rips her hand from her panties and laughs. "Mmmm I need dinner," she mumbles and climbs off the bed.

"You're both fucking dead!"

I grab his phone and flash it over his face to unlock it. My fingers fly over the screen as I message Lance.

"Lance will be here in an hour. Maybe he can finish you off."

We grab our things after throwing clothes on and leave the room. As I pull the door open Nate's velvet voice stops me.

"Tonight was going to be our night. Everything you ever wanted was going to be laid bare. I was ready to finally show you my soul."

I cringe and crinkle up my nose. *Have I crossed the line?* I look over my shoulder at him but he shakes his head.

"Oh save that regret. The games have only just begun."

Chapter 24

"Y ou're really not going to come with us?" Mom leans on the outside table with her hands splayed flat on the surface. I shake my head no, staying firm.

I keep my eyes hidden behind my large, black sunglasses. I don't trust my eyes right now. Nate thinks they give away every emotion I'm not yet ready to tell.

Mom stands straight and rests one of her hands on her hip. She is in a pair of long white, linen trousers and an off-the-shoulder blouse. It's the most casual she has been in a long time. She purses her lips, sun rays hitting the nude gloss she has on. I let out a sigh.

"Greece won't be the same without you," she murmurs after a moment's silence.

"Yeah, I won't pretend I'm not jealous. I just need to figure out what I am doing with my life," I mumble and turn my head toward my leg that is resting up on a deck chair.

"We can make a plan when we get back." She begins to stride off before she pauses. Without turning back she says, "You know, I am trying to be understanding. But me showing you how much I love you is making sure you have your future set in stone. Do you think I would have this life and all this to give you if my parents didn't do the same for us?"

Once she's finished she walks through the French doors. Bradey comes outside and pats me on the top of the head. His brown scuffs scrape against the wooden panels as he moves around me and sits in front of me. He rests his elbows on his knees, with his hands fisted under his chin. Deep lines wrinkle around the corners of his eyes, and deep purple bags occupy the space beneath it.

"You look like shit," I say slowly. He pulls his polarized sunglasses off his head and puts them on, so his eyes are shielded.

"I'll be clean when I get back," he assures me. But it doesn't come out with confidence.

"I really hope so, Bradey. All this shit and Nate sacrificing his place in our home has to be worth something?" I say but it comes out as a bleak question. My throat burns as my tears try to come out.

"I will talk to him when I am back. He's my fucking best friend. There's nothing we don't know about each other and nothing we wouldn't forgive each other for."

I swallow and clear my throat. I can guarantee he doesn't know about the sick and depraved things we have been doing with each other. "Well, you are lucky to have a person in your life that would give up everything for you."

"Sara will come round. You'll see. Girls just hold grudges a little longer than males."

I pluck a piece of ice out of my tea and throw it at his face. He swipes at it, letting it hit the ground by his feet before he laughs.

"Well, have fun house sitting while I am in Athens."

"Ohhh I can go to parties without you looming around, scaring everyone off."

"Mmm you'll still have one brother in town, telling everyone to fuck off. You forget, we are males. We know what goes on through their heads. We've saved you from a lot of losers."

"No honestly, I absolutely love being everyone's baby to look after and order around."

"Heard you and the Hawk boy called it quits?"

"Yeah and what?" I say, growing a little flustered when he brings up Leith. I still haven't heard from him.

"It's for the best. He's not as cute as he tries to portray," Bradey says and stands. "Catch you on the flip side, my little baby." He farewells me while tapping me on the shoulder. I roll my eyes, but can't help but giggle at the insult he throws back at me by using my own words against me.

An hour later, I float around the pool, with water ebbing and flowing around me. I can't help but wonder what Nate is doing. My messages to him this morning have gone unanswered. I don't know why I'm surprised because he ignores me at the best of times and I may or may not have crossed the line last night. I don't normally cross lines. I stay well away from any line that could make me look bad or hold any negative consequences.

Letting go of the overthinking and people pleasing me is hard. I get moments of agony in my heart that makes me believe embracing the dark side and letting anger fuel my actions is a good idea, then when it's all said and done, I'm the same person that cares too fucking much. Leith, Nate, Bradey, Sara, Kirsten, Mom and Dad swirl around in my brain, never letting me forget that I royally fucked up. I hear rustling to my left and look up to the camelia hedge that frames our pool fence. I frown when I see food being thrown over the greenery and get snagged on loose twigs. A bag of crisps balance on a pink flower, making the stem bend dangerously. Then Kirsten comes hurtling over the edge, landing on the wood chips with a thud.

"Fucking hell, you could have just answered the door or your phone!" she screeches, turning on to her all fours and then climbing up straight and piling her food into her arms. She cradles crisps, dip and chocolate carefully while marching over the cobbles and dumping them on the table beside my phone and cold drink. She kicks her scuffs off, loses her shirt and then dives into the pool.

As she comes up, breaking water with her head, she swipes the water off her face and smiles at me. I shake my head.

"What the fuck just happened?"

"It's officially summer break. What are we doing today?"

"I was going to float around in the pool for hours on end."

"Good plan. The cheer girls are going to a party tomorrow night. You should come!"

I flop onto my back again and close my eyes. "No thanks. I'd rather feel sorry for myself and spend the night on my own."

Water gets splashed over my face, causing me to begrudgingly open one eye and glare at Kirsten.

"That's stupid. You need to rip the band-aid off. I reckon try explaining your side to the girls again and then we can all have the summer of our lives."

"I'm not ready yet."

"Mmmm I will take that as a maybe. So have you heard from the dark and mysterious brother of yours?"

I sit up and paddle around in the deep end.

"Should you be calling him 'my brother' after what happened?"

"Brother, brother, brother..." she sings loudly, ending with a mischievous giggle.

"No, I haven't heard from Nate." I wipe a single water droplet off the tip of my nose before continuing, "What do you think he meant when he said let the games begin?"

She waves her hand in the air, showing me how unserious she is about his warning. "He's a bad boy. But he's not that bad. He will probably wank all over your face when you sleep."

"Okay, ew."

"Orrrrrr hot?" Her voice is high pitched.

"God, you're kinkier than I ever realized."

"Haha, sexually comfortable, girlfriend."

We float in the water, letting silence wrap around us. It's a comfortable silence. My leg floats effortlessly on top of the water, relieving it of the strains.

"What do you want to be when you have finished college?" I ask, breaking our tranquil silence.

"I want to travel. See the world. I am so sick of living in Burke Town where it's freezing in the winter and smells of lake weed in the summer with a sprinkle of mosquitos."

I can't disagree with her description of Burke Town. Everyone knows everyone here, and civilians fall into an easy comfort in life. For most people, they are born, raised and stay here. There are a handful that get claustrophobic though and want to seek out more in life. Kirstin is one of those larger than life people for sure.

"Where do you think you will head to first?" I ask.

"Well if I have my teaching degree I could take up overseas teaching contracts. Maybe Japan first, then Vietnam. Otherwise, if I flunk out, I could always hit the party countries first and work in bars." She sounds at ease.

"Do you not get anxious about not having a plan?"

"Nope. I think having a plan and shit with life happening, changing my course would send me into more anxiety." Her words weigh heavy on me. I face her and frown.

"It feels like every worry and sleepless night has been a complete waste," I say then grunt in frustration. "God, all the fun I missed out on. Seeing all you girls being confident and free makes me so jealous because now I'm a complete nutcase with no sense of belonging."

"You have time, my ginger friend." She giggles, knowing full well I hate being called ginger. "Now let's go make cocktails and eat chips while finishing the last of Elite."

Chapter 25

I stroll around the house in my daisy duke shorts and white singlet while testing the movement of my knee. My toes carefully touch down on the tiled floor repeatedly without issue, giving me confidence. My knee feels better every day. Music blasts through the small Bluetooth speaker as I indulge in me living alone for two whole weeks. The steady thumping of the drums bounce off the walls and fill the void in my head I like to pretend doesn't exist. As I grip my phone in both my hands, I message Nate. I'm so sick of waiting for him to contact me.

I end it with an eye rolling emoji, trying hard to downplay the mess I created. But by gods it felt fucking good. A few dots appear on the screen then it goes dead. I chew the inside of my cheek and frown at the phone when nothing comes through.

Kirsten told me what we did was nothing compared to what he and his friends did. If we were to compare the list of illegal actions, Nate would go down harder because he has breaking and entering, kidnapping and physical abuse against a female. We purely used and abused him, so just sexual assault if we want to put labels on it.

Yet somehow what I did feels worse. Nate, although terrifying, anyone would expect it from him. Me? I'd be shunned by every person.

It's only ten minutes later when I am making a blueberry smoothie, that Nate messages me.

> Nate: Meet me in the reserve tonight by the lake. We can talk then. 10pm sharp

> Why don't you just come round home.

> Nate: I'll see you there.

> I won't come.

> Nate: I look forward to seeing you Paisley.

A soft knocking sound follows when I place my phone down on the marble benchtop. If he really wants to see me, he can come here. I pour my smoothie into a tall glass then after taking a sip, I place it down. I pull out my favorite cupcake recipe book and flick through the pages. I fan through them to find my favorite orange cupcake recipe.

I pull everything out of the cupboards and look over all the ingredients proudly. After turning my speaker up another level, I pour flour into my Pyrex bowl, then carefully measure the sugar and baking powder. I grate a whole orange and toss the rind in the bowl then add in melted butter, eggs and a squeeze of orange juice.

While mixing the contents I ponder about what my family is doing. I know they have landed in Greece. They're probably sleeping as they would likely be jet lagged.

I slowly tip the wet mixture into the muffin tray and slide them into the oven. I don't really know why I bother with the recipe book because I can almost do them all by heart.

Eight minutes later I pull them out of the oven and place them on the airing rack.

I mix up the buttercream icing, that I know I can do off the top of my head now and place a few drops of pink coloring in the batch then fold it through. While I wait for my cupcakes to cool a little more, I flick through my music playlist and turn on All American Rejects, Gives You Hell. I turn it up and lean my hands on the benchtop while hanging my head in heavy thought.

My hair curls over the crevice of my shoulder in soft spirals. When I let it air dry after a swim in the pool it normally gets a nice, natural wave through it.

After about five minutes of embracing the upbeat electric guitars and thumping drums from one of my favorite guilty pleasure bands, I fill my piping tube with the light pink icing.

Once it's all stuffed in, I squeeze the end tightly and make perfect swirls on top of my orange cupcakes. When I have done them all, I crouch down and look at them all carefully, inspecting my decorating job. Perfect. Picture fucking perfect.

I lift the entire tray, slam my foot on the pedal of the large stainless steel bin and tip them all into the bottom of it. With a thud, I throw the tray into the deep, granite sink and stomp out of the kitchen. I need to get ready to meet Nate and see if he is forgiving me or playing with me like his own little toy. Trick or treat.

Chapter 26

The last of the sunset skims across the darkened sky. The strips of dark pink contrast against the ever-growing blackness. This could be romantic or it could be really creepy. I hug my sweater around me a little tighter as a shiver runs over my skin.

I walk down the stone path to the picnic area, only the crunching of my feet on the ground can be heard now. Any boats that were on the lake are long gone. Trees grow thicker as I weave my way deeper into the reserve. I pull my phone from the back of my jeans pocket, flick my light on and hold it in front of me while my eyes search the surrounding trees. I don't know why I gave in and fucking came here.

Actually I do know. Because I am utterly insane. I have my whole speech repeating over and over in my head. I need this man to breathe. I need this man to function. I want to get on my knees and tell him I have been in love with him from when I was a little girl. My protector but more so, my support in my life that leaves all his judgment at the door.

With him, I can show him all my ugly feelings and emotions and know they are completely safe with him. Maybe if he sees me confessing my love to him, he will show me all his ugly emotions, all his emotional scars and know that I will take them all and surround them with love. We can build something new, something that isn't trying to live up to these insane expectations everyone has of us.

I round the corner and see a tall, solid figure looking out over the lake. His broad shoulders and long back are covered in a dark sweater, with faded jeans and messy hand brushed hair to match. He doesn't move as I close the distance between us in the clearing. I'm not quiet. I'm slow, but not quiet.

Birds burst from their roosting branches with loud squawks and frantic flapping of their wings. Stones ground underneath my feet, pushing deeply into the dry, dusty soil. Trees surround me on either side now, with only the water visible directly in front of me, where Nate is.

I clear my throat loudly when he doesn't move. I am starting to feel awkward, whatever I was expecting I am not sure this is it. He still doesn't move as I edge closer. I can smell him now. That same strong, spicy scent that always makes me drunk. Tentatively, I lift my hand up and very lightly touch his shoulder.

"I know you are mad at me..." I start to say but he steps away from my touch and spins around, finally facing me. His jaw moves as he grinds his teeth together before he speaks. Tilting his head slightly, he opens his mouth.

"That was our night and you took that away from me."

Growing confused, I shake my head and take a step back. I can feel the malice wafting off him now. There is nothing friendly about him. "What do you mean our night?"

He steps closer to me and wraps his hand tightly around my neck, showing me the deep betrayal in his eyes.

"I was about to open myself to you. It was going to be me and you against the fucking world. No one knows you like I do. No one would ever protect you and care for you like I do. I was going to show you how much I fucking love you." He whispers the last sentence while he strokes the soft part under my chin with his thumb.

His hand is still firm around my neck. My fingers squeeze his wrists while I frown at him.

"You kidnapped me. You started this."

He clucks his tongue and then runs his tongue over the front of his teeth with a smirk following the motion. "No, you see I was righting the wrongs in your life. You? You started a game I fear you had no part in playing in."

I've pushed him too far and fear turns my veins into ice.

"You belong to me, Nate. No fucking games," I breathe while still battling with his grip.

"Oh yeah, you're my fucking person. I belong to you and you belong to me, Princess. Now let the games begin," he growls and shoves me back. I stumble, rubbing my throbbing neck and frowning deeply at him. I slowly shake my head with tears stinging the corners of my eyes.

"Nate what are you doing? This isn't what I came here for."

"Run..." he snarls, nearly inaudible. I shake my head again, showing the pleading in my eyes. This isn't going how I wanted it to.

"Run Paisley. And don't let us catch you...." he says quietly with a grin touching his lips at the end.

Us? Who the fuck is *us*? With my hand still rubbing my neck, my eyes catch movement on either side of Nate. Lance and his swim partner step out from behind the tall trees.

"I'll call the cops..." I threaten, growing distrustful.

He snickers and pulls his black hood over his head. His face is no longer visible to me, apart from his full lips. They are confident lips, tugging at the corner, telling me this isn't a game I can opt out of. I've pissed him off. I bruised his ego. His cocky yet mysterious demeanor is what he is most proud of from what I have experienced.

"Sorry Princess, You have fallen in love with a monster. You wanted me to bare my true self to you, so fucking feel free to indulge in it. *Run...*" The last word comes out in a casual whisper. It makes it scarier. My soft checkered jacket no longer keeps the breeze off me. The summer breeze that normally brings relief to the humid weather brings a haunting whistle through the trees. I take a step back with fresh tears burning my eyes.

His two friends flank either side of him as I step another three times back. I don't dare take my eyes off them and I hope I am still on the path that brought me to this clearing. A crisp twig snaps under my sneaker as I take a larger stride back. One hand raises in front of me, as if it can save me from them. The other frantically waves at my back, searching for any trees I might be about to collide with.

Nate isn't violent. I could never believe he would truly hurt me. So what does he gain from this game? I dampen my lips with my tongue while retreating further. He needs to win. Whatever game we have started between us, he needs to win. He wants to scare me off, he wants to have me concede and play innocent Paisley again so he looks like the tough scary boy from college that no one fucks with.

No one at college crosses Nate and so far, I am the only one that I know of that has. My cheeks puff out as I blow out a long breath.

"You will never ever win this game you started. You have power over everyone but me. *Brother*..." I taunt him, knowing damn well I have lost my mind. Fear seems to do something different to me these days. It makes me completely fucking insane and downright stupid.

He tilts his head, purple hues behind him giving him a menacing aura. The three silhouettes look like they could be grim reapers from a horror movie. Yet still, I don't feel like they are going to kill me.

"I thought I told you that you and I"—he flicks his masculine index finger between us—"have never been brother and sister."

I mouth *brother* silently, growing wild and insane. I spin on my heels and use all my adrenaline I have running through my body to push me forward. I keep my breathing even as I surge forward in a fast sprint but within seconds my knees buckle and I falter. I grind my teeth together, with sweat beading on my forehead when the pain threatens to drop me then and there.

It's dark but I can see the path enough to know where to go. Within a moment of cockiness, my heart begins to race as crashing starts behind me. Even though I believe they aren't secret serial killers and my tickets are about to be punched, being chased through the woods in the dark still scares me beyond anything I have ever experienced. It's a rush I no longer desire.

My legs pump in long strides as fast as I can manage and force myself to keep going. My track teacher would be so proud of me right now, my doctor, not so much. My loose jacket slips from my shoulders as I run like I have never run before. Two figures run through the trees on either side of me. There's no sunset behind them, so they only look like shadows. They don't run ahead of me, or behind me, always beside me. I know they could catch me if they wanted to, but they like this game.

A deranged chuckle from one of them drives this point home as it shoots an icy shiver up my spine. My chin trembles as I divert my eyes back to the path in front of me. He can win. I don't like this game anymore. My jacket flaps behind me. It has now slipped further down my arms and—I get ripped back mid-step. Nate clenches my jacket, pulling hard so I'm pulled back against his hard chest. As the edge of his black hood rubs against the side of my face, his heavy breathing brushes against my neck.

"Don't tell me you are surrendering to me that easily."

"I'm over these sick little games. I'm going home," I sneer at him as my nipples harden. I am well and truly over these games. I am a sick bitch that still has a body that will grow hungry for this man, even if he is holding me captive in a dark forest. He clicks his tongue before running it up my sweaty neck. His hips thrust roughly, rubbing his hard cock up the small of my back.

"Run faster because if I catch you next time, I'll be shoving it in your ass dry. And trust me, you won't want that," he warns me.

My eyes widen and I try to rip his arm from around my waist but it's a strong barricade. His menacing chuckle fills the silence between us. I swing my head from side to side, trying to pinpoint his friends. I know they are there, silently watching us, but I can't see them. Nate's arm drops from my torso and I lurch forward, not wasting any more time.

I can hear Nate behind me the entire time. He's so much faster than me. This is a stupid game. I change tactics, hoping that my eyes adjust enough to the dark so I don't knock myself out and dart off through the trees. I go on a diagonal line toward the lake where I know I can find my way with my eyes closed if I can just get there. Every shadow that comes into view, I leap over, hoping I clear whatever it is.

I hear a stumble and crash behind me and I grit my teeth harder, feeling more determined. I don't know which one fell over but it makes me happy knowing I have lost one. I zig zag as much as I can, darting through trees. Soft moonlight creeps through the leafy gaps now it is high in the sky. I use it as a guide, running toward where it seems to be lightest in this dark and dense forest. "Oh fuck!" I hear someone grunt out after a loud thud, letting me know someone has hit a tree. It sounds like Lance. I suck in a long breath and keep pushing forward.

I dart off to the left, changing my tactic and try to head back to the path. I have run so far, if I can get back on the path I mustn't be too far from the car park. As I weave left and keep jumping and striding forward, a tall dark figure steps out from behind a tree and I run straight into him.

"Better. But still not good enough," Nate says over the top of my head while both his arms hold me firmly against him.

"Where's your little minions?" I ask between loud huffs.

"It's me you need to worry about."

Chapter 27

"You left me high and dry at the chalet. Do you think you need to remedy that?" he asks slowly while keeping me in place against him so I can feel every hard line on his body, even the one stabbing my stomach.

"You literally came into my bedroom at night and kidnapped me. You also choked me till I passed out."

"Oh but I thought you were so desperate to get to know me. Isn't that what you keep saying to me? Don't tell me you don't like what I have shown you. Geez I may get hurt feelings," he says mockingly that makes me forget the feeling of running for my life.

"This isn't the real you though. This is a fucking front. You know what pisses me off the most about me and you?" I snarl, growing angry.

"What would that be my angry little kitten?" he asks. I try to ignore his hips that still rock against me.

"You want to help me, be my support, you want me to be vulnerable around you and by fuck I have my whole entire life! Yet you always act so perfect, so strong, like nothing can ever get to you. A cool and calm composure yet deadly aura around you that lets people know you will cut them down in an instant if you need to. But when have you ever been vulnerable around me? To tell me what you are actually feeling? That's the real you I want to get to know!" The last comes out in a shaky screech.

Nate pulls back and rips the remainder of my jacket over my wrists. It flutters over my bare legs. "Your legs move well now for someone that couldn't walk a week ago."

"Pain doesn't register when you're scared out of your mind...I have no doubt I have torn apart my knee and will pay for it for the rest of my life."

His eyes are lost, yet focused. Lost to reality and the words that leave my mouth, yet focused on what his hands are doing in front of him. He pulls my white babydoll top and tugs it over my breasts, leaving them bare. I don't exactly fight against him but my body still quivers where I stand.

"I've grown up admiring your strong legs as much as I fantasized about your smart mouth." Nate almost whispers. Crunches from twigs and stones sound behind him then dark silhouettes come into view as well.

"This is insane and toxic. I don't want to be a part of this anymore," I murmur while taking a subtle step back. He matches my movement, always my mirror yet the opposite reflection. He's tall, dark and gloomy. *Strong.* I'm short, pale and wear oversized ribbons in my hair. And *weak.*

"Would you let me fuck your ass in front of them?" He finally pulls the hood away from his head. Loose strands of his hair dip over his glazed eyes while his wicked lips part slightly to let out his heavy breaths.

"No, I honestly don't want this," I say, feeling stronger with my words. I keep my even stare on Nate's face, trying not to let my mind drift off and obsess about the fact that the moonlight is leaving a soft twinkle effect in his possessive gaze that sends my affection for him into overdrive. He's a beautiful fucking god, and I've been in love with this man for too long. Yet it's toxic and never right between us. Right and wrong. It doesn't make sense yet that's exactly what it is.

His thumb swipes over my erect nipple and I close my eyes, angry that it sends an electric shock straight to my needy vagina. My need for Nate could almost make this heartbreak worth it. I have wanted him for so long, but not like this. Everything is a fucking mess. The last month comes crashing down on me. I bend down and pick up my jacket and wrap it around myself once I have pulled it on.

"You win Nate. You always fucking win," I say before turning and walking toward where I hope the pathway is.

"Paisley fucking stop!" he calls after me but I ignore him and keep walking. Right on cue my knee begins a deep and deadly throb. Tears stream down my cheeks and I frantically try and swipe them away. There's noise behind me, and my face scrunches as I realize I can tell it's not Nate just by the way the person walks.

"He sent his little playthings to bring me back to him?"

"Nah just making sure you get to your car. Don't want you falling into the lake."

It's Lance's voice. The tall parking lot lamp comes into view and I sigh with relief. I nearly had my horror movie kink played out in real life. But when it came to it. It's not me. I cross the lot, pacing toward my car.

Hands wrap around my wrist as I reach my car, causing me to halt.

"He doesn't know how to love, you know."

I snort and rip my arm away from him. "Oh because he opens up to you and only you. Do you guys chase loads of girls through the woods?"

"He doesn't open up to me. It's just obvious. He started out in a house that didn't show love. And yeah, we do fucked up shit and fucking love it. You wanna be with him? You need to expect him to show his passion for you in some eccentric ways," he says then turns and walks off.

I stare at his back, feeling frustrated. Eccentric? It's crazy. I thought it could be fun to let go, but this is walking on the knife's edge of jail time or the looney bin. But most of all that keeps floating through my brain, is yeah, Lance is right. He started his life off with parents that treated him like trash and didn't show him what pure love was.

I guess all he has is his twisted love ideals in his mind. I open my door and sink down into my seat before I fire my car up and speed out of the parking lot. There's too many questions, not enough answers and one toxic fucking love between Nate and I.

Chapter 28

After I'm showered, I stroll into my room, grimacing slightly when my weight bares down on my knee tentatively. I have my first therapy session on it in two days and I'm worried they will look at it and ask, "Have you been running through the woods at night? Running from three men you fraternized with previously?"

I roll my eyes to myself and throw my towel into the laundry basket. It leaves me naked while I berate myself for being stupid. I will be the only one in the therapy room that knows of my erotic shenanigans. Knowing they are sick and inappropriate to say the least makes me feel like I somehow look different.

I stop when a loud tapping steals me from my insane thoughts. I look toward the source of the tapping sound to see Nate sitting in my armchair, tapping his solid thumb ring against the wooden arm rail. I lock eyes with him and he leans back a little further as he tilts his head. His eyes are like granite but give me nothing of what is going on in his head.

His tapping turns into a steady beat, as if he's pretending he's playing the drums. Is this another game? Will he try to take me again? Could I not have made myself any clearer? I cross my thighs as much as possible and hug my bare breasts with my arms as I keep watch. His stalking eyes flick over my naked body, following my movements before he matches my stare head on once more.

"No more games Nate," I say with a tremble in my voice.

He stands tall as soon as the words leave my mouth and stalks closer to me. He nods once and pulls me to him.

"No more games," he whispers against my ear then pulls my arms away from my breasts. I'm vulnerable and exposed in front of this man once more, but in a completely different way. It's just us this time. No games. Just us.

"Games are fun, but I'm over this bullshit. I'm sick of trying to tell myself you're better off without me, yet needing to be the one to protect you. I wanted you to be with someone better than me, but I also can't stand back and see another man take you to your appointments, care for you when you are down and be your shoulder to cry on. I need it to be me." He brings our lips together.

His full lips press into mine with a possession I never thought possible. He has finally said everything I have always hoped he would say, everything I always hoped he felt. I relax into his hold and press my body against his while holding his lips to mine.

Nate breaks our moment and stares intensely into my eyes.

"No one else, Paisley. Don't touch anyone else again. I can't handle that."

"And what about Lance?"

He smirks and traces my bottom lip with the pad on his thumb.

"He's a friend. He knows I have been in love with you since the day I turned up on your doorstep as a pimple face kid. We had fun together but it's always been you. Remember I have saved my virginity for you."

I scoff and pull back. "A virgin? You need to stop calling yourself that."

"No girl has ever been able to do it for me. No girl has ever touched my fucking cock until you let your friend abuse me. The only pussy I have ever wanted is yours."

My brows furrow. "You know there's a chance you might not even like pussy after having men for so long."

"Never. Let me prove it to you." He pulls me back to him and suffocates me with a kiss that makes my knees go weak. My heart thuds in my ears as he forces my lips open then he slowly massages my tongue with his own.

His hands slide down my back and grip under my ass cheeks, where he then grasps them hard and lifts me up onto his hips.

While keeping a perfect rhythm with his tongue he walks us to the edge of my bed then lays me on my back. His body rests on top of me, caging me in, but I don't mind. There's no erotic thoughts mixed with fear. It's just need and love. It's perfect. It's just us.

Nate slowly rubs his hips against mine while my legs stay firmly wrapped around his hips still. His hard cock through his sweatpants massages perfectly against my swollen clit. I moan against his assault on my mouth while pleasure builds inside of me. His dark strands of hair brush against my wild red hair, his dark eyes burn into my pale ones, we are fire and ice. Always have been and always will be. Together we are a storm of wild love, passion, possessiveness and fractured souls.

His hand reaches between us, gliding down my stomach and sending goosebumps over my skin. His long fingers find my clit and rub it firmly in circular motions. I raise my hips against his touch, needing more of what he is giving me. I will never have enough of this. I would happily die feeling this way.

I suck my lips in and breathe deeply through my nose while his fingers rub in precise movements. I claw his back through the fabric when the intense pleasure becomes too much and my body combusts as I reach the crest of my orgasm. A whimper leaves me while I still claw at Nate's back, as if I need to hang on for dear life so I don't fly away. I rest my forehead in the hollow of his shoulder while a new shudder runs through me.

"This is different," is all I can say through heaved breaths. It's different and so much fucking better.

Nate looks down to his pants where a fresh wet patch runs down the front.

"I'm never washing these pants again," he growls then stands straight as he slowly slides them down. I sit up on my elbows and watch him. His arms tense and thigh muscles bulge when he kicks the pants to the side. I see Nate as Nate. Sometimes I forget he's an athlete that works out every single day.

He lifts his singlet over his head and drops it where he stands. He drops to his knees in the next moment, gripping my thighs, he pulls me to him and licks the wetness from my inner thighs.

His tongue, painfully slow, runs up my soft skin and then over my sensitive lips, where he tastes the remains of my orgasm.

I place my hands on either side of his head and pull him up to me. He hovers over me, with dampness still on his lips. I pull his head down to mine and trace his lips with my tongue.

"I want you in me now," I breathe against his face quietly.

"I wasn't planning on waiting any longer." He agrees with me and spreads my thighs wider apart with his hips. His large tip nudges against my pussy, almost begging to be let in.

"Ready?" he asks in a strained voice.

"Now," I beg him.

He grips his cock between us and guides it in. It stretches me wide and I whimper loudly. He thrusts it all the way in to the hilt and holds it there. His tense body holds still and he towers over me.

"I think your pussy is squeezing the life out of me."

"Sorry," I apologize as if I've done something wrong. He frowns down at me and pulls his hips back then ever so slowly and glides it in deep again.

"Don't be fucking sorry. It's the best feeling in the fucking world."

He pulls out all the way to the tip, then thrusts forward quicker. Lowering himself a little more, he wraps one arm around my thigh and lifts a leg up so it's over his shoulder while the other is wrapped around his hip. He holds my leg there while thrusting into me over and over.

I cry out in pleasure, understanding why he moved my leg the way he did. He can penetrate deeper, reaching a g-spot inside of me I never knew I had until now. Every time his pubic bone grinds against my clit, electric shock waves pulsate through me. A deep, primal groan comes from Nate as he glides in and out of me at a steady speed.

The hard ripples of muscles covering his body tense and flex with every movement he makes. Sweat beads along his chest and begins to drop down onto my breasts, mixing with my own perspiration. Veins bulge in his neck, causing me to zone out on them as my whole body ignites with an overwhelming pleasure.

Nate leans down and pulls my nipple into his mouth, sucking on it with force.

"I'm going to come," I cry out and dig my sharp nails into the skin on his broad shoulders. He rams into me with force again and again and then penetrates deep as he reaches his own climax. My muscles clench around his hard cock, milking the last of his pleasure. Our foreheads rest against each other while we lay there tangled around one another. His sweat drips down onto my flush cheeks, but neither of us are able to form words yet.

After a few minutes, he rolls off me but pulls me with him so he has me cradled against his chest. His arms stretch around me protectively as his chin rests on the top of my head.

I try to fight it but a yawn escapes me. I want to do more of what we just did, but it's well into the early hours of the morning now and after running for my life earlier, I'm exhausted.

His chest vibrates against my cheek while he chuckles.

"Sleep princess. But don't be surprised if you wake up to a cock inside you."

It's my turn to giggle now.

"I don't think I will mind waking up like that at all. What are we doing tomorrow?" I ask while fighting my eyelids that are trying to close.

"I'm going to show you the real me of course," he says with a hint of teasing.

"Of course," I mimic his last word with sarcasm before sleep pulls me into its dark embrace.

Chapter 29

The birds chirping in the large maple tree in front of my window should have been the first thing I awoke to. Instead I lie on my side, eyes firmly shut and a thick sleep fog suffocating my brain, I slowly realized I was rocking my hips back against Nate. His deep, primal grunts were close to my ear as his strong hand holds onto my hip bone while he thrusts in and out of me. My nipples harden when the blanket slips away from me, causing the fresh morning air to brush over them. I take a deep breath in through my nose, smelling sweat, sex and Nate's cologne.

His hand slips from my hip and finds my clit, massaging it gently as he thrusts in and out. I clench instantly as the motion sends a shrill through my body.

"Tell me how you need me to do it for you..." he groans. He wants me to tell him what to do? He's a sex god that can probably make me cum with one look. I close my eyes again and listen to my body, feeling his fingers on my clit. His thrusts grow rampant, building a sensual sensation in me.

"I want you to rub up and down faster," I whimper. He changes the movement of his fingers and uses the tips of two fingers to rub up and down, pushing against my g-spot every time he pushes downward.

"Like that?" he asks me, sounding stern.

"Yeah like that," I cry out when it becomes too much and I climax.

He presses his hips hard against my ass cheeks as he fills me with his cum and his large splayed fingers on my hips hold me in place.

"I need to get the morning after pill today," I say groggily when I have the ability to form words again.

"Agreed. But first breakfast and I want to give your knee a massage after a shower."

"You going to be my therapist now?"

"Well ya see I kinda feel guilty for chasing you through the woods, but in my mind the night at the chalet was going to be the night I get on my knees and show you how much I love you. You took that from me so I was a little angry." He almost sounds dismissive about it. Like the toxic shit we did over the last couple of weeks was nothing.

"I'm going to choose not to get into that right now because it may lead to a fight and I want a massage."

Half an hour later I'm lying on the couch with my legs over Nate. His fingers work their magic, gently massaging into my knee. I glance at the small closed holes around my knee where they had performed keyhole surgery, before flicking my eyes back up to Nate's serious face.

"Do you think we're sick for falling in love with each other?" I ask quietly.

He snorts then leans back on the couch and lifts an arm over the back of the couch so it's stretched alongside me.

"No, you're not my sister."

"True but we share the same last name now. You became my brother when Mom and Dad officially adopted you."

"Moot point because we will share the same last name when we get married anyway." he states with cockiness and runs his thumb over my bottom lip lightly.

"People will talk if they see us together. Mom and Dad will say all sorts of things."

He lets out a long sigh and then picks up one of my hands. He runs his fingers over the back of my hand softly. "A, I don't care what people think and the sooner you stop giving a fuck, the happier you will be. B, your parents have done a lot for me and I wouldn't be in college or living a stable life without them. But they are also narrow-minded and selfish."

"So pretty much fuck what everyone says? That's the answer to everything?"

"Fuck what everyone says will stop you from having so many questions and ponderings in the first place."

I shake my head and let out my own sigh. I guess they do say opposites attract because I am not like that. I do care what everyone thinks and I like having a large social group around me.

"I can't just switch it off like that. My brain gets so loud with intrusive, self-sabotaging thoughts bouncing around erratically. If I could have slowed my thoughts and made better decisions from the start, Sara may still want to be my best friend."

Nate's eyes fill with sadness while he listens to my confession. "I think she's an immature friend that is angry at you for her own selfish reasons. But if it's weighing heavy on your heart then I will support you with needing to make amends with her. Just not today. Today I get you all to myself. I think I have waited long enough, don't you?"

I blush and rest my head against his arm that still rests beside me. He rubs his thumb over my cheek, eyes locked on the fresh pink blush that must be coating my skin.

"Did you know I used to listen outside the bathroom door when you showered? No idea what I was listening for, but any moment I could get to secretly admire anything about you, I took it."

He gives me a cocky smirk before he runs his tongue over the front of his teeth.

"I used to sit on the edge of your bed and jack off to you into a handful of tissues while you made cute sleep noises."

I suck in a breath and gasp. He can't be serious? His face looks like he is indeed very serious.

"When?" I wheeze with eyes wide. I'm internally screaming at myself that it is so wrong but so fucking hot.

He shrugs then runs his hand over my bare leg playfully.

"Heaps of times. I was a horny little teenager okay? Now get your ass in my car, you're my passenger princess while I show you what the mysterious Nate gets up to during the day," he says, mocking me slightly. We have always been close, yet at an arm's length so I am more than curious. I crave to know. But now, I have a feeling he's somehow going to get the last laugh. He always does.

He slips out from under my legs and holds his hand out to me. I take it and he pulls me to a standing position before he grabs me around the back of my head and pulls me into a kiss.

Nate pulls back and rubs the tip of his nose against my own. "Let's go."

Chapter 30

We pull up to the college car park. Being summer break, it's nearly empty aside from a few random cars spread out through the expansive area. I push open the door, but Nate bolts around the hood of the car with a mischievous grin and finishes opening the door for me. He helps me out of the car and smacks me on the ass as he slings his gym bag over his shoulder and leads me into the side entrance.

It's close to where the pool is. Nate already told me in the car the college swim team are here for training and also a meeting with their manager to go over their national competition that is a few weeks after we are back at school. As I trail behind Nate closer to the side door I admire him from the back. He reminds me of a stallion. Tall, deadly, protective yet fucking beautiful. He's wearing a thin school singlet with his name in large print on the back, and his usual black baggy basketball style shorts. He can literally wear anything and make it look like it's straight out of a supermodel catalog. His spicy cologne has me sucking in my bottom lip. I really thought finally doing the deed with Nate would sedate some of my dark desire toward him but it has only made it worse. Memories from the school pool come swarming back to me and it reminds me of Lance. I was so stuck in our little bubble that I forgot about his boyfriend that wasn't his boyfriend.

"Is Lance swimming today?"

Nate doesn't miss a beat and with ease, pulls me through the threshold and keeps walking with my hand securely in his. I like him leading our way. It's a new level of protectiveness I have never felt.

"Yeah he'll be here. That man needs to work on his back-stroke." He chuckles the end bit. He's not phased about the sure-to-be awkward run in at all. I will never get a handle on this guy.

I try my best to cover my growing panic attack. "Nothing you need to work on then?"

"Hell no. You know I'm perfect at everything."

I can almost hear his eye roll in the tone of his words. The large aluminum doors burst open when Nate shoves them with his rough hands. Heads swivel our way and we're both greeted with a firm lift of the chin from Nate's swim team.

His hand slaps against Lance's, showing their brotherhood over top of their standard swim team relationship.

Lance looks past Nate's shoulder, locking eyes with me. The corner of his lips twitch while he tilts his head slightly, as if I've become even more interesting to him. Was I not interesting enough when he chased me through the park or kidnapped me from my room?

"Nice to see you Princess," he says quietly then turns and walks back to the group of young men.

"Why do you—" I start then pause briefly before continuing, "And now him calling me Princess?"

Nate flicks his hair out of his eyes and laces his fingers on top of his head while casually walking backwards toward the group.

"Conversation for another day. Go sit," he says with a cocky smirk. He turns, leaving me to watch his back as he walks away like he has done so many times before.

I head over to the viewing seats and perch on the gray plastic seat then throw my feet over the one in front of me and cross my feet at the ankles. I let myself glance at the scuff marks on my white Reeboks before I pull my phone out and check my messages. *Princess? Would a princess wear scuffed shoes?*

I have a flood of memes from Kirsten that has my eyes bug-ging. They involve brother and sister relations. My fingers fly over the screen as I reply to her dark humor.

> I could never look at Bradey that way! Gross

> Kirsten: Ima frame the adoption papers and put them on your wall so every day you wake up you feel like a brother fucker

> Ha-ha! You're sick. What are you doing today?

> Kirsten: The cheer girls are having drinks. You should come?

I re-read the message a few times, my mood becoming solemn. I miss my team, I miss Sara and I miss my old life. My teary eyes go from my phone to Nate. He's in his swim shorts, seeming like he's about to climb into the pool but he's paused, staring at me. Fucking man being able to read me so well. He bunches his eyebrows, while clearly debating whether or not he should come to me or get in the pool. I give him an encouraging smile. I know it doesn't reach my eyes but I need to be supportive today.

He asked for one full day of just him. I settle back into the uncomfortable seat as he nods back to me and jumps in the pool. I want my old life back, but with Nate as my boyfriend in it, I don't understand why I couldn't have both.

I quickly reply to Kirsten, letting her know I'll skip the get-together. Me and Sara will be having a conversation one day soon. She can't hate me forever. I watch Nate swim lengths, warming up. I've watched him swim casually and in competition for years and years. I know his routine.

His coach walks in with another man in ironed suit pants and a button up dress shirt with half the buttons undone and the cuffs rolled up to his elbow. They stand shoulder to shoulder, heads leaning in talking closely. The coach then stands straight and claps his hands loudly.

"Timing sprints for freestyle first. Two laps. Then we'll be doing butterfly."

Nate, Lance and the others climb out of the pool and stand on the diving blocks in each of their lanes. Coach stands to the side with the man in the formalwear and blows on a loud whistle. They all dive in smoothly, showing how well trained they are. They stay underwater for what feels like the longest time before they glide up and throw their athletic arms at a fast pace.

They are all similar speeds until it comes to the end and they do their tumble turn over under the water. Nate and Lance get a slight advantage over the others and get a small lead. Nate pushes hard, his arms showing how powerful they are as he sets a pace that even Lance can't seem to keep up with. By time he gets to the end of the lane and slaps the end of the pool edge he already had a meter on Lance and meter and a half over the others. Now all lined up, ready to start their next sprints, their chests move, almost like they're synchronized with them heaving heavily in and out.

Once they have caught their breath, they climb from the pool and prepare to start all over again. This time in a different style.

I watch them dive in, precisely at the same time, technique can't be faulted.

Twenty minutes later, Nate is out talking closely with the coach and the well-dressed business looking man. I slide my feet off the seat and skip down the stairs toward him. He turns to me as he slings the long, black strap of his gym bag over his shoulder. When his eyes fall on my face my heart feels like it skips a beat.

Water beads at the ends of his strands, before it trickles down onto his cheek bones. His swim team seem to happily leave the pool, walking in front of us. They haven't given me any looks of disgust. They are probably scared of Nate and will prefer to do it behind my back. Nate throws his arms over me and drapes his hand off my shoulder so we are walking side by side back out to the car park.

I squint into the summer sun as it hits my face as soon as I step outside. I swear I can feel my freckles growing like a wild mob every time I'm in contact with the UV rays. While thoughts spew into my rampant mind, I cling on to one that should have been at the forefront.

"Oh! Who was the guy in the fancy clothes you were talking to?"

Nate opens my passenger door for me and slaps my ass as I climb in. I can't help but give a surprised giggle. Nate jumps into the driver's seat and throws his pickup into reverse before he finally answers my earlier question.

"He was a scout for another college. He usually does the rounds to small town colleges to see what swimming talents are out there." He plays down his answer but this is massive news. I turn to him and curl my knees under me at the same time.

"He watched you more than the others..." I reply, my heart racing. Why is he not excited? I'm excited for him. Maybe more excited.

Nate snorts and shrugs his shoulder while flicking his indicator on and turning left so we are on the main road in Burke Town.

"And? I'm not moving to the other side of the country and going to Stanford."

My jaw drops. "St-Stanford University?"

"Yeah but stop looking at me like that. Firstly, he said well done at training but getting into Stanford this late in your studies is hard and second, I'm not leaving you so forget he was even there."

"He might come back to you though and offer you something. You're a really good swimmer."

"Yeah but there are a lot of good swimmers around that also have lots of money and parents that give nice donations. I'm living with my kind of ex-boyfriend and my adoptive parents don't want me." He gives me a panty-dropping smirk and pulls into the parking lot at the pancake house. I look at the large banner across the roof and raise an eyebrow to him. "Gotta eat, Paisley."

"Maybe he will offer you a scholarship," I mumble quietly as we both climb out at the same time. Nate comes around the hood of the car and laces his fingers in mine. I look around, worried about who may see us.

"Stop stressing. Everyone we need to worry about seeing us is away on summer break. And on the off chance I get offered a scholarship, I won't be leaving you. Remember..." He trails off.

***

An hour later we are lying alongside the lake where we used to go fishing as kids. But it's now overgrown with large trees and the small beach area has been washed away from storms so it's now a deep drop off. I haven't come back here in years. I got sick of the boys telling me it was too dangerous for a girl to fish here now.

It has been untouched for so long that, although everything is overgrown and scruffy. The water is so clean here. The gentle sway of the water hitting the bank is like a relaxing white noise to my frantic mind. Nate rolls on his side and starts running his finger along my jawbone, tracing the outline of my face.

"You really still come here?"

He lets out a steady breath and rolls back onto his back. "Yeah, it's nice here."

"Why did you never tell me? Or Bradey? He would have probably come here with you."

"I like coming here on my own. Away from people's bullshit. And Bradey would rather be with his girlfriends and the ballers," Nate says before he falls silent.

He doesn't need to say it, but I know he also means Bradey would rather be around anyone with drugs.

"Why did you never tell me?"

"Because you would have come and hung out with me every single time and I couldn't do that to you."

I sit up and look down into his face, blocking the sun and casting a shadow over his handsome face.

"That's the point isn't it?"

He rubs his hand over his eyes then lets his forearm rest on his forehead.

"Paisley, I've wanted you my entire life. But I come from a fucked-up home and some of the trauma I have been through has altered my brain. I'm not wired like all the good rich boys that would love to have you as theirs. You deserved a chance at a normal life. The one your parents always wanted you to have. I wanted to keep my distance so you could fall in love with someone that deserves you. But turns out as time went on and any horny fucking teenager made whispers of wanting to fuck you or take you out, I lost all coherent thoughts and scared them off anyway."

I can't help but giggle, although it sounds like a slightly insane laugh.

"Yeah, a few weeks ago I was so mad you wouldn't talk to me, hang out with me yet you also never let me date either. I was a little confused."

"You and me both, Princess," he replies with a smug look on his face.

"Why do you always call me Princess?" I ask him. His lips purse with a slight red blush staining his cheeks. Oh no, he isn't avoiding this. The flush on his face has made me more determined. I throw my leg over him, quickly straddling him. He raises his hands to push me off him but I quickly grab his wrists and plant them on either side of his head, leaning down. It's now my turn to smirk into his face.

"Why?"

He shakes his head a little, saying no.

"Why? Or I will never fuck you again. And remember that time you promised me one question and one answer?" I warn him. He frowns then looks away from my face.

"Well that's not fair. I only just got your fucking pussy so, as if I am going to let you take it away from me."

"Why Nate?" I repeat my question.

"Fine, when we were younger you were watching an animated Disney movie. And, well, there was a fucking red headed princess on there with freckles and blue eyes and I remember looking at you then the TV then you again. And well, you know my fucking little lovesick brain thought that they had made a movie about you so you must be a princess."

I fall back, rolling off Nate, laughing my ass off.

"Wait, so my nickname princess is because you thought I was somehow an actual princess?" I ask between laughs. I rub hysterical tears from my eyes.

Nate rolls on top of me now, pinning me down with his body.

"Fucking hell Paisley. Well obviously when I got a little older I realized I was being stupid. But the name stuck. I don't ever want to talk about this again," he growls down at me.

"Oh no we are going to be talking about this a lot."

He grinds his hips into my crotch and I pause my laughter and look up into his brooding face. "Bring it up again and I won't ever fuck you again."

"That's not fair. You can't use that against me now," I argue with him. He rolls his growing erection into me, rubbing my clit firmly through our thin bits of fabric. I suck in a breath, trying hard to not give in and moan from the growing pleasure. He leans down and nibbles along my jaw while he rolls his hips into me again.

"Fine, you win."

"Good, because I have thought about fucking you here too often. I would hate to have to get up and leave and be moody for the rest of the day." His voice is full of sarcasm. He pulls his shorts down, while I tug my panties to the side. He thrusts straight into me, groaning as soon as he's as deep as he can get.

"How many orgasms you want, *Princess*?"

"Endless," I breathe into his face before he covers my lips with his own.

Chapter 31

The next day I dangle my legs lazily in the pool at home. I adjust my black sports cap on my head while I sway my legs through the relaxed current. Nate swims toward me, bursting out of the water with his arms smashing into the water in the next instant while he practices his butterfly. As he nears me, he smirks and then rests his muscled forearms on my bare legs.

"Have you heard from the scout?"

Nate starts using his wet finger to draw random designs over my legs, water dribbles down the side of my thigh and onto the cobbled ground beneath me.

"Told you it doesn't matter."

I grip both sides of his face and lift his head so our eyes meet.

"It does matter. Promise me, if you hear from him you will tell me?"

He searches my eyes with his own while he bites his lower lip. He then nods once and floats back into the pool, away from me.

"You joining me?" he asks slowly. When his voice goes low and drawn out like this my body aches for him. There's something alluring yet menacing about it.

"I need to make some phone calls first."

A frown ripples across his forehead as he hears my words. "Can't be that important."

"Why would you say that?"

"'Cause you're here with me. School's finished and your parents are away on holiday..." he murmurs as if they are facts. To him they are facts. I shake my head slightly and sigh.

"I have dreamt of being with you for as long as I can remember. Now we have been together, it has given me a clear enough head to realize I need to right my wrongs. I want us to be together and everything else in place too. I want to make it up to my cheer squad and then I guess we need to figure out what to tell my parents."

His arms caress the water slowly as he keeps himself afloat while his eyes burn into me.

"Those girls don't deserve your fucking loyalty. And easy I'll be telling your parents the day they fucking land that you're mine. They can like it or fuck off."

"You always say shit like that and make it all sound so easy." I wave my hand out in front of me to empathize.

"It is that easy," he states.

"We are two different people. I care about different stuff. I have so much anxiety over them not talking to me."

"Fine, you sort that shit. I'm going to shoot hoops with some of the boys. Tonight you are mine," he growls slowly and swims toward the steps of the pool. As he climbs out water runs over his body like a waterfall. *Matching the intensity of my wet vagina,* I think to myself. He closes the gap between us then hooks his arm around my waist and pulls me up to him in a possessive hold.

"I mean it. I don't like sharing you. Never have, never will. You have until 5pm. I'll be back then and your addictive ass better be here."

I smile at him, wrapping my arms around his neck as I do. I get up onto my tip toes and kiss him carefully on the lips.

"See you soon," I say, assuring him he has me tonight. My stomach does a backflip as my heart races. I'm fighting all my willpower right now to not jump up onto him and tell him to take me to my bedroom.

If I knew we could isolate ourselves away from the rest of the world and just have him to myself selfishly, I would probably be happy. But we can't do that, and in the real world my friends and family matter to me. My life that I have worked hard for matters to me.

✱✱✱

It's midday when I stroll into the arcade to meet Kirsten. As soon as I see her I pull her to me in a hug. Her babydoll perfume envelopes me, along with her perfected heat styled blonde curls softly sliding over my shoulder.

"Hey skank!" she greets me in a friendly way. A soft giggle leaves my lips as I draw back from our embrace.

"Hey number one partner in crime!" I return the greeting that jokingly describes our interesting meetup a few nights back.

"So don't be mad at me but." She pauses and puts on determined puppy dog eyes. I frown at her, growing anxious. If she starts with that, it usually means I will in fact get mad. "I invited some of the cheer girls to hang with us."

"Fuck's sake Kirsten," I panic and hiss at her. My hands start to weep with anxiety-induced sweating and my heart pounds against my chest.

"They wanted to come. It's just Erin and Sascha, they want to see if you are okay," she insists and bends her head slightly so her hoop earrings sway to the side with her long hair. Her eyes skim past me and over my shoulder. *They're here.*

I take in a long breath through my nose and blow it out through my pursed lips slowly, but it comes out with an audible shake.

Kirsten sighs and I can see she regrets her decision. She feels bad and now I feel bad that I made Kirsten feel like shit. I blink rapidly, willing my fresh tears to stay hidden and the corners of my lips slowly morph into a friendly, yet fake, smile.

My dry mouth makes it impossible for me to swallow so I give up on the impossible task and casually rub my bare neck, in the hopes it will relax my neck that feels weighted.

"It's okay. I guess these panic attacks are new to me. I want to run or scream. But I'm trying hard to do neither of those," I admit to Kirsten in a trembling voice.

"I hate seeing you struggle so much. You're usually like the big bright sunflower in our friend group. You are vital to us all.

We need your sunshine, rainbows and cute cupcakes. It breaks my heart seeing you as a wilted flower." Her words hit me to my core.

Not long ago I thought maybe Nate was right and I was chasing friendships that don't deserve my time because they could never care as much as me. But now I see, we are all pieces of a big puzzle. We need each other to be complete. They need me as much as I need them. I give her a slow nod and let out another long breath, although this one doesn't feel as fragile. I grip Kirsten's hand and spin around, pressing my foot onto the sticky juice-stained carpet with purpose as I march toward Erin and Sascha. They're both holding slushies, eyeing at me warily as I get closer to them. When I am directly in front of them, I give them a tentative smile.

"I thought you would have gone away for summer break?" I ask in a friendly tone, trying to keep it casual and unawkward.

"We're off in a few days. My parents are already at their beach house but I am heading to Erin's family cabin. Her mom is just making sure all the yard maintenance is done before we go away for a month," Sasha says then takes a slurp on her blue slushie.

"Oh yeah I get that. Cabin sounds like fun." And I mean every word. I went there two years ago for team building time. It's deep in the mountain on a private subdivision. The swimming hole in the river is only a small walk from the cabin, which makes it the perfect secluded summer home.

"How's the knee?" Erin asks and steals a glance at it. She winces briefly when she sees the small plasters over the incisions.

"It's actually really good. I've been trying not to overdo it. But I have no idea if I will be cheering again," I admit and clear my throat when I remember me sprinting through the woods from three male swim champs, thinking I was going to get fucked to death.

I feel the fresh warmth in my cheeks and I know it's not from the heat. It's from the thought of them taking me in the forest and the freshly discovered, messed up part in me enjoying it.

Both girls step forward with sullen looks and rub the tops of my arms.

"It's okay Paisley. You can definitely cheer again. We can just feel it in our bones," Erin encourages me. Guilt washes over me when I realize they have assumed my rosy cheeks are from sadness at my admission about my blurry future with the cheer squad.

I pat both their hands and grin at them. "It's okay. I'm starting to make peace with it. Well, as much as I can," I say and Kirsten leans her forearm on my shoulder while flicking her hair over her shoulder.

"Let's have a bowling game. Then the watering hole has our name on it."

Chapter 32

It's been two weeks of absolute bliss. It's been quiet with me hanging with Nate and Kirsten. Even a few nights of drinks and dinner with Lance and their friend, Harley joining us. I'm fairly certain Kirsten, in a buzzed state, has bed hopped and visited Harley but I chose not to ask her about it. There's still that massive piece of the puzzle missing though. Every single time I smiled or laughed, I would mentally tell myself that Sara should have been in all of my new memories. Not missing from them.

I wipe the last of the crumbs off the bench and into my waiting hand when the door opens with a click.

"Paisley, we're home..." Mom's voice sings through the house gently. Vacation must have done her some good. I shake my hands off into the sink and turn around to face Mom, Dad and Bradey as they come through with their suitcases rolling behind them. They have the sun-kissed glow. All except Bradey. He looks pale and sick.

He looks like he has lost nearly half of his body weight. My heart completely shatters when I take in the sight of him. He was meant to get clean. He said he would be okay. This isn't him being okay.

"Hey guys. How was vacation?" I ask warily.

"It was good. We missed you though. And Bradey ended up with a terrible tummy bug. He was in his room sick most of the time with high fevers and body chills."

My eyes go from Mom's worrisome face and straight to Bradey's. He looks away from me and focuses on the fruit bowl on the countertop.

"That really sucks. Doesn't sound very relaxing," I murmur quietly. I pace to Dad and peck him on the cheek then give Mom a gentle hug. I didn't know what I was expecting. I had my emotional walls up, expecting animosity and World War Three. I may have made peace with a portion of my cheer squad and finally landed the man that has occupied my dreams for as long as I can remember, but home has a long way to go. The cracks run deep between us and I wonder if we'll ever recover.

Nate and I had said we would tell Mom and Dad tonight that we are a couple but now I'm wondering if we should hide it a little longer. I don't want to keep secrets anymore but this really doesn't seem like the right time. Bradey turns from me and starts walking up the stairs, toward his bedroom.

I follow closely behind him in silence. My emotions are solemn and overwhelming, causing any words I may have thought about speaking to become lodged in my throat. I follow him into his room. I cleaned it while they were away. I cleaned the entire house. I really wanted to sweeten the mood before I told them I had fallen in love with my brother. He looks around and then drops onto his bed without uttering a single word.

"You look like crap," I say slowly. May as well speak my mind. He would if roles were reversed.

"Yeah well going cold turkey would do that to you." His muffled words get caught in his pillow.

"You said you had it under control, like it is no big deal."

He rolls over, flopping onto his back while he kicks off his scuffs. He swipes sweat off his forehead with the back of his hand and snaps at me. "Well can't say I have ever been a druggy before. Lack of experience and all with this shit. Can't all be perfect fucking Paisley."

I retreat backwards so I'm standing in the open door frame. I plant one hand on the framing, hoping it will ground me somehow. I sniff, desperately trying to keep my wits about me and to control my unshed tears.

"I won't take what you say personally right now, because I know you are not yourself. But know this Bradey, no one in this world is perfect, especially not me," I say calmly, maybe a little too calmly.

I pace up the hallway, fighting the urge to look into Nate's old room. So many of his belongings are still there. He never opened the door to his room while he stayed here. He always came straight to mine. I jump onto my bed and fold my legs under me, while I carefully tuck my linen skirt down so my panties aren't on full display. Picking up my phone, I text Nate and tell him that we can't tell my parents yet about us and I give him a very watered-down version of Bradey's current state.

Within a moment I get a reply from Nate and I can't help but grin ear to ear. I get butterflies in my stomach every time Nate's name pops up on my phone.

Nate: Okay, try not to jump my bones when I knock on the door then

Before I even get a chance to frown and reply with a *'what the heck are you talking about?'*, the doorbell chimes through the house. I slide off the bed and by time I pace to the top of the staircase, I hear Mom and Dad's voices greeting Nate. They sound sincere and certainly like they were expecting him.

Curiously, I head down all the while I tell myself they don't know about us. But what if someone told them? Not many people know, and the ones that do are good at keeping secrets, but we also were out in public in our small town. We tried not to be handsy when we were around people, yet the thought of someone seeing us in his ute kissing does cross my mind.

"Hi," I mumble awkwardly when I get downstairs. Nate's head whips around to me. His eyes slowly dip to my bare feet, then even slower as they crawl up my body until they land on my face again. His face holds a knowing smile then he gives me a small nod. He crosses his arms over his near bare chest. He has a thin muscle top on and basketball shorts, but his thin straps still show me most of his chest. My eyes catch the gleam of his silver ring around his thumb when he leaves it out from under his armpit and taps it on his bicep.

"Sooo what do I owe the pleasure?" he pointedly asks Mom and Dad, his attention now back on them. My cheeks redden but I cheer myself on inside. Go me for being brave, facing this head on and not jumping out my bedroom window into my garden.

"We want to have a family talk at the table," Dad says.

"Family talk?" Nate asks, sounding skeptical and a little salty still. I can't blame him with how he was treated.

"Can we just sit at the dinner table?" Dad says a little louder, sounding exasperated.

"I will get some drinks," Mom chirps and swerves off to the kitchen while we follow Dad into the dining room. I feel my hair move from my shoulder and a shiver runs over me. Nate is directly behind me, so close now his fingers brush over the nape of my neck softly. We enter the dining room and Nate drops his hand but still stays close. Bradey walks in and heads toward Nate. Their hands clap loudly as they greet each other with one of their handshakes.

"How was vacay bro?" he asks Bradey.

"It was okay, probably better if I wasn't sick. But shit happens," Bradey sighs.

"Yeah true," Nate says and ends the conversation. Nate knows so much about Bradey's habits and holds so many of his secrets. Our time together we didn't discuss much about Bradey and my parents. If I had asked, would he have told me anything I wanted to know?

I get a little jealous, knowing they have this solid bond with kept secrets and so many moments from their teen years that only they will ever know about. Nate was always my protector when I needed him but they still kept me at arm's length because to Bradey, I was the annoying sister.

We sit down at the dining table. I expect Nate to sit down at the far end with Bradey but he pulls the seat out beside me and sits down. He keeps his casual, dark demeanor and leans back, with one leg kicked out in front of him and his arms crossed over his chest once more.

Dad clears his throat as Mom places beers down on the table for the men and hands me a juice. I frown and feel my shoulders tense while she takes a sip of wine and sits next to Dad.

I can live alone for weeks on end but they still don't want to share an adult drink with me. I ignore Bradey's gaze on me and

Nate. If I look at his face, I'm sure it will be full of questions about why Nate is next to me and not him, and I will crack.

"Firstly, Nate, we want to know the truth. Do you take drugs? Or were they for someone else." Dad starts the conversation.

Now I fight the urge to look at Bradey again, but for a completely different reason. At least now Bradey's attention is on Mom and Dad. The chair he sits on creaks loudly as he shifts nervously.

"No, I am not a drug taker. I have to drug test for my sport so I would have been caught a long time ago don't you think? And no the drugs weren't mine." Nate pauses, as if fighting the urge to say more but nods slowly, letting Mom and Dad know he was done talking.

"Okay, well once we had the chance to calm down and talk about it, we did think it seemed far-fetched. We apologize for jumping to conclusions but the fact remains our house is a drug-free zone. You are all adults now, but you still live in our house while you're at college and we won't tolerate drugs at home." Mom steps in and says.

"Fair call," Nate murmurs.

"Well," Mom says, then takes another sip of wine. She must be very nervous. "We missed you both on family vacation. It just wasn't the same, and with Bradey being sick the entire time, I guess we got lonely and realized that we may have been a bit harsh with you. With you both." She meets my gaze. I raise my eyebrows at her in surprise. Who the fuck kidnapped my parents and replaced it with these caring impersonators?

"Paisley, we are sorry with how we acted with the cheerleading. We truly believed that pushing you to achieve your goals was what you wanted. We always thought it was your dream, but maybe now we see it became our dream for you along the way and we really missed the part where you grew into your own person that may want different things now."

I swallow thickly as a strong wave of guilt washes over me.

"Mom, cheer is what I have always wanted. But when I became injured, I realized I have nothing else. I am lost without it, and the years of you and Dad pushing me will be for nothing. I'll never make it to the top like I wanted. Or like you both wanted. Feels like a waste of my entire life so far." I nearly whisper. Nate tilts his head slightly so he's looking down at me with concern.

"You have reached the top. You cheer for a college team that wins numerous competitions. You didn't make captain but everyone knows if you didn't injure yourself and have your little mishap at the last game you would have been captain."

Little mishap? I think she means my mental breakdown in front of everyone and being boycotted by my team.

"The injury can be a play it by ear thing. See how your recovery goes. But the point of this conversation is." Dad looks to Nate. "We want you to come back home and you three live under this roof while you finish up college. It was always the plan and we would still like it to be the plan."

"Oh," I gasp, thinking this was left field and unexpected. But Nate stays quiet, like he's processing what they have said. He can't mean to say no and stay with Lance? I feel Nate rub my bare leg with his foot then he smirks. I try to hold my straight face.

"I would like nothing more than to be sleeping under this roof again if that is okay with everyone. Paisley, is that okay with you?" He turns to me and rubs my ankles. I splutter and cough loudly.

"Yes, why wouldn't it be?" My voice comes out squeaky.

"Well this is a cute conversation. Let's go get your shit Nate?" Bradey speaks loudly now. Nate stands and looms over us.

"No time like the present I guess," he replies. Looking at Mom and Dad, he quickly adds, "Thank you."

Bradey stands and paces out of the dining room toward the front door with Nate following close behind him.

"I am going to go to my room and do my knee stretches." I stand up and take off up the stairs then grab my phone. I furiously message Nate, telling him they better not be buying drugs for Bradey.

I stare into my screen intensely, waiting for Nate's reply. But he doesn't message me back.

Chapter 33

The moon shines bright through the small gap in my curtains. I haven't left my bedroom. In fact, I haven't left my bed. I look toward my window, wondering if Nate and Bradey are awake in the next room getting high on narcotics.

This time of the night was often peaceful for me. I would use the time when the house was quiet to go over my goals, make plans and meditate. But right now I'm left feeling grim and I want the night to be over as soon as possible. How quickly my brain and heart have switched on me is insane.

I keep telling myself Nate would never do that to Bradey when he knows he needs to get clean, he wouldn't do that to me. Yet something in me is also second guessing and insecure about the possibility that I may have Nate all wrong.

I let out a long, slow breath and rub my temples to ease my growing headache. I'm so confused that the tense pressure is now building up to a migraine. I keep breathing. In and out. In and out.

I've never had so much anxiety before and as of late it feels like it has a chokehold on me and controls my life. I hold my breath as I hear my door slide open, the plush carpet brushing against the bottom of the timber. My bed dips with a new weight on it. I know it's him. I can smell his aftershave. He crawls up the bed and lies against my back, then wraps his arm around my waist and pulls me to him.

"Someone might see you."

"I don't care. You do. But if it pleases you, everyone is fast asleep."

Something in me breaks and I start to sob hysterically. "Hey, it's okay," he whispers against my ear in a soothing voice.

"I'm a nutcase. Something is seriously wrong with me," I whimper between sobs.

"Everything will be okay. You will be okay Paisley. You're strong. You're okay." He repeats the mantra.

My heart goes from a fast hammer that feels life threatening, to a decent canter but nothing that is making me feel like I'm not dying of a heart attack. "I don't like feeling like this. What's wrong with me?"

"Nothing's wrong with you. You do have a lot going on at the moment. Your body is telling you that it needs a break now."

"But how?"

"I honestly don't know. Hopefully our fuckwit brother can sort his shit out soon and you parents finding out sooner rather than later would take away a lot of your anxiety."

My heart starts picking up its pace again and I suck in a large breath, scared it may be my last. Nate moves his hand from my stomach and holds it over my ribcage, where my heart bashes against it.

"Do you feel me breathing?" he asks quietly. I try to still myself as much as I can and feel his chest against my back. Closing my eyes, I take the time to focus solely on his chest moving in and out, slowly, pressing against my shoulders. With everything I have I force myself to match the same rhythm. My heart takes a lot longer to cooperate. But eventually we both lie against each other, in complete darkness, aside from the moonlight filtering through.

"I already miss you sleeping with me all night," I admit selfishly.

"Me too. More than you would ever believe. Let's get Bradey on the straight and narrow and then we'll have time for us to be out and proud."

"I like the way you talk to me so openly. When you're around other people you go back to being a man of little words."

"That's because most people bore me and I don't care to talk to them."

I snort at his brash admission. "You also don't sugarcoat things."

"Don't see the point in that either. Now go to sleep in my arms and I will leave before the sun comes up."

***

The sparrow on my window ledge catches the first of the chilled morning rays, waking me from my slumber. Smelling the remains of Nate in my sheets leaves a regretful pain in my stomach. Secrets, lies and deceit still own my life right now, but it has love, belonging and kindred spirits at the core of it. As I spread my arm over the space where Nate lay only mere hours ago, I find it hard to hate the fact I have this whopping secret for the time being.

I have a plan, this one makes sense. It's not a selfish plan, it's for the better good of everyone around me. My brother needs to be better. Completely. Not the fake better that I can see through. Mom and Dad have had some kind of awakening and that is also something I want to nurture them a little before I drop this bomb on them. With all the wrongs over the last few months, could a happy family be too much to ask for?

There's a lake party starting this afternoon. Sara will be there but Kirsten and the other cheer girls have told me Sara hasn't said anything bad about me in weeks. It makes me hopeful that tonight we may be able to have the long overdue conversation and mend our fractured friendship. I slide out of bed and push the velvet blinds fully open and smirk at the small bird that stays in its place on my windowsill.

Its small, soft head tilts as it studies me. I pause, studying it back. I ponder the fact that its biggest problem today is probably trying to find a shaded tree to perch in when the sun gets too hot, or find a deep enough puddle of water to swim in. I sigh and walk out of my room. *In my next life, I want to come back as a sparrow.*

I tread down the staircase and walk into the dining room. Everyone is already up and all four of them are seated around the table. My heart does a backflip and I can't help but smile. *See, some secrets are okay for now.*

I pull out a chair opposite Dad, next to Bradey and two seats over from Nate. But as I go to lower myself onto the seat, a bowl shatters on the ground. My head whips around and my eyes land on the white porcelain on the tiles. Fresh raspberries scatter amongst the shards.

"Oops, my mistake," Nate says, filling the silence.

I look across to him. When our eyes meet he raises an eyebrow at me.

"I'll just clean that up," he murmurs while casually tapping his fingers on the backrest of the spare seat beside him. Understanding dawns on me and I openly roll my eyes but a dark warmth fills me.

Grumpy, possessive man. The one thing that will get me acting like a princess is Nate being his moody self.

My mind races as I try to figure out how we can make this look casual because all of a sudden I feel like we're deers in the headlights and the attention around us has grown wary.

"You're so clumsy Nate. I swear I don't know how you became such a good swimmer because you were born with two left feet and butter fingers to match!" I scorn him, acting pissed off. *Too much, Paisley. Laid that on way too thick.*

I hear a cough then a deep inhale. Nate's face is bright red with a tight fist covering his mouth. Mother trucker is smothering a laugh.

"Paisley. That's not very nice. Is it that time of the month?" Mom says as her seat scrapes across the floor as she stands up.

Now it is my turn to go bright red.

"Yeah sorry, bit mean of me. I woke up on the wrong side of the bed," I mumble. Mom comes around with a half broom and shovel and starts cleaning up the mess. Embarrassment takes hold of me and I step backwards a few paces.

"I'm going to shower," I say and ignore Nate's fiery frown glaring in my direction. I bounce up the staircase and hear Nate's voice behind me.

"I will just go see if she is okay," he voices. I don't look back and fling the bathroom door open. As I go to close it, Nate's large hand slams on it and forces the door back open. He slips in and then shuts it behind him.

"Two left feet and butter fingers?" he asks with a snicker.

"Well you were making it obvious."

"No, I had it handled. You on the other hand..." He slowly shakes his head with mocking sarcasm. Nate steps hard up against my body, reaches behind me and turns the shower faucet on. The echoing of the water spray fills the small bathroom. "You on the other hand told everyone my little secret. My butter fingers are my greatest strength from memory." He whispers the last of his words against my ear and slips his hand down into the front of my pajama shorts. His fingers sink into my wet pussy. He forces two fingers as deep as they will go so his knuckles graze against my clit.

I suck in a breath and let out a soft moan.

"That good, Princess?"

"Yeah..." I breathe out, losing any ability to think straight. He hooks his fingers upward as he slides them in again and then slowly drags them out again. I shudder in pleasure as he strokes my g-spot. He pushes in again while bringing his free hand up and grips the back of my neck. His grip is tight making it impossible for me to move my head. He brings his face closer, nibbling on my ear lobe gently while he increases the pace of his fingers in my pussy. His fingers are drenched in my desires for him causing it to coat the inside of my thighs.

"I'm going to come," I whimper as quietly as possible.

"Do you want it faster or slower?"

"Faster..." the words come out in a rush telling Nate how desperate I am for my release.

His fingers move faster inside me, brushing my g-spot with perfect precision.

"Harder or softer?" He breathes against my damp ear.

"Harder," My voice hitches as I reach the crest of my orgasm. His fingers thrust into me harder and I moan when my muscles grip his fingers. Nate lets go of my neck and covers my mouth now while holding me tightly against his chest. "Shhhh," He chuckles against my thick hair. Slowly, he pulls his fingers from my pussy and presses them against my lips. "Open," he orders me. I open my lips and he pushes them inside my mouth. I suck my juices off his fingers before he finally removes them. Nate lets me go and moves toward the door. I turn around, facing him with a new rosy glow on my face. Embarrassment and fresh pleasure.

"Mom and Dad probably heard us." I say looking past him toward the closed door.

He shakes his head and smirks at me. "They don't pay attention to shit. Isn't that obvious?" He remarks while his hand finds the door handle. I rush to him and pull on the material of his shirt. He pauses, looking down at me with curious interest.

"For someone as inexperienced as you, you sure know how to use those fingers of yours." I say playfully then tip toe and kiss him on the lips. He licks his lips slowly, tasting the orgasm he gave me.

"I know your body better than you know it. Every summer when you get new freckles, I memorize them. Every new curve and laugh line, it's stored up here," He taps his temple before finishing. "I'd be really fucking worried if I didn't know your body well enough to be good at giving you orgasms," He says with confidence. Fuck I love him.

Chapter 34

Kirsten walks straight up to me when I climb out of Bradey's jeep and pulls me to a hug. Nate jumps off the back and throws his towel over my shoulders, causing me to pull from Kirsten and frown at him.

"Nice to see you again Kirsten. Still got fuck all clothes on I see," he murmurs as he looks over her basic triangle bikini.

"Luckily I'm comfortable in my body and like showing it off huh." She throws back at him confidently. She links her arm in mine and pulls me away from the jeep. I look over my shoulder and see Nate standing there with arms crossed over his chest and lips turned down at the corners, showing me he isn't impressed at all with Kirsten's smug comeback.

Bradey rounds the jeep and nudges him in the ribs then hands him a bottle of beer. I turn back to the front and let Kirsten lead me toward the cheer girls with a satisfied smirk on my face. She really is a fucking queen and I love her.

As we head toward a large tree by the clearing that has all the girls huddled underneath drinking, I see Sara off to the side, sitting with her legs crossed under her. I suck in a deep breath and blow it out slowly, causing wild strands of red hair to float in front of my face. I keep my steps even, with twigs crunching under my converse shoes. My hand slides up my side and I tug at one end of the towel, pulling it off me and draping it over my free arm.

"You will be okay Paisley. We got this shit," Kirsten says in a hushed voice just before we get to the perimeter of the group.

"Hey guys," I greet them after clearing my throat. Fake it till you make it.

"Hey Paisley," Sascha replies and looks me up and down then smiles. "Cute fit!" she exclaims. I look down at my floral, fitted wrap dress and adjust the hem that skims my bare thighs.

"Thanks, can you believe I got it from a thrift shop during the year?"

"How did you luck out like that? The times I've gone in there have been next to nothing in my size or that looks half decent."

I giggle and drop my towel to the ground and sit on it with my legs folded under me.

"Well the time before that I got a vintage denim jacket but it was in the men's section. I just have to roll the loose sleeves up a bit but it looks cute. I will take you next time and see if I bring you better luck."

"Deal! I will hold you to that," she says. They all dive straight into small separate conversations. I lean back on my hands while I fight happy tears that seek their way to fall from my eyes and destroy my confident nonchalant demeanor I try hard to keep up with. I tilt my head and look up as a shadow casts over the side of me. Sara is standing over me and it feels like my world has stopped. I don't know if all the girls stop and stare, but it feels like all has fallen silent. I don't dare take my eyes from Sara's as she looms over me.

"Want a drink?" she asks and holds out a plastic cup.

"What's in it?" I ask slowly and tentatively take it from her outstretched hand.

She shrugs and smiles. "One of Erin's secret concoctions. Vodka being the main ingredient."

"Sounds about right. Thanks."

"No probs," Sara replies and turns to start walking back to the other side of the group.

"Sara," I start. I don't really know what and if now is even the right time. She turns her head to me and gives me a sad look then keeps walking though. Not the right time or place I guess she made the decision for me.

She has offered me a small olive branch and for that I am thankful. We may not be talking yet, but it has broken the ice enough that I don't feel like I am going to hurl at the thought of being near her. I take a sip and grimace then face Sascha and Kirsten and join their conversation.

"Erin really comes through with the craziest punch mixes," I chuckle.

"Yeah she really does." Sascha giggles and covers her mouth with her hand when her punch threatens to spill through her pursed lips.

I can't help but let my mind briefly drift from our conversation and look over my shoulder toward where Nate and Bradey stand. Nate is laughing at something funny another basketball player has said. But he then takes a sip of his beer and glances at me over the long bottle. His dark eyes, only slightly shown through the dark strands of his hair, heat the blood running through my veins. I like knowing that no matter where we are and what we are doing, he is still alert to me. My teeth clamp onto my lower lip as I force my view back to my friends. He truly is a dark angel.

"Paisley..." Kirsten forces my mind back to the current conversation. "Sorry, what?"

"Let's go in the water."

"I'm in!"

Kirsten, Sascha and I walk past the girls and weave through the growing crowd of college students. A group of boys I recognize from Bradey's basketball team drag large logs into the center of the clearing. There are still a couple of hours of hot daylight left, but I know what they are prepping for. I don't know firsthand, but I have heard. First it's the fire, then it's the alcohol and large speakers, then the madness begins. Bradey and Nate have never let me stay. If I ever tried to argue about it they would throw my cheerleading goals at me. *If you get drunk and make a mistake, do you think the coaches will want you as captain? Do you not think the future cheer captain needs to have a squeaky clean college record?* Those comments would get me every single time. God I was weak. Maybe I still am? Bradey and Nate haven't mentioned what time I should go home and neither have I. If it comes to that, we will see how much I have changed or how little.

I stumble on a tree root, which causes me to run into the back of Kirsten. My hands land on her bare back with a loud slap.

"Fuck sorry."

"Too busy looking for lover brother?" She chuckles once she has caught her balance again.

"Kirsten, not so loud."

"No one heard me, calm down."

I look around purposely and know she is right. Sascha is already pushing her inflatable into the water and wasn't in ear shot. My heart settles down and stops feeling like it's trying to escape through my rib cage. After I throw my dress onto the small bank, I grab a spare inflatable and can't help but grind my teeth together as I drag the baby blue blow-up plastic into the water. The cold water sways around my legs, dancing around my bare thighs as I get deeper. Water splashes against my back as I throw myself on to it.

"Who picked the colors for the inflatables this year?" I mumble while letting my hands float on either side of me in the water.

"It's kind of funny, the guys reckon they are going to fuck girls on them later," Sascha says, almost sounding wishful.

I choke and sit up coughing. My legs hang over either side of me now, kicking slowly in the water as we float further out.

"That's sick," I reply and the moment I do I remember what sick really is and my cheeks grow red.

"Ohhhh yeah you are right. That is so horrendously sick," Kirsten chimes in mischievously.

Sascha laughs and holds her stomach. "You are way too girl next door Paisley. But we love you for it. To be honest, I wouldn't mind having two hot brothers cockblocking me."

"Yeah, because it has been so much fun my entire life."

"What happened to Hawk Boy? He was hot. We heard you went to one of his parties even thought you were becoming rebellious."

An anxious, but brief silence spreads between us before I answer, "It just didn't work out."

"Shame. Blue looks good on you."

"I think I suit maroon," I say, letting my lips tug at the corners into a sly smirk.

"I think you also suit dark colors," Kirsten says and I look down at her lying flat on the plastic inflatable, giving her a 'shut the fuck up' look. Her eyes twinkle, showing me she isn't done yet with the teasing.

"Black looks really good *on* you!" I kick my legs out instantly and send Kirsten's inflatable flipping over in the water. She lets out a scream before she goes under. Kirsten resurfaces and coughs while pushing her blonde hair back and out of her face. A wide grin spreads across her face then she climbs back on.

"Here I'll hold it," I say as I throw my leg out, letting it land on top of the inflatable.

"My cute friend is actually evil."

"Being good is boring. You should know that."

"I'm going to swim back in and get a drink. It's fucking hot," Sascha says and starts paddling toward the shore on her plastic inflatable.

"I actually need a drink too. You coming in?" Kirsten asks me. I look toward the shore and see Nate leaning against the tree closest to the shore. His shoulder rests casually against the trunk but his eyes burn on me. The water bobs around us, sending us further out each time we stop paddling. Lance hits his arm and nods his chin toward where they are all drinking on the logs but Nate shakes his head and looks back to me.

"Nah I will come back in soon. I'm enjoying it out here," I tell Kirsten

"Okay, I'll bring a drink back for you soon if I can find some bottles."

I watch Kirsten paddle back in and then as I look past her, I can make out the confused look on Nate's face before it turns to a deep frown. Oh yeah, Mr Protective is worried about my safety and is not impressed I am out here alone. I wiggle my fingers at him innocently and lie back on the inflatable, letting my hands float on either side of me once more. The sun beams down on me, but it's nice. I hear nothing but the gentle slapping of lake water against my plastic inflatable and some jet skis in the far distance. As I lay quietly, I allow myself time to process some thoughts that cause my mind to feel overwhelmed.

Bradey seemed a little more focused today and had some color in his cheeks. Mom and Dad have come back from holiday with a new attitude but I wonder how much of it is organic and how much they are forcing themselves to act and say things so they feel better about themselves. Because I still don't understand how they really can't see how much Bradey is struggling and that he has an active drug addiction.

I'm mad at myself for not knowing sooner, but I knew he was off and knew something was going on with him. I just didn't know exactly what. I let myself feel a glimmer of satisfaction that some things seem to be getting better when I lift my knee and bend it a few times. It really is feeling good. I have had a few physio appointments, otherwise hanging out in the pool with Nate has clearly helped a lot.

I sigh and sit up again when I think of the few weeks we had, basking in each other's company and letting ourselves be obsessed with one another. My heart jumps and eyes grow wide when I realize how much I have floated away from shore. Nate's still standing in exactly the same spot, focused on me and my lone inflatable. I must look like a small dot to him now, because I can't work out any details on his facial expression like before. But I can feel his angry aura from here. I roll over onto my stomach carefully, so I can paddle back toward the bank but disappointment greets me when I feel how deflated the plastic has become.

"Cheap fucking shit," I curse to myself as I let my angry words toward my inflatable mask the fact I'm starting to grow anxious. I'm a good swimmer. But not that good.

I look up while my arms paddle in long smooth strides. Nate has pushed off the tree and is standing on the edge of the bank with his arms crossed over his chest. Am I truly broken that while I quietly fight for my life, I still think he's pure sex and if any girl tries to touch him now, I would probably end up in jail for murder?

I paddle a little quicker, but water pushes against the front of the inflatable now it has lost most of its air and pulls the front down, causing lake water to wash over my chin. *I don't want to yell for help.* Causing a scene and having everyone standing on the edge of the water staring at me fills me with a horrible shiver. *Maybe I will just quietly sink in the lake, dying a true death instead of dying from embarrassment.* I start to morbidly giggle to myself while I look around the lake some more. Nothing but water. *Fuck my life.*

The inflatable sinks a little more so the water is now brushing over my back and shoulders. I push myself off it and lay my arms over the side of it so the rest of my body bobs in the deep lake. I glance at Nate as he rips his singlet off and drops it to the side of him. *Oh hell no, he's not coming to save me...*

He takes a long stride and dives off the high bank into the lake and starts swimming toward me.

Yeap he's coming to save me. I could just sink right now so I don't have to face him with my red, freckled face. But my will to live is stronger and I sit there anxiously as Nate swims closer and closer to me. He makes it look so easy and seems like he puts no effort into the distance he can cover in a short space of time. He reaches me in mere minutes and I shy away from his furious face.

"And how were you planning on swimming back?" he bites out, while leaning on the pathetic excuse for a floating device.

"I'm a good swimmer," I all but squeak.

"No you're not," he growls at me and rips the inflatable away from me. He tosses it to the side and pulls me to him.

"And don't fucking float on something this color again. If you want to float in the middle of the lake you can float on my cock."

I gasp and punch him in the shoulder. One arm is locked around my hips while the other moves up my body and wraps around the back of my head like a vice.

"And thanks to you, the secret you wanted to keep is well and truly spoiled now." His words slip from his angry lips. I chew the inside of my cheek as I look over to the lake bank. There is a line of our friends watching the lifesaving events play out.

"Well damn, you didn't have to save me."

"So you admit, I was saving you?"

"Don't get a big head," I murmur and stare directly into his broody eyes.

"Already got a big head. Or have you forgotten already?" he says and pushes his hips against me. Luckily my arms are paddling in the water, trying to keep me afloat so I can't be greedy and wrap my fingers around it.

"We need to head back." I settle on saying. His sly smirk says all I need to know. He knows exactly where my thoughts had gone. He rolls over and pulls my hand over his shoulder.

"Get on my back."

"Oh no, you can't be serious."

"Paisley, for fuck's sake. Get on my back or I will drown you myself," he scorns me. My dignity is long gone now I suppose. I float onto his back and hold onto his shoulders while he starts to breaststroke toward the shore. I reach back and grab the plastic inflatable and he pauses.

"Paisley..." he warns me.

My breaths come quick and my throat burns with the feeling of someone stomping on it.

"I don't want to litter in the lake."

Nate slowly starts swimming again and his back vibrates against my chest.

"Of course you don't. It will be the first thing that goes on the fire later."

Chapter 35

Swimming back was a lot slower than it was when he came to my rescue. Yet somehow when we start to get closer to the shore and our feet make contact with the pebbles on the lake floor, he doesn't even look like he's tired. I place my hands on my hips as we walk toward the waiting group and take in oxygen down my burning, dry throat. I side eye Nate and make contact with his broad, bare chest then flick my eyes back in front of me.

"You aren't even breathing heavily. Are you human?" I mumble under my breath.

He scoffs and leans into me a little, making me halt my steps. "I am so disconnected from society that I sometimes think no. And I am glad about it." He adds on the end as he stands straight. I roll my eyes and smile. Of course he'll find a way to make himself still seem superior to the ones that have their shit together.

"Babe are you okay?" Kirsten skips through the water and meets me when the water is mid-thigh height now.

"Yeah stupid inflatable went flat on me,"

"Oh my god thank god Nate saw you in trouble."

I can almost feel his arrogance and smugness rolling off him in waves.

Bradey and his basketball team go ankle deep in the water and a few clap Nate on his back. He stands tall but he looks uncomfortable at the touch.

"You okay sis?" Bradey asks me as he stands directly in front of me.

"Yeah I'm fine everyone. Just the inflatable deflating on me. No harm done."

"Why did Nate come get you?" he asks, looking between us two. I suck on my bottom lip while my mind goes blank. Is he really starting to see that our relationship has changed?

"Just being a caring brother. You should try it sometime," I say in Bradey's face, trying to act nonplussed.

"Thanks Nate," I say over my shoulder as I exit the water. I will thank him properly later when we don't have an audience. But as my feet touch the safety of the grass, Nate strolls off up the bank into a different direction.

"No worries. *Sis*," he yells over his shoulder as he retreats. Did he really think now would be our time to confess our love for one another in front of everyone? He knows the situation at home needs sorting out first.

I watch his bare back as he walks away, feeling a mixture of guilt, shame and something entirely different. Bradey throws his arm over my shoulder and walks with me out of the water. I shake my head slightly, telling myself that the sick tingle I got when he called me sis is disgusting and needs to be put in my return to the sender box of emotions.

"I can get someone to drive you home now?" Bradey says casually. Here it is. Pivotal moment.

"Where are you sleeping tonight? You've been drinking so can't drive. In fact, no one here can drive from what I can see."

"Paisley don't start. Me and Nate crash wherever we end up, in the back of the jeep or we get a ride to a house with someone sober. It's no biggie."

"No biggie. So I think I'll do that tonight as well."

"Yeah and Nate will spend all night thinking he has to protect you from guys and not have a good time."

"Aw but you won't? I'm hurt," I say sarcastically.

"You know what. Do as you please Paisley. But if you wake up with regrets, don't come crying to me." He slides his arm from my shoulders and heads back to the middle of the clearing. His shoulder lifts when he tips his head back and downs the last of his drink. I sigh with exasperation and walk with the girls to the cooler that has the punch in it.

"I'm so sorry for leaving you. If I had stayed we could have both floated back on my inflatable."

"Don't stress Kirsten. Who was to know I would get stuck in the middle of the lake," I laugh, already feeling more relaxed over my near-death event. I pick up an empty cup and hold it under the tap then turn the nozzle. The peach-colored liquid streams out and I let it fill the cup to the brim before I close the small plastic nozzle. The cool liquid greets my dry lips when I take a sip. As I remove the plastic cup from my mouth, I catch Nate glaring at me from across the clearing.

While his eyes bore into my own with a coldness that could make anyone wither where they stand, my soul jumps up and down, as if it wants out to be across the clearing with his own. He's angry at me, for multiple reasons, but the main reason is me claiming him solely as my brother in front of everyone.

Nate leans his head to one of his friends when he is tapped on the shoulder, while listening intently to his words, his eyes still seek me out. How can a look so cold threaten to burn the entire world down around me? I swallow thickly and raise my glass to take another mouthful to sedate this increasingly painful sandpaper mouth. I'm so lost in this feeling toward Nate that my limbs become cemented and my tongue feels swollen. I force more punch down then watch Nate walk off with his friend that he has just conversed with.

Kirsten slips her delicate fingers into mine and tugs at my hand, bringing my attention back to her. Abruptly I am reminded that we are surrounded by half our school and me and Nate don't live in a magical world with just us and our taboo feelings.

"If you want it to stay a secret you really shouldn't stare at him like you're going to eat him."

"I can't help it. Sometimes I actually hate feeling like this." I tug at a long tendril of my hair, watching the water droplets roll down my stomach.

"What exactly is your plan with him? Fuck him for a bit then go back to being siblings? Or marry him one day and fuck everyone else."

"I honestly don't know. But I'm sickly obsessed with him. It's deeper than love. It's like he owns my soul. It's honestly as if gravity moves differently around us when we are together and I am addicted to that feeling."

Kirsten blows out a long breath and links her arm through one of mine.

"I feel sorry for anyone that tries to break the rules and touch you because he seems more obsessed with you."

"Break what rules?" I look to my side at Kirsten in confusion.

"Sara just asked me what is going on with you two because she has heard from one of the guys that Nate has told everyone if they touch you tonight, he will dismember them and then throw them into the lake for the fishes," she says with a grim tone in her voice.

"He won't mean it literally." I get defensive, but I don't know if I really believe my own words.

After the words leave my mouth, I look out to the trees where Nate's walked off into.

"You know those games we played with the swim team was fucked up but a little fun. But truth is, I think Nate has it in him to do some really bad stuff. No game playing, just bad, bad stuff."

"Kirsten, you don't know him like I do. He has been there for me in a way that no one else was when I was a mental case."

"I hope you are right."

"Can we change the subject?"

"Good idea," she agrees with me then leads me toward the growing group around the fire pit that has just been lit.

The large speaker gets put off to the side, and as the sun starts to set and more drinks flow, the bass thumps through the group.

An hour later, my cheeks hurt from smiling and orange sun streaks intertwine with gray skies. I desperately try to ignore the urge I have to glance around the crowd to try and spot Nate. Sara's loud voice rings through the drunk crowd while she tosses a bottle and catches it over and over again. Her lips dance at the corners, showing her confident yet teasing smile. It's contagious. Always has been.

Her tanned skin is so perfectly sun-kissed that it almost has a shimmer to it under the last of the daylight. The clinking of her fingers heavily dressed in rings against the glass bottle every time it lands echoes along with the music.

"Who is down for some spin the bottle?" she asks loudly so everyone can hear her.

I keep quiet and hunch my shoulders a little. I'm always down to watch but have no desire to play.

"Let's go!" Bradey's best friend says loudly with a fist pump raising at the same time. Bradey pushes through the crowd and squeezes in next to Sara. He gives her a cocky grin then slides his tongue over his teeth and throws his arm over her shoulders playfully.

"I will play and hope it lands on you," he says smugly and winks in her direction. Gag.

She slaps him playfully and turns back to everyone.

The next song starts, the drum and bass pumps out of the Bluetooth speaker, with neon flashing lights illuminating from it in sync.

Sara spins the bottle and with a flash of green glass with the orange from the flames bouncing off it, it slows down, before it finally comes to a stop on one of our cheer friends. A long slow whistle rips from one of the basketballers then his head swings between the two.

I snicker under my breath and shake my head as I look around the group seeing how excited the guys and girls are right now. Sara gives our friend a lopsided smirk then confidently, stands up and marches around to her. As she stands, Sara grips onto either side of her face and pulls her instantly into a passionate kiss. Excited chants come from everyone while I watch in amusement. *I guess that's one way to start a game.*

"That may be the best kiss I have ever had," she screeches and sits back in her post beside Bradey.

He snorts and tosses his hair back from his face. "Yeah, that is because you haven't hooked up with me yet."

"Yet," she repeats slowly and rolls her eyes. I should probably care that my drug addict brother is trying to get in with my once best friend that potentially still hates me, but I really think there are much bigger things in this world that people—including myself—can spend more time worrying over.

Sara tosses the empty glass bottle across the pit to the girl she has just made out with. She catches it and places it on the twig covered floor. Following a giggle, she delicately spins it in her fingers and it lands on one of Burke Towns football players.

All bulky five feet eight of him stands up and lifts his chin to her. Ew. When did these guys get so arrogant and unattractive?

Chase tenses his muscles and curls his biceps as she prances over to him. She kisses him delicately on the cheek then sits back down, leaving him standing there dumbfounded. I can't help but let out a loud cackle as I imagine in his head he was about to sweep her off her feet and make her swoon all over him. *Classy, I like that.*

She tosses him the bottle and he grips it in his strong hands while he still stands.

"You don't know what you're missing."

She shrugs and rests her chin on her hand while she perches on the edge of the log. "Jocks just don't do it for me." Everyone laughs, making him angrier.

His cheeks grow red as a pulsating vein spreads across his forehead. He sits down in a heap and spins the bottle roughly on the ground. It spins furiously then slows down. As if the world stops around me, I see it slowing more and more as it turns my way. I already start shaking my head and grab Kirsten and try to pull her more into my seat.

Right as it stops in my direction, the footballer grins at me. Sweat beads on his veiny forehead.

"Naw, Paisley the lil' virgin Mary, looks like it is your lucky day!" he announces, as if I would be the luckiest girl ever to be able to kiss him. I shake my head again and put my palms up.

"I'm just watching. Kirsten can have my spot," I assure him and everyone else.

"Oh I don't think so. I will be the first in the school to taste your sweet butt." As I start to shake my head again and argue with him, a black figure flies across the group, over the fire and straight into him.

"Nate what the fuck are you doing!" I scream when I realize Nate is on top of him on the ground, beating the crap out of him.

"Fight! Fight! Fight!" half the group chant loudly over the music, while a small fraction stand back, watching with shocked looks and another few try to break them apart. My eyes are wide in shock as I keep looking around. My heart hammers so hard that I can feel it in my throat. They both throw punches in each other's direction as they roll through the clearing toward the bank.

"What did I fucking say?! I made myself real fucking clear!" Nate growls loudly while he lands another punch straight into his jaw. Blood pours from Chase's nose while he coughs and still tries to throw punches back. But Nate is faster and stronger, considering he isn't as bulky as this guy. I push my impressed thoughts for his fighting skills aside as I follow the tumbling pair closer toward the lake. Nate straddles him and wraps both his hands around his neck, squeezing tightly. Fuck.

Bradey starts beating at his back.

"Fucking stop! You're taking this too far!" he bites out through his gritted teeth. Nate doesn't stop though. He squeezes harder while Chase's face grows red and his eyeballs swell. I push through everyone, slamming my elbows into any-thing I can connect with without thinking. There's no time to think.

I crouch low and wrap my fingers around his wrists, trying to loosen them. "Nate stop!" I say, tears on the rims of my eyes.

"He was going to kiss you. He thought he could," he mumbles while fixated on the choking man beneath him.

"Nate fucking stop or I will leave you and never look back!" I cry desperately. His eyes flip across to mine and he frowns.

"You would leave me?" he asks and I hear a wheeze start beneath him. Good, he has loosened his grip.

"If you kill a man? Yeah I would."

He blinks slowly then nods his head and releases his hands.

"He was going to kiss you. No one can touch you," he mur-murs. I can now feel the weight of the stares from the partygo-ers around us. *Now,* our secret is out.

"Nate I'm not fond of sharing either. There's no me without you. So please get off him. I can't bear to lose you. Ever."

Nate shuffles off him and glares at me through bloodshot eyes. I stare back, watching the remarkable thing of his human-ity coming back to him. His morbid, chaotic self calming down and the cool calm and collected Nate returning to me.

He looks around then stands up, holding his hand out to me. I grip it and let him pull me to my feet.

"You have got to be fucking kidding me. You're fucking my sister?" Bradey gets up in his face and yells at him.

"None of your business brother," he says calmly. He towers over Bradey, looking down at him, meaning business. Bradey scowls at him and shoves at his chest.

"It's disgusting. Not only are you two related, but you're my best friend so it goes against bro code."

"Not blood related and again, none. Of. Your. Fucking. Business," he draws out then pulls me away from the group. He drags me through the trees toward Bradey's parked jeep.

"Nate, stop. Are you okay?" I ask, feeling unsure. The repercussions of this are going to be bad.

He spins me around and presses my back firmly against the jeep's hood. The silver ring on his thumb rubs against my chin when he strokes the tip of his thumb painfully slow against my bottom lip.

"You have a split lip," I breathe against his thumb. My eyes lock onto the small amount of fresh blood that beads on his top lip. I follow the movements of his tongue as it snakes out and licks the blood off it.

"I would have killed him. For you. I will do anything for you."

"I know but I don't want you to kill someone for me," I sob and rake my fingers over his smooth black hoodie. I fist my hands on it and pull his hard body against mine. "Don't ever do that again. Trust me enough to know I wouldn't have kissed him."

"I do trust you but the image I still have in my head overwhelmed me. I don't like guys thinking that they even have the right to touch you." His hand grips me around the back of my head possessively. Showing me exactly what he means. I am all his, and he is mine.

"Well I think now they all know they need to stay clear of me. I don't think anyone will even want to talk to me now."

Nate slides his free hand purposely up my bare thigh, raising my dress at the same time. Goosebumps erupt over my skin. His finger hooks around the waistband of my bikini bottoms and tugs them down. He doesn't say another word, just his heavy breathing tells me what he wants. What he needs. I need it too. I know what shit I'm going to get for Nate's demonic outburst but I still would happily lose everyone as long as I had him.

As my bikini bottoms drop to my ankles, I lift one foot out of them and lift my leg up onto Nate's hips. He holds it there while he pulls his hard cock free with his other hand. He lines it up to my entrance and rubs it a few times against it. He covers his mouth with mine and pushes his warm tongue into my desperate mouth. I welcome it and return the same assault on him with my own. I break our hungry kiss and stare at him. "Call me your sister. Just one time."

The head of his cock massages the inside of my pussy as he rests it just inside. "I told you, I have never seen you as my sister."

"Please just one time," I beg him, letting my kinky brain do all the thinking now. My fingers walk up his baggy hoodie, trace the outline of his jaw carefully and then grip either side of his head.

I can see him fighting his demons even as I beg him to give me what I want.

"No barriers. No hiding the ugly," I whisper with a pleading expression.

He runs his tongue over his white teeth and drops his head down to mine so his hair covers his face. His fingertips painfully dig into my thigh and he rams his cock deep. I cry out as I move my hands around the back of his neck and hold him tight against me. He thrusts into me painfully but I don't want him to stop. It feels too good.

"This what you want, sis? You want your big bad brother to fuck you hard?" he groans.

"Yeah..." I whimper loudly. I clench my needy muscles around his cock, squeezing as tight as I can.

"You like that little sister? You want me to punish you better than your parents can?"

I moan as his cock stretches me and hits my g-spot. His pelvis rubs against the front of my clit with every thrust. We are so close together that our bodies are rubbing all over one another. Every touch, every movement sets my body on fire.

"How's that Paisley? How does it feel getting fucked from your delinquent brother?"

I can't speak. All I can do is hang on and whimper as I get closer to coming. Wetness coats my thighs and it excites Nate even more.

"My sister's nice and wet for me. Do you know how many times I watched you sleep when we were younger, wondering if your tight pussy would get this wet for me. Wondering if it tasted good. Wondering if it tasted even sweeter because it wasn't meant to be mine?" He breathes harshly. He slams into me and groans loudly as his rock-hard cock pulsates deep within me.

"I always wondered if fucking my little sister would be the best fuck in the world because she's the one person that is meant to be off limits." He says so quietly as the peak of his orgasm finishes.

"And?" I sigh with my eyes closed and resting my head on Nate's shoulder.

"You're my addiction Paisley. There will never be anyone else."

"We are toxic together Nate."

"Toxic together but broken apart," he replies.

Chapter 36

O nce we have caught our breaths and are clothed, I immediately reattach myself to Nate. This time in a more needy, loving way. He's my home. *Toxic together, but broken apart.* His words replay through my mind as I rest my head against his comforting chest. His arms wrap tightly around my shoulders to hold me right where I am. The feel of his hands rubbing up and down my back gently helps me fall into a calmer space. My head gets so loud when I am overwhelmed. It scares me. I don't ever want to go back to how I felt when I thought the only choice I had was to run away from everyone and everything. I want to find coping strategies so I can be stronger. Nate is my coping strategy it turns out, but I am okay with that.

I can still hear music weave through the thick trees, darkness now blankets all around us. Subtle crunches of twigs and stones become louder and louder with conversing voices. Male and female. I knew we would have company sooner rather than later.

"So my dear brother and innocent lil' sis are doing the fucking dirty?" Bradey's voice is the first I hear. I tense against Nate and he feels it. His arms protectively grow tighter around me.

"Not really how we had planned on you finding out," Nate replies. His voice is deep, leaving a rumble vibrating from his chest against my resting head.

"Blood relation or not. It's still fucking sick."

"I would suggest you stop talking, before you say something hurtful toward Paisley which I won't tolerate. We have been through a lot, you and I. We both hold a lot close to our chest, so let's not be judgy," Nate growls out over top of my head.

"Wonder what Mom and Dad will have to say about this," Bradey says, sounding bored now. He is trying a new angle to fuck with Nate.

"Paisley will decide to tell them when she is good and ready."

I pull back from Nate and stare at Bradey. "The whole town will know soon. Everyone at college officially knows. We have to tell them," I mumble and swipe away fresh tears that soak my cheeks.

"You think I would have learnt the first time not to have secrets. But I honestly thought I was doing the right thing," I continue as I gaze at Sara who is standing behind Bradey. She averts her eyes and finds something interesting to look at in the dark overgrown forest.

"I think I want to go home now. Party seems to be over for us," I murmur and huddle against my safety blanket once more.

"Yeah, let's leave and walk out to the main parking lot. I'll get us an Uber," Nate agrees.

He steps away from me and holds his hand out with a cocky smirk on his face. His face is perfectly calm and dangerously handsome. I tilt my head as I reach my arm out and lace my fingers in his. He winks at me and then leads me past Bradey and Sara.

"Don't think cute cupcakes will make this better, sis," Bradey scorns me as I walk away from him.

"They may help though," I reply without missing a beat. I will find the better me, the stronger me and most of all I will be happy again soon. My voice needs to be the first thing I work on.

***

I wake up groggy the next morning. I delicately brush my fingers from my face while I assess the scale of my hangover.

Sure, I sobered up pretty quick when the drama unfolded but prior to that I was still drinking a lot of punch. I close my eyes and hold them shut while I placate the pounding behind my eyes.

But now with my eyes closed I envision myself stranded in the middle of the lake, and Nate's beating the crap out of someone who was playing spin the bottle. It's been a long time since I have gone out and had fun without dramas and lies. It's what I need but the universe is slow on the delivery.

Nate stayed with me last night and left in the early hours of this morning. I hate when he leaves, the bed feels cold and empty without him. As I slowly open my eyes, I gingerly slide out of bed. My body feels like it has run a marathon and as I pull an oversized tee on, I chuckle about the fact I kind of did while nearly drowning then getting painfully fucked.

I open my bedroom door and I stop short as Nate's tall, toned body waits at the top of the staircase. His hip leans against the top of the rail while he casually uses his thumb to scroll on his phone. He is dressed in loose fitting jorts, crisp white crew socks and a baggy black singlet. His dark hair skims his ears while his head stays slanted down, looking over his phone still.

"You sleep well?" he murmurs and starts typing a message.

"Average. You?"

"Like a baby," he replies and I can hear the humor in his voice. "Ready?" He finally slips his phone into his back pocket and stands straight.

"No... yes... maybe..." I shrug as I stand side by side with him. We both descend the stairs. My toes only just touch the cool tiles when I see Mom putting her MacBook in her work bag.

"Where are you going?"

She presses her glasses higher on her nose and frowns at me. "Work emergency I need to sort out. One of our trauma kids isn't doing well."

"Do you have time to talk? I really need to tell you something." *That's an understatement. I plan to unload a lot,* I add on mentally.

"I can't sorry, Paisley. They really need me at work."

A swallow gets stuck in my throat as I try to hold back a sob. "Mom, please I really need to talk to you. It is important."

"Maybe you should hear her out," Nate insists from beside me.

She shakes her head and lifts her bag. "I will try to get home early tonight, we can talk then," she says and rushes toward the front door. I rake my long nails over my scalp and keep my hair in a messy ponytail style while I glare at the front door in disbelief. Mom's car starts up and then the engine becomes quieter the further she gets down the road.

"I told myself today was the day. I would have my voice. I would be strong. What the fuck just happened?"

"Don't do this to yourself, Princess. Deal with it when you can. Your voice will still be there when the time is right."

Nate tugs his phone out of his back pocket and reads something on the screen then puts his phone away once more. I search his face a little, trying to decipher the strange expression he has. I can tell he's seeking to be his calm nonchalant self but there's a slight difference there. I just don't know if it is positive or not.

"Who's got all your attention on the phone?" I ask.

"No one important. You feel like going to the Grizzlies house party tonight?"

"You hate parties, and I'm not fond of them," I answer him. He lets out a big sigh and for once I notice how tired he looks.

"No secrets right? Your brother got high last night, he hasn't come home and I'm certain he will be there tonight getting high again. I need to make sure he is okay."

"How long have you been looking out for him?"

"Since the day he became my best friend. Things are fucked up at the moment. But when we were little kids that were inseparable we had each other's backs. We held each other's biggest secrets and he listened and took the time to understand when I told him about my dad. No one else did. My best friend is still in there somewhere. He's just lost right now."

I blink rapidly and chew my bottom lip as I turn my head away.

"Don't cry. Just tell me you will come to the party as my date tonight."

I turn my head back to him and force a hesitant smile at him. "I would absolutely love to come to a party with you, where everyone will gossip and stare."

He coughs and puts his large fist over his mouth. The wrinkle at the edge of his eyes warms me and soothes some of my anxiety.

"Good because I would have hated to tie you up and throw you in my car trunk if you had said no." A mischievous smile plays on his lips. We have moved on from games, but I know from experience sadistic games are not above him when he feels they are warranted.

"Hmm I don't know if I should be scared about the fact you admit that so freely, or if that the image I now have in my head doesn't seem so bad."

"Fucking hell Paisley! Get that sweet ass of yours in the pool so I can fuck you and then cut some lengths!"

***

We pull up alongside the curb in Nate's large truck. The roar of the engine cuts off abruptly as it turns off. I'm dressed in a basic black satin skirt and royal blue cotton singlet. Mom wasn't home when we left and Dad was watching the NBA with the neighbors so I took that as a sign that being here, paraded as the freak is better than being the isolated depressed girl at home.

My eyes flick to the side as Nate opens his door and I inwardly sigh. He's dressed so casually yet still looks like the most edible eye candy here.

"Come on Princess," he says, opening my door. I grip his hard shoulders and giggle when he lifts me with ease from the high truck and swings me around once before placing me down again. I get up on my tip toes and pull his head down to mine. Our lips lightly touch, so delicately our skin grazes each other while leaving a searing heat in its wake. We pull apart and I can't help but smile. "How do you, Nate, become the only thing that makes sense in my life?"

"And soon my love, we will make a new life that makes sense with us in it—together." His fingers brush over my lips where he had just been.

I don't know what he means by that. Confusion ebbs within me but I force it away and mentally make a note to ask him about that later. Our fingers intertwine and we cross the road that is becoming busier. I lift my chin a little more than normal to really fake confidence. Nothing like ripping the band-aid off.

Chapter 37

My nose twitches, fighting the potency of musky cologne when we pass a group of college men who are by the glass stacker doors as we enter the house. The house is single level, but still covers a lot of square feet. It's a light creme color with tinted glass paneling along the front and a well-kept lawn and basic straight hedge along the front yard. My white and black Nikes squeak on the wood panel flooring when we come to a stop in the entrance. Nate scans the room then tugs me and leads me through the crowd. I see Kirsten beside the large speaker as she dances around the small space she has found. I smile and pull on my hand to get Nate's attention. He looks over his shoulder at me and raises an eyebrow in question.

I nod my head toward Kirsten and he follows where I am directing him. He shakes his head and tries to keep walking. I pull his arm again and this time he turns around and looks down at me.

"I want to go say hi!" I say.

Nate drops my hand and crosses his arms over his chest with a deep frown creasing his forehead.

"Every time you seem to leave me, you find trouble," he grumbles. It isn't loud but I can make out his deep words. It's taken years of practice.

"I will be fine. We are confined to a house with people we know. What could go wrong?" I reply.

He snorts and looks around slowly before his eyes land back on me.

"Yeap and now you have done it! Something is definitely going to go wrong."

I grin and tip toe before putting my hands around his neck. He stands like a statue, not removing his arms from his defiant chest position. "I will be okay and I will come find you soon."

"Go see her then, I will find Lance but I won't be far."

"I'm sure you won't be," I say sarcastically. I know him well enough to know he will still be in viewing distance. I drop my hands and go to walk toward Kirsten when a vise-like grip captures me from behind and pulls me against a rock-hard frame. I close my eyes and lean against the wall I know is my man. His distinctive cologne envelopes me. Nate's head leans down and his lips slowly kiss my neck then his lips softly move against my skin as he talks. "I love you, Princess."

"I love you too," I sigh with a happy smile. He pulls back from me and slaps my ass as he turns and walks off through the crowd. I can feel lingering eyes on me. I take a little peak at the faces that openly stare and I can't work out if they are confused or disgusted. *Probably both*, I decide as I focus my attention back on Kirsten. Fuck 'em.

"You came!" Kirsten shrieks and pulls me to her in a warm embrace.

"Of course I came! I mean I absolutely love parties because they always seem to go so well for me," I reply and squeeze her back.

She giggles against me and lets me go. "Well tonight will be different. You'll see."

I smile at her but inwardly cringe. I have a deep pit forming in my stomach that I try to ignore while keeping my face straight. "Of course," I agree with her weakly and run my fingers through my long hair to try and act nonchalant. I make a loose curl with a large piece of my hair as I twirl it tightly around my finger then drop it, so it lays loosely over the front of my shoulder. Kirsten hands me a bottle of cheap wine, I press it against my lips and tip it back. The strong potent taste makes me wheeze with my fisted hand over my mouth.

"This on special or something," my strained voice forces out when I feel like I can breathe.

Her eyes wrinkle at the sides and her nose scrunches as she giggles and takes the bottle back. "One of the girls got given a whole box of it for next to nothing,"

"Well that makes sense. I think you guys were given expired wine."

She shrugs one shoulder lazily and purses her lips while she starts body rolling in front of me. "Still does the same thing at the end of the night doesn't it," she teases me and spins around happily while still dancing. It's contagious. Being happy with my friend is contagious. I start dancing with her and hold my phone up, recording all the good parts I can. No more moping. Every moment that has passed recently I have felt stronger and stronger with every breath.

Getting knocked down doesn't have the same weighted anchor to keep me down now. I can now brush it off and stand back up, taller than before. I lean to the side and pop my hip, rolling it in a snakelike way while Kirsten cuts shapes and shuffles perfectly in front of me. She has always been good at shuffling.

We both crack up when a plastic cup is dropped beside her and she doesn't miss a beat, kicking it as she dances and goes back to tearing up the space around her. Sara walks past us and gives us a soft smile. Feeling powerful, I grab onto her forearm and meet her curious gaze.

"Can we talk later?" I ask, feeling hopeful.

She tilts her head, causing her long hair to flop to the side and run down her arm. "Yeah I would like that," she agrees and I can feel she really meant it.

I pull her into a hug and she hugs me back. I can't hold in the single tear that runs down my cheek. "I've really missed you."

"Me too. Life doesn't make sense without you being my best friend." She pulls back. "I will come find you later okay?" she continues with a soft, heartwarming smile. I nod and bite my bottom lip so she can't see I am fighting to stop my lip from quivering like a baby. She slips off through the crowd and I see her walk toward Bradey and whisper something in his ear. He kisses her on the head and I frown. *Since when did they get together?*

Bradey looks over toward me and winks. I scowl at him. He better not be getting with her just to get back at me and Nate.

I refuse to let it get me down, thinking positive, I swallow and keep dancing, mentally telling myself they may really like each other or be down for a fun summer fling. Not overthinking things I have no control over, and letting the anxiety suck the happiness from my soul really has to be top of my priority list. It feels unnatural but maybe with practice eventually it may just become part of who I am. A new and improved me.

I grab the bottle of wine from Kirsten and back away from her with a smirk.

"I need a breather," I say and hold up the bottle. "Thanks!"

"*Biarch!* Don't choke on the sour wine!" she laughs at me loudly.

I turn and head for the front door. The house is a lot busier now. Nate catches my eye off the side not far from the door. He's talking to Lance as he leans against the wall while sipping on a beer. I hold the bottle of wine up and smirk at him. He frowns deeply, looking nonplussed. I openly roll my eyes.

I'll be back in a minute, I mouth at him.

His eyes flick back to Lance as he listens to what he's saying but he's already pushed off the wall standing straight. I know he will come find me. But I don't mind. I step down the concrete steps and onto the grass. I take another large mouthful of the wine and then get nudged to the side.

"What the fuck man—" I start when Bradey keeps walking across the grass. He pushed past me and he didn't even bother to acknowledge me. *Asshole.* He really *is* butthurt over me and Nate being with each other.

Bradey slips off down the road and I step forward so I can get a better view down the footpath. He stops beside a car I recognize. It's dark but I would recognize that car anywhere. It's the one I lost my virginity in. Leith steps out of the backseat and hands Bradey something, then without having a conversation, he turns to climb back into the car. Bradey's already walking back with his hands stuffed in his jorts pockets and head down. Does he think that will make him invisible?

Leith pauses as he sees me. He stares angrily at me for a moment, sending an ice-cold shiver down my spine. But what leaves me feeling like I have been touched by the devil is the malicious smirk that tugs at the corner of his mouth. He slips back into the car and it takes off down the road.

Bradey tries to slip past me and I grab onto his hoodie.

"Why were you seeing Leith?" I ask, but already knowing the answer. It's a truth I wish wasn't real.

"Fuck off Paisley. You have no leg to stand on with your judgmental opinions."

"Don't speak to her like that Bradey. And what have I told you about getting gear from them?" Nate's deep voice floats over my head. I can feel him at the back of me, just slightly pressing up against me. My pillar of support every single time. With him at my side I feel like I could go to war with anyone.

"Well you my dear brother, have stopped everyone in our town from selling to me. It's your fault."

Nate scoffs and wraps a hand around my waist then rests his lips against the top of my head. He speaks against my head to Bradey. "Yeah no it's totally my fault. Sorry for always trying to look after you," he says then pulls us away from Bradey. Bradey stomps off into the house and leaves us standing on the grass. Nate wraps both arms around me now, standing at my back. He drops his mouth to the nape of my neck and kisses it.

"Is that the secret you had on Leith? He was dealing drugs to my brother?"

Nate sighs against my neck, the warm puff of air floating over the hollow above my collarbone.

"Yeah, they deal drugs and steroids to fuck loads of people in our town. Pisses me off."

"Why didn't you just tell me?"

"You didn't know about Bradey's addiction then, and I was a little chaotic in my feelings about him fucking you if you remember."

I feel the heat grow in my cheeks, like a tornado sending vivid images into my mind. I remember the night with Leith, the pool, the forest, the whole lot.

"God we've done some messed up shit."

"It was foreplay to our lifelong relationship."

"So that's how you sleep at night."

"I tell myself whatever I need to without any guilt."

"I know," I giggle and turn in his arms.

He kisses my forehead, then slowly moves down to my nose before he moves lower to my lips. He kisses me painfully slow. A speed I am not used to with him. I open my lips, welcoming his soft tongue as he invades my mouth and massages my tongue with his own.

He pulls back and gives me one last soft peck on my lips with a smug grin that follows.

Awkwardly fumbling his hands in his pockets against me, he pulls out his phone, looks at the screen then slips it away again. He clears his throat and runs his thumb over my lips. His ring scrapes my chin, sending a shudder up my spine. I clench my needy muscles and wonder how I can be brought to my knees by a single touch.

"I need to tell you something," he says, causing me to open my eyes and search his face for answers before I speak. His face is blank and unreadable like usual.

"That is never a good start to a conversation."

"If you think it is a break up talk, you are very wrong. You just need to make a decision on behalf of both of us."

I try to step back but he holds me in place. "Don't fucking put those walls up. Just listen to what I have to say."

"Fine," I say sulkily and know I sound immature.

"Listen and don't speak until I am done, okay?"

"Mhm."

He shakes his head slightly with a smile.

"I got scouted from that swimming day you came to. Stanford University have offered me a scholarship program to start in the new semester. I can just transfer everything I have done so far over to them and carry on my studies."

"My gut told me that day that something was going to come of that visit... Stanford is amazing!"

"Yeah it is, but I won't accept it unless you come."

I hold my breath and drop my gaze and stare at my feet. As I slowly blow out my held breath through my lips.

"What would I even do there? I doubt Mom and Dad will pay for me to live with you and I can't afford my own tuition."

"You could talk to them. Your college fund should be your college fund no matter where you choose to study. And I can get a job. If we want it to work, it can work."

"Nate..." His name comes out on a trembled breath. "You can't turn an opportunity like this down no matter what I decide. But I need time to think about what I am doing. My whole life is here."

"Well it's simple for me. I'm there with you. Or here with you. There's no other option."

"You'd be giving up your dream for me."

"When are you going to understand?" Nate whispers and rests his forehead against my own. "My dream is you. The only dream I have ever had was to have you. I need you like humans need oxygen to live. There's no me without you, Princess."

Chapter 38

Nate leads me back inside after we agreed we would sit down and talk it through tomorrow. My mind is reeling. I'm happy for Nate, he does deserve it, especially if he can make his own name for himself. But I don't know if I want to leave Burke Town yet. It could work but I don't know if I am ready.

The thumping of music vibrates under my feet, running up my legs and adding to my nausea. I take a mouthful of the wine that is now clenched tightly in my frantic grip. Kirsten meets me halfway and tugs at the bottle, coaxing me to give it to her. I loosen my fingers and let it slip into her grasp.

"You okay?" she asks.

"Yeah just another fucked up night. How did my life go from plain jane boring to mind blowing manic?"

"I can't even answer that myself. It's like watching a mind-fuck thriller movie."

"You're preaching to the choir. Maybe one day I can write a book about my life."

"Don't leave out the spice with Mr Dark and Twisted. Everyone falls for the red flag."

I burst out laughing and nod in agreement.

"Yeah what can I say. They have bigger dicks and know how to use them."

"I will take your word for it." She wiggles her eyebrows at me suggestively.

"Hey where's Sara? I want to talk to her before she gets too drunk,"

"Ah, she went out back somewhere with Bradey..." Kirsten says slowly, trying to read my reaction.

"When?" I ask, confused.

"When Bradey came back inside." She shrugs. My face pales because I know why Bradey was outside in the first place. Could my brother really be dumb enough to get Sara into drugs as well? *Sara does know better than that*, I try to silently tell myself.

"I'm going to try to find her. I'll be back," I say as calmly as possibly but my heart hammers frantically against my rib cage. I slip through crowds of party goers, saying hi to everyone I know from school when they make eye contact with me. I slowly open doors as I move through the house and re-close them when I don't see Sara. I walk up the wide hallway that has basic gray white tones and bright abstract canvas paintings on the walls. I open another door, look around the large bedroom then pull the door shut when I declare it's empty. I pass a couple of drunk women and stop them.

"Have you ladies seen Sara?" I ask, trying not to sound alarmed. They shake their heads and apologize. I grip another door handle and try to open the door but it's locked. "Sara?" I call out.

"Paisley?" It's Bradey's voice replying.

"Yeah, where's Sara?"

Silence.

"Bradey open the fucking door. I'm getting over your shit seriously. You need help!" I feel the door unlock. I chew the inside of my cheek and push the door open. The scene before me causes me to gasp before a loud sob burns from my throat.

"Sara?" My croaked cry makes the word nearly inaudible. I look to Bradey who stands there with his cock out, white powder dusting it and tears streaming down his cheeks. I look back down to Sara who lies lifelessly on the ground with powder on her nose and white foam at the corners of her mouth. Her lips grow more purple the longer I stand in place. I drop to my knees and crawl to her.

"No, no, no, no," I say over and over again. I grip her shoulder and hopelessly shake her although deep down I already know. *She's gone.*

My fingers press into her neck that doesn't seem warm enough. Her skin isn't cold but it doesn't feel as warm as Sara normally is. I can't find her pulse and streams of my tears fall on to her hair as I hover above her.

"She's gone, she's really gone." The choked words burn on my throat. I suck in a deep breath and sit down on my ass with a loud heartbroken cry ripping from me as I let my breath out.

"I'm sorry, we were making out and I thought it would be hot if she did a line off my cock. She was okay for a bit then just fell," Bradey spits out.

I almost forgot he was there. It feels like an impossible task right now, but I peel my eyes from Sara's still body and glance up to Bradey.

"You!" I yell through my clenched teeth. "You promised you would get clean, that you had it under control." I then look back to Sara and brush her perfect, shiny hair down as more tears flow.

"My lies. All of this because of my lies. I should have told Mom and Dad the day they accused Nate of taking drugs. I should have ended it instantly. This is on me," I sob then scream. Bradey breaks behind me and starts weeping while he pushes his cock inside his pants. Nate flies into the bathroom and takes in the scene around us.

"What the—" he whispers, shocked. He drops to his knees and pulls his phone out. I can feel myself going cold. Shocked. Lifeless just like my best friend.

"We need an ambulance," Nate says but I'm focused on Sara. The rest of his words fall on my deaf ears as I block out all the commotion around me. The bathroom threshold becomes jammed with more people. I don't know what they say and if they shed as many tears as me. I just stare at the color changing in Sara's face. It's so slow, yet fast at the same time.

"Princess, we have to step back. The EMTs are here."

"I won't abandon her again." I grip Sara's hand quickly. "Don't make me," I say stronger this time.

Nate tries to take my hand from Sara's but something in me snaps. My other hand flies toward his face and I punch him on the jaw. "Leave me alone!"

His expression doesn't change, he doesn't even flinch. Why is he always so understanding and kind to me?

"Ma'am you need to move."

There's a new voice. Deeper, older. My swollen eyes look up and I see the dark blue uniform. "I don't want to leave her. I'll never see her again," I cry loudly, unable to care about how I look or sound.

The EMT crouches low beside me and rests a hand lightly on my shoulder. "Is she your friend?"

"My best friend."

He nods once and rubs my shoulder slowly. "I promise we will take really good care of her. We won't hurt her," he says soothingly. His voice aids me. I squeeze my fingers tightly around Sara's floppy hand. Her heavy rings make dents in my fingers and knuckles. I carefully slip a ring from her finger with one hand so I don't alert everyone to what I am doing. I wiggle it carefully and as it falls from the tip, I quickly fist it against my palm.

I stand shakily, my legs threatening to give way under me. The EMT stands with me and goes to put his arm around me but Nate steps in between us.

"I got her," he says and pulls me against his chest. At first I wonder what he is doing, but as we slip through the doorway and past the massive crowd that fills the hall wall to wall now, I understand. He's sheltering me from them all.

Two cops push past everyone and Nate pulls me to the side and has me against the wall as they walk past. Once they have gone through, he keeps walking us away from the most horrific scene I have ever seen. We step out into the lounge area but it's crowded as well. More officers are there with a notepad and pen each, talking to partygoers.

Bradey is already there, on the couch with a blanket wrapped around him. Anger grows in me further. Why does he get a warm blanket while Sara gets zipped up into a body bag?

I'm wrapped in Nate's warm arms, like a blanket, but all I feel from that is guilt. Not comfort. I will ruin his life too. What I touch, rots.

I push against his chest and swipe away my tears that still slip over my cheeks. An officer steps toward me. "Are you Paisley?" he asks me.

"Yeah I am."

"Are you the one that found Sara and Bradey in the bathroom?"

"Yes."

"We need to ask you a few questions."

"No, this can wait. I want to get her home." Nate starts to argue with the officer but he gives him an exasperated look before speaking. It's more to me than it is to him.

"We have a fatality in this house, the questions will not wait and the suspected crime scene needs to be processed."

As if the consequences of the events slip through my heartbreak from losing my best friend, I look past the cop toward where Bradey sits, still shaking underneath a blanket. *Crime scene*, the words keep tapping against my overwhelming grief. What will this mean for Bradey? Then I slowly focus back on the officer. What will it mean for Leith, who sold them the narcotics? The sadistic smirk on his face flashes behind my swollen eyes. I square my shoulders and sniff loudly.

"I will answer some questions," I say shakily. My voice isn't strong but I know what I have to do. Tell the truth. It's what I should have done a long time ago.

***

In a messy blur I spend the next half an hour going over the full night of events. I tell them about Bradey's addiction, but repeat more than once that he's not a killer. It was a terrible accident. But I also make it very clear that Leith and his friends have been selling him drugs for a long time now. I give them Leith's details before they say they are done with questions for me. For now.

Nate is still at my back, rubbing it over and over again in an attempt to give me strength. But as my lungs feel constricted and my heart aches from slamming against my chest, all I can feel is more self-loathing and guilt toward myself. I don't want to be comforted. I don't deserve his love. This could have all been avoided if only I was a better person. He tries to pull me against him now that the officer has gone back to Bradey but

I fight against it. It feels unnatural, a feeling that will probably haunt me for the rest of my life, but I need to be a better person.

I create a small distance between us so we are no longer touching. It feels unnatural.

I raise my head and we make eye contact. I don't look to his eyes for strength or love, I look to his dark black eyes for confirmation that he is too good for me. It feels unnatural.

I lick my lips and quickly swipe away my fresh tears. Nate frowns at me with a worried look in his eyes.

"I will help you get through this," he whispers in a deep, velvety voice. It shatters me. I feel the last tiny fragments left of my soul disintegrate and float away. I shake my head once and he tilts his head. His dark hair drops over his forehead. My god, his black hair that I spent most of my life lusting over. His dark eyes that I wanted to be on me. My mind is not matching my heart right now. It feels unnatural.

"You need to go to your new college and make the most of this opportunity you are being given. Live your life away from this shit."

He steps toward me and I instantly step back.

"Paisley you know we go together or not at all. You have just lost your best friend. Don't be rash until you have had time to process."

"I don't need time to process. I need you to go. Everything I touch turns to shit."

"I'm not leaving." He raises his voice. His jaw moves as he grinds his teeth together.

I need to be stronger or he won't listen to me. I need to be believable.

"Listen to what I am saying. I don't want you anymore Nate and I certainly don't want us living together. Take this as an opportunity for you to start a new life. You will find someone else. I don't want to ever see you again," I argue back.

"Paisley..."

I put my hand up and then hear my parents' voices and other parents coming in the house now.

"Go, and don't come back."

Mom comes running over to me and pulls me into a tight hug. I lose it and cry against her. My back aches as I struggle to breathe and gasp in air yet it doesn't feel like it is filling my lungs.

"Paisley. Through your nose and out your mouth," Mom says gently. I risk looking up, watching Nate's back disappear through the large glass doors. It feels unnatural. I feel dead.

Chapter 39

Time means nothing when you feel nothingness within yourself. Time flies by you, yet you're stuck in a space of time that doesn't move. It goes fast, yet it goes slow. It's a feeling that can never be put into words. Just felt. Just experienced. And for some, they may be lucky enough never to be caught in this time warp of being the living dead.

I lie in bed. The sun peaks through my curtains, the sun goes away, the moon comes out. My room is in total darkness. Night times are cold, lonely. They remind me of him. They remind me of her.

Chapter 40

"Paisley, it's the first day of school. Please just give it a go. All your friends want to see you," Mom says close to my face.

She's kneeling beside my bed, patting the hair down on my head. I pull the blankets over myself. Darkness finds me again.

Chapter 41

I sit at the bottom of the shower as Mom washes the shampoo out of my hair. Bubbles surround my naked body.

"It's Sara's six-month memorial service at school next week. I can come with you. Even if we sit at the back away from all your friends. I think it will be nice to do it for Sara."

I bury my head in my knees. Her name. It kills me more and more every time she says it.

I can't speak. So much time has passed and yet words fail me still. I close my eyes and cover my ears with my hands. Darkness finds me again.

Chapter 42

The smell of the gym and over perfumed students makes me nauseous.

Abruptly I stop, unable to find the strength to walk any further through the crowds of people. My throat feels like it's swelling up, yet I don't think an epi pen will help me today. Mom grips my hand harder and squeezes it tightly.

"I—I can't," I breathe. Mom's eyes grow wide. I haven't spoken since that night. Six months ago I spoke more than enough words.

Mom's features smooth over and she pats my shoulder with her free hand. "Yes you can. Believe in yourself."

She tugs at me and leads me to some spare seats. I feel fragile as I sit down. I no longer allow myself to look in mirrors. I have lost so much weight. I know I don't look right.

Kirsten and a few of my friends catch my eye. Lance too. They all sit in the second row but have turned toward me. Their eyes hold so much sadness so I divert my gaze.

"Go and sit with them," Mom insists beside me but I shake my head. Endless time passes from when the memorial begins. Sara's parents get up and speak, teachers, our cheer coach and squad. They all say the nicest things. They all talk about how much they miss her and how sad they are. Sad?

For the first time I look up and stare into the large framed photo of Sara that is placed beside the microphone. Sad? This is unbearable. Why can't people openly talk about their feelings and emotions? It's something I should have done a long, long time ago.

"Does anyone else want to speak?" the principal says as he stands behind the microphone. Nobody makes a move to stand up. I look around as the principal starts to close the memorial. I don't give myself any longer to think on it. I stand up.

"I will." I shake a little and lean on the chair in front of me.

Mom stands. "Paisley you don't have to."

"I need to. I'm okay," I say and nod at her. I walk up the middle of the two rows and ignore the whispering. I grip the microphone and keep my stare straight ahead. If I look down at my friends who I have ignored for the last six months, I may lose my nerve.

"Grief is more than just feeling sad and missing someone. It's layered with a lot of emotions no one dares talk about. Grief can be emptiness from that special person not being in your life anymore." I swallow thickly as a fresh lump forms in my throat. I close my eyes and then slowly open them again when I feel I have the strength to talk once more. But as they focus at the back of the gym again, I see him. He stands in the doorway, leaning one shoulder against the door frame and hands shoved in his pockets. He doesn't smile, or wave. He just stares, his soul drills into my empty core. Does he recognize that there's nothing in me anymore? I am lost.

I cough, clear my throat and speak as strongly as I can.

"It's feeling lost. Not knowing what you feel. Not being able to put it into words or explain to anyone around you that is trying to comfort you. But you feel completely lost, from the moment you wake up to the moment you fall asleep. Grief can be unexplainable bouts of happiness when you think of good memories or something triggers you to smile, then you are left ridden with guilt. You shouldn't be able to feel happy when you are grieving right? Just sad."

"Grief can have you riddled with anger. You tell yourself you can't be angry. That person is dead now. They are gone forever, only a cold heartless person would feel anger." I take a glimpse over my friends' faces and see some slight nods. It encourages me to keep going.

"So we purely don't speak on it. We don't tell each other how we really feel, what layer of grief we are currently feeling so we never truly support each other. We all grieve alone, with our private emotions that we feel like we shouldn't have. But we all have them. I am angry. I am so fucking angry that I didn't force Sara to make up with me when I first fucked up," I say loudly and I hear gasps from the teachers. But I don't want to sugarcoat this.

"I feel self-loathing because I kept my brother's drug addiction quiet and if I hadn't, my best friend may still be here. I am mad that Sara should have been cheer captain this year and she never got the chance. I feel completely broken." My voice hiccups and I swallow again as I fight the tears. My heart is in my throat as it attempts to block my words. The next words come out in a whisper.

"I feel utterly broken and I don't know how to mend myself. Sara, you were really one of the best. My childhood would have been a dull existence if it wasn't for you. You were a bright shining star on the earth and maybe when I am brave enough, I will look up at the sky and find the brightest star because I know that one will be yours. Sara, please forgive me for my fuckups, I promise I am going to be better. I am going to do better. And by better, I mean being more honest to everyone and myself about who I am. You were always authentically yourself and for that, I was always in awe of you."

I lock eyes with Nate, no matter how much it hurts.

"I promise I will be happy. Truly happy." A shudder runs through me as I fight a painful sob and I make my way back to Mom. The whole row where Kirsten and our friends sit stand as I walk past and clap gently with tears in their eyes.

"It will be okay," Mom says and pats my knee.

"Yeah Mom, I think it will be."

After the closing speech from the principal, two buckets are passed around. One for Sara's parents and one to be donated to drug and alcohol counselors and a new program that has been set up in Sara's name. It's an anonymous service for any students to use at the college if they are struggling with addiction. It's bittersweet.

"Mom, I need some space. I'll be home later," I say to her and leave the gym without waiting for a reply. I don't see Nate again at the gym. I make my way in my car to the lake. I park in a small car park and look down the long gravel path. Carefully,

I step out of the car and slowly walk down. So much of my innocent childhood was spent here fishing. I walk down to our old fishing spot and sit under the big tree. The ebbing of the water slapping against the rocks becomes rhythmic and almost tranquil. Therapeutic in a way.

I hear the rustling of grass before Nate appears and sits down next to me. He bends his knees up and rests his forearms on them as he looks out beyond the lake like myself.

"How's your new college?" I ask.

"That's really all you have to say to me, Princess?"

I start crying and cover my eyes with my long sleeves when his nickname for me leaves his lips.

"College sucks. Turns out I'm not good at living without you, Paisley."

"Turns out I can't even exist without you. So you're doing better than me."

He scoffs and picks at a blade of grass in front of him. "Oh I doubt that."

"I'm sorry for what I said. I didn't mean it."

"You were very convincing. But whether you meant it or not you know I don't take no for an answer. I'd never actually leave you."

I turn my head to him and see he's really serious. I know from experience kidnapping isn't past him.

"You did leave though."

He shakes his head once and throws the blade of grass back onto the ground. "No, I was giving you a bit of time while I set shit up at our new college. Your Mom kept me updated on you. And I was there when I needed to see you for myself."

I feel confused. "What do you mean?"

"I'm selfish and completely in love with you but I could see what you needed in that moment when you spoke those hurtful words to me. You needed your mom and complete silence. I wanted you to need me but you mean so much to me that I took a step back for a little while and took the back seat. But in no fucking way was I ever going to leave you forever. I told your mom about us. Your dad too. They were mad, but when they saw how empty you have been, they kept me updated on you and said if it is me that will bring you back to life then that's all they care about. The rest doesn't matter. But even then, their words were purely just words. I took a step back but it felt like I couldn't breathe or live without seeing you, feeling you, knowing you were okay. I came back, coming into the house at night like I have so many times and watched you sleep. But you were never okay. It's like you have withered away in front of me."

I gasp at his truthful words. "I can normally feel you. But this time I couldn't. I was so lost in the dark and felt nobody."

He wraps his arm around me and rubs my shoulder. "I know but it doesn't mean I would leave you alone. Even if you can't feel me there. If your heart is ever broken, I would happily give you mine. If you felt your soul was lost, I would walk with you in the darkness and find it for you. My whole life has been about protecting you. And that's something I don't plan on changing any time soon. You just have to let me be your protector and lover. I don't deserve you, you are too good for me. But I also don't fucking care. Like fuck anyone is getting you. You're spending the rest of your life with me, Paisley. Fuck what anyone says or thinks."

I cry harder and his hand brushes my cheek and turns my head toward him. "Hey, pretty girls shouldn't cry," he whispers while brushing away my wet tears.

I lose myself in his stare. "You said that to me when I hurt myself when I was little."

"I will always be your protector. Always have been and always will be."

"I think I want to leave this town and be with you now. Can we leave together? I don't want to be here anymore."

"Princess, I already have our place all set up."

His lips find mine and I tense. He pulls back mumbling "I understand if you're not ready. I will be patient."

I shake my head slightly and look out toward the still lake. "You look the same. Me? I am a skeleton. I know I don't look right anymore. Walking past mirrors frightens me." I admit to him.

He grips either side of my head and forces my face back to his. "No you don't look the same. Your body frame is smaller. But your eyes today when you spoke looked the most alive I have seen in a long time." One of his hands runs down my neck and settles on my chest. My heart is thumping rapidly against his palm. "This is what I need to be healthy. Sleep and cupcakes can fix the rest." He then winks with a smirk. Tentatively, I smile back.

Fuck I love him.

One Year Later

Nate

I roll my shoulders and crunch my neck side to side as I pace across the road. For a second, I glance up at the tall towers around me before my eyes settle on the small cupcake shop in front of me. Paisley's Cupcakes.

The corners of my lips twitch as I fight a smirk. Not very original but Paisley seems to think it's perfect. The small, forest green cafe almost gets swallowed by the towering buildings around it, but slowly over time, Paisley's small shop has become more popular.

How people can enjoy frosted cupcakes so much, I will never know.

I push open the door and listen to the usual bell ring that announces all her new customers.

"One moment," she calls out. Her head is lowered as she writes something on her notepad on the oak counter. I grin and cross my arms over my chest while watching her work. I may not understand the love for cupcakes but seeing her happy, truly happy, makes me not give one single fuck. Her auburn hair hangs loosely from her green ribbon. Paisley raises her head slowly and her gaze settles on me. She arches an eyebrow, her sky-blue eyes twinkling in the natural light that shines through the window.

"Oh carry on, no hurry," I assure her while my eyes dip to the top of her breasts that just slightly peek through the lace lining on her dress.

"Turn over the sign on the window to closed. I am done for the day," she orders me and places her pen and notebook under the counter. My dick throbs painfully in my pants every time she orders me around. She will always be the only person in my life that can tell me what to do. I turn slightly, and spin the sign on the window while looking out at the steady hum of the city. Our city.

Paisley wraps her arms around me from behind and leans her head against my back. "How was training??"

"Good. Big cardio session before lengths but worth it if I make it into the Olympic team this year."

I pat her hands and then unlink them so I can pull her around to the front of me. "How was the bakery today?"

"Good. Sold a lot more orange chocolate cupcakes than I normally do so I will make a bigger batch of them in the morn-ing," she says with a satisfied smile on her face.

"That's good. But we need to get a move on. The kids will be waiting for you."

She tiptoes and kisses my lips softly. "Yes and I have promised them that the quiet scary man will say hello to them today."

Fucking Paisley. Making promises she can't keep because I won't be talking to any little screaming girls. My brows furrow while a war wages within me. Satisfy the pain in my pants or the pain in my head with the thought of having to smile at strangers. Without any more hesitation I grip her ass and swiftly lift her then put Paisley down onto the edge of a small table. I use my hip to edge her legs apart, so her skirt rides up and her bare thighs rub against my own. A soft giggle leaves her perfect lips followed by a content sigh. "We don't have time for this..." She tells me, but not very convincingly. I move my hips slowly, rubbing my hard cock up and down her covered pussy.

While running a lone finger over her cleavage I say, "I will make you a deal."

She pushes against my chest and then crosses her arms over her ample breasts. My cock flinches against my track pants when I gaze at her pouty lips. "Making deals with you is like making deals with the devil," Paisley insists.

"Probably worse." I whisper and use my index finger under her chin to push her head up to face me. "Let me fuck you here and now and I will smile today," I finish.

"That's so fucking unfair. And what if someone peaks through the window?"

"They won't. It's getting dark and you have all your fucking posters covering the view,"

I slide my hand over her breasts and down her stomach then into the front of her panties. I carefully rub between her saturated lips. "Oh your mouth doesn't line up with what your pussy wants," I chuckle. She sucks in a breath as I push my fingers in deeply.

"I will make a deal with you," She moans seductively. *This should be interesting.*

"Mmmm?" I ask while pulling my fingers out before pushing them in again.

"Turn around and block my poor customer's view and I will suck your cock dry, just the way you like it. In return, you smile today and tomorrow,"

I snort and shake my head. But my cock spasms at the new image I have in my head and she smiles at me when she feels it. How does she always win?

I pull her off the table and spin us around so my back is toward the windows.

She drops to her knees and tugs the waistband down on my pants, letting my pained cock spring free.

The cold breeze brushes against it, causing my balls to tighten. I wrap her long hair in my fist and guide her head onto my cock. She opens her mouth while gripping the base and runs her lips over my shaft until they hit her hand. Intently, I stare down at her, watching Paisley work her tantalizing mouth when I notice her free hand slips into her own panties. Her hand subtly moves up and down as she plays with her pussy, pleasuring herself while she pleasures me. I use both my hands now, to grip the back of her head and start fucking her face harder. My balls tense as pre cum slips from the end of my cock. My breathing becomes ragged as I thrust in and out of her mouth. She gags loudly causing a groan to slip from my pleased lips. I'm getting close.

"Ah fuck!" I grind out when I cum down her throat. She swallows all of my pleasure and then pulls away from my cock while she closes her eyes and rubs her fingers over her clit. I can't tear my eyes away, and why the fuck would I want to?

Her fingers move faster while Paisley whimpers loudly. Her cheeks grow flush and she lets out a slow moan as she reaches her own climax now.

She stands straight again and puffs into my face showing me how breathless she is. I take her hand, and use my tongue to clean her wet fingers.

"Let's carry this on later Princess." I tell her.

We step out of the shop and I lock the door behind us. The door rattles as I turn the handle and push on it, double checking I have locked it correctly. My nightly routine, because if anyone dared break into Paisley's shop and cause her any heartbreak I would have to kill them. That would be a shame. In terms of the law anyhow.

Paisley's phone rings as we cross the road and find my truck.

"Hey Mom, I'm just heading to cheer practice," she says in her chirpy voice.

She listens for a moment as I press the button on my keys and unlock the truck. We climb in and she keeps speaking on the phone. "We were hoping to see Bradey on the weekend too. We can make a day of it?"

I turn the truck on, it roaring to life instantly. I go to pull out of our park and a man runs out in front of us. I slam my fist against the horn, making him jump out of his skin.

"Stupid cunt. Whose fucking idea was it to live in this shithole city again?" I growl and slam my foot on the gas pedal. I take a deep breath in and then take the risk to look at Paisley. She's glaring at me, still holding the phone to her ear. Then she starts laughing. At my expense of course. *Girl is going to be the death of me.*

"Nah, just his road rage. We are good. I have to get to the little tots' cheer class. I'll talk to you later Mom. Love you."

She places the phone down into the center console and pulls her work shoes off. I already have her sneakers in the back seat for her to change into. Along with her bike shorts and sports bra. The last of the afternoon rays bounce off Sara's ring that Paisley still wears every single day.

"We seeing the bro this weekend?"

"Yeah, it sounds like it's a family day for everyone."

I nod and take a right hand turn toward the gym. Bradey is in prison now, but his time is nearly up. When he gets out he has a lot of community service to do. But he got off lightly compared to the Hawks fuckers. Leith, Tucker and a few others got a lot more jail time for selling and distribution. Turns out Leith also laced the cocaine he gave to Bradey with some other shit on purpose so he got extra time.

I sometimes think I should feel guilty for fucking Leith off so much, but he was well mixed in the drug world before I came along. Getting beaten and abused by my own family has left me with wounds time won't ever heal. I don't feel empathy like normal people. I see the world and people alike through hardened eyes. I just can't be fucked letting anyone in aside from Paisley and at one time in my life, Bradey.

I pull up out front of the small community center and smirk at Paisley. "I'll find a parking space then head up."

"Okay see you soon. Remember the word hello when you come up." She giggles with her gym clothes in her hand and jumps out of my truck before I can say anything. I want to yell at her for stirring me up but as I see her run up the stairs and into the center where she teaches primary aged kids cheerleading, I lose all motivation and anger. Selfishly, I hated how much she put into cheerleading and her friends. I was so lost and unhappy that I wanted her to be focused on me all the time. I inwardly cringe at the memories of her endless sleepovers with Sara where I would put my ear against her door and listen, wondering how Sara could make her laugh so beautifully. I was so jealous. I scoff and shake my head at memories from the journey we have both gone on to be in a place like this. She glows as she disappears from sight. She really is *happy*.

While still parked alongside the curb, I think back to my childhood. Bradey as a skinny school kid throwing his arms around my shoulders when I turned up to the local skate park with a fresh black eye from my Dad. He said to me, '*come live with me, we can be brothers.*' Because of him I have a life I could have only ever dreamed about. Had it not been for him, I wouldn't have finished high school or become a swim champion. Because of him, I wouldn't have Paisley. Bradey was always firm on the fact we had to scare off all the high school and college men because she deserved someone better. Bradey got it into his head that all college men were drug addicts that fucked around every weekend just like him.

He didn't want her to be with someone like *him*. I turn my indicator on and pull away from the curb while blinking away tears. I don't cry. I never fucking cry. Dad always told me crying was for pussy's. But while a lone tear rolls down my cheek I can't help but feel sorrow and regret and I can only hope that Bradey finds his own happiness too.

The End

Acknowledgements

Thank you to everyone who supports me on this journey while I learn, grow and write stories that make my heart sing. You all know who you are.

A special thank you to Zoe, Liv and Kai for helping give this book an extra sprinkle of deliciousness. You're amazing.

About the author

Talia Atkins is a proud Aotearoa author. Fairly new to the author world, she mainly writes dark romance and dark thrillers with a sprinkle of spice.

When not writing, she is a mum to five busy children, taxi driver to their many sporting events and working full time.

Want to follow Talia on her socials?
Check them out here.

Also by

The Monsters Within Us Duet
Darkened Souls
Darkened Hearts

***

Claiming Kenna

***

Harlows Plague

***

The Haunted Past Of Birdie